Readers love
LUCIE ARCHER

My Paradise Is You

"This was a sweet, fast little romantic adventure in Bermuda that I thoroughly enjoyed."

—Love Bytes

"I really enjoyed reading about Ian's struggles to come to grips with who he is and what he wants out of life. It was not an easy journey but it turns out amazing in the end."

—Gay Book Reviews

Taming the Wyld

"It's definitely a feel good tale, and Jake and JD's reunion at the end made everything worth it."

—Joyfully Jay

"If you are looking for a novella with romance, intrigue, suspense, and a bad boy that falls head over heels, then this is your story!"

—Diverse Reader

"This is a great read for anyone who wants a super-cute love story, in a short amount of book time. You'll fall in love with the reformed playboy Jake—and root for JD."

—Alpha Book Club

By LUCIE ARCHER

Love Wins (Dreamspinner Anthology)
My Paradise Is You
Past the Breakers
Taming the Wyld

Published by DREAMSPINNER PRESS
www.dreamspinnerpress.com

PAST THE
BREAKERS

LUCIE ARCHER

Published by
DREAMSPINNER PRESS

5032 Capital Circle SW, Suite 2, PMB# 279, Tallahassee, FL 32305-7886 USA
www.dreamspinnerpress.com

This is a work of fiction. Names, characters, places, and incidents either are the product of author imagination or are used fictitiously, and any resemblance to actual persons, living or dead, business establishments, events, or locales is entirely coincidental.

Past the Breakers
© 2017 Lucie Archer.

Cover Art
© 2017 Brooke Albrecht.
http://brookealbrechtstudio.com
Cover content is for illustrative purposes only and any person depicted on the cover is a model.

ISBN: 978-1-63533-398-5
Digital ISBN: 978-1-63533-399-2
Library of Congress Control Number: 2016962555
Published May 2017
v. 1.0

Printed in the United States of America
∞
This paper meets the requirements of
ANSI/NISO Z39.48-1992 (Permanence of Paper).

For Camille

ACKNOWLEDGMENTS

A HUGE thank you to everyone who made this book possible.

CHAPTER ONE
CASING THE JOINT

CASEY USED to love the color red, but the fire engine parked outside his restaurant—lights flashing and hoses on full blast—had him rethinking that. Or it would have if his brain had bothered to register anything other than *It's gone*. Because life as Casey knew it was over, burned to ashes like the first soufflé he ever made, and he had bad luck and a little faulty wiring to thank for it.

A strong waft of smoke punched him in the gut, and he fell to his knees as he struggled to catch his breath. He vaguely registered his girlfriend, Isabel, at his side before the paramedics ushered him to an ambulance. His vision started to blur, and he did his best to listen to what the paramedics tried to tell him, but his body felt as if it was in revolt.

"C-can't… breathe," he kept repeating, pawing at the collar of his shirt trying to hold off the boa constrictor tightening its hold around his neck. His chest ached, and he thought he was going to suffocate or have a heart attack. He blinked his vision clear and saw Isabel talking with one of the paramedics before the doors of the ambulance shut.

"We're taking you to the hospital as a precaution, Mr. North," said one of the paramedics. "Just try to take deep breaths. Everything's going to be fine."

But that was a lie; nothing would ever be fine.

Cinder was everything to him, his livelihood, the dream he'd spent nearly his whole life working toward, so the late-night call from the police informing him of the fire had turned his blood to ice. Then they'd pulled up and he couldn't believe his eyes. The flames had devoured it.

He made Isabel take him back to the restaurant after the hospital released him, but what he saw when they arrived almost had him in need of a return trip. The fire had gutted the place, the burned remains filling his heart with a sadness mixed with the bitter taste of failure. An electrical fire had started in the restroom and quickly spread, taking the whole damn restaurant with it. The police tacked up yellow caution tape all around it, but little to nothing remained to salvage—of the restaurant or of himself.

Isabel vowed to stay by his side and assured him that the insurance company would pay for it all. He felt so thankful to have her support that he went out and bought her an engagement ring as soon as he could. He'd decided to wait for the right time to propose, but with every day that went by, the right time felt like it slipped further and further away.

Casey was in his therapist's office when he got her two-word text: *it's over*. And yeah, that pretty much summed it up.

Two months after Cinder, Isabel left him because of a different kind of faulty wiring, the kind that made it difficult for him to pull himself out of bed most mornings and mocked him from inside his own head. He couldn't blame her for leaving, not when he let himself go. He'd gained twenty pounds in that time and didn't bother shaving anymore, his jet-black hair growing in thick on his face.

When it became a chore to turn on the faucet for a shower some days, how could he turn on anyone else? But a little common courtesy would have been nice, instead of a text and a covert mission with her friends to pull a Grinch. She even took the lightbulbs and the toilet paper from their shared apartment.

Depressed, dejected, and utterly destroyed, he packed up what little Isabel hadn't slithered off with and pointed his car north toward Land's End. He had a sister there, older by a year and a half, but they had grown apart when he moved away. He thought he had two nephews, and he hated himself that much more when he called from the road and she corrected him: three nephews.

"WE'RE ALMOST there, Jasper," Casey said, eyeing the cage strapped in the backseat.

The cat meowed a pathetic reply.

The serene drive up from LA to LE took a toll on both of them. Land's End sat almost halfway between the Hollywood Hills and Seattle, nuzzled against the Pacific Ocean. The sleepy little coastal town had bed-and-breakfasts lining the shore and tiny shops where visitors could go antiquing in the afternoons when the sun got too hot to sunbathe. The fish place down by the docks stood as their biggest restaurant, which contributed to his skipping town as soon as he'd gotten the chance.

His dream had always been to own his own restaurant. He left home at seventeen and moved across the country to the Big Apple for culinary school. There he worked his way up from a dishwasher to a well-respected chef over the span of four years. When it came time for him to spread his wings and venture out on his own, he took the opportunity to move to Los Angeles. Even though New York had treated him well, the West Coast ran through his veins.

But the trip home to Land's End signified him giving up, throwing in the towel and admitting that life had beaten him. He'd lost, and now he had come crawling home empty-handed with his tail between his legs and nothing to show for his twenty-nine years on earth. He felt like a total loser, and the Welcome to Land's End sign mocked him on the drive-by.

Rachel had convinced him to stop in and say hi before heading to his temporary home, but the drive had worn him out, and he wanted to sleep before he had to deal with family. What was he supposed to do with three nephews and a sister he hadn't seen since their mother's funeral? With that in mind, he made the decision to pass by the turnoff to her house and continue on.

Soon he pulled up to the house he'd rented with what little savings he hadn't dumped into his restaurant. He'd have to make do with what he had until the insurance check showed up. The one-story dwelling looked smaller than it did in the online listing, but he was in no position to be picky. Powder-blue awnings on the exterior walls blended in with the sky, as did the white trim around the doors and windows, but he kind of liked the effect.

Jasper started to stir in his carrying cage when Casey turned off the ignition. A few sporadic meows here and there marked the extent of his protest about the long car ride, but Casey knew he should take the little guy inside. They both had a desperate need to stretch their legs.

Isabel had brought Jasper into his life when they moved in together, but she obviously rejected him too. Casey didn't consider himself an animal person—his hectic job didn't allow for much free time outside of work—but some days the marmalade tabby felt like the only friend he had in the world. They had a sacred bond.

Most days the feline gave him his only reason to get out of bed, and a shitty one at that. If he didn't empty the litter box at regular intervals, Jasper would leave wonderful "presents" all over the living room to show his appreciation. His therapist said it was good he had some semblance of purpose in his life, even if it only consisted of picking up the fur ball's excrement.

Casey didn't know how long he spent sitting there trying to will himself to get out of the car, but a sharp rapping on the window startled him from his thoughts of despair. His heart leaped into his throat as he clutched his chest, the organ doing double time as he flinched and turned toward the noise.

On the other side of the glass stood an old woman, at least sixty or so, with snow-white hair and a suspicious scowl on her hardened face that looked like it took masons a thousand years to carve out of stone. Maybe she was a lot older than sixty. In one hand she held a wooden cane that she had tapped on the glass, and in the other a brown leash that led to a small yet round puffball of a Pomeranian. He could hear her mumbling something, so he rolled down the window.

"You live here or are you just casing the joint?" the woman asked, her eyes narrowing even more with every word.

"Uh, neither. I'm renting for a while," Casey replied.

"Just the driveway?"

Casey wanted to bite back with a sarcastic comment, but he held his tongue. "The whole house. I just had a long drive and needed a moment to collect myself."

"Do it from the inside, then. You're gonna rile up all the neighbors."

She turned to leave, but he felt the need to introduce himself. "I'm Casey, by the way."

"Mrs. Walton," she hissed back over her shoulder, tugging on the leash to get her dog to follow. Just what he needed: an old curmudgeon for a neighbor. He'd arrived in the town five minutes ago and already made an enemy.

He sat there for a few minutes longer, watching as she limped up her sidewalk to her front door. Her bright green house—almost lime— seemed in complete contrast to her dreary personality. It didn't suit her in the slightest. As if she'd read his thoughts, she sent a glare his way as she opened the door before disappearing into the house.

Casey rolled the window back up and pushed the door open to step out. The smell of salty air always brought him comfort, and he was glad to finally escape the confines of the car. He stretched his arms above his head and groaned at the feel of his muscles loosening. His head lolled back so that the sun shone down on his pale face, warming his cheeks, which had spent the last several hours weathering an assault from the air conditioner.

After a minute or two of warming up his muscles, he walked around the back of the car to unbuckle Jasper's carrier from the rear passenger's seat. Casey accidentally jostled the carrier when he pulled it out, much to Jasper's displeasure. "I know, buddy. I'll let you out in just a minute. Just hold on a little while longer." He set the carrier down for a second to get one of his bags. Once he'd secured it over his shoulder, he picked up Jasper again.

He chanced a glance at Mrs. Walton's house and saw her curtain move as he walked up the sidewalk. It didn't surprise him that she'd been watching him, but he couldn't do anything about a nosy neighbor, other than hope he didn't have to interact with her much. He had his own problems to deal with, and he didn't need anyone or anything else making his life harder.

The man he'd rented the house from told him he'd left a key in the mailbox. Casey had to put Jasper down to fiddle with the door. After a brief struggle with the lock, he pushed it open. He deposited Jasper on the other side of the threshold before closing the door and opening Jasper's carrier so he could stretch his stubby legs.

The house smelled lemony upon entry, thanks to a Lemon Fancy geranium on the table by the door. He'd been given instructions on how to water it, though he'd had plenty of experience keeping an herb garden. He knew a lot about edible plants used for cooking, so he had confidence he wouldn't kill it.

The front door opened into the living room, and he dropped his bag in a nearby chair on his way to explore the rest of the house. The sparse furnishings appeared clean and sleek and made the house look modern while still managing to have that quaint beach-house vibe. The walls matched the exterior, with pale blues and yellows with white trim. Casey couldn't decide if he liked it, but it would have to do.

The two bedrooms sat on the left, with a guest bathroom and the laundry room between them. A small office area sat in the corner by the front door and opened up to the living room with the kitchen just beyond, complete with an island and huge windows that gave a nice view of the ocean. He should've loved it.

The open concept would allow him plenty of room to move around while he cooked, but the thought of doing so turned his stomach. Every time he stepped into a kitchen, he smelled the burning of his hopes and dreams as pictures of the scorched remains of Cinder flickered through his mind. As a result, his recent meals consisted of cheap takeout or frozen foods he prepared in the microwave, even though he hated how junk food took up residence around his middle.

He peeked his head into the first room. It looked pretty standard and had a queen-size bed. He didn't need two bedrooms, but he couldn't find a one-bedroom that had beach access. The second room was the master, with a california king canopy bed complete with sheer white curtains tied to the four posts. It looked romantic; he hated it.

French doors led from the master out onto the deck, where a barbeque grill sat. He didn't know if grilling would cause the same visceral reaction that a kitchen did, nor if he had the balls to find out. But the infinity pool looked tempting enough, the blue water seeming to blend right into the ocean as they both stretched into the horizon.

Casey needed to bring in the rest of his things and get Jasper settled before he could indulge in a nice swim. He considered his lack of material possessions a plus, as he only needed two trips to unload the car. He'd been too distraught to bother with his kitchen gadgets. A friend of his, one of the sous-chefs who worked for him, insisted on holding on to them until he worked things out. He tried to tell her to keep everything, but she insisted he would want them when he got his life back on track. *If* he got his life back on track.

He put his bags in the master bedroom and braved the kitchen for a drink. It took a few tries before he located the glasses, but he quickly filled one with ice and water from the refrigerator-door dispenser. He took a few sips, then made sure to fill a small bowl for Jasper. While he drank, he leaned a hip against the marble countertop and pondered aloud where he could put the little guy's food and litter box.

"How about the guest room? No, might be too messy… and I don't want to leave the door open all the time. Bathrooms are out too. You'll get litter all over the place, as we learned the hard way…. Hmm, any suggestions?" He paused and looked down at the cat, who was lapping up water at his feet. "You're really no help, Jaspy."

He finished his drink and set the glass on the island. Then he scooped up both Jasper and his bowl of water to take into the laundry room. It would work for the time being. With that decided, he made one more trip out to the car for Jasper's things: his bed, a half-empty bag of food, his dishes, the litter box, and a few toys. He caught sight of Mrs. Walton peeping out her curtains on his way back in. That had already gotten old.

Once he had Jasper's things situated in the laundry room, he went back into the bedroom and unpacked his own. It was almost time for dinner when he'd finished putting away his clothes, but the hypnotizing sound of waves beyond his bedroom door had made him sleepy. He decided to take a nap first and then order pizza from the place he'd worked at the summer he turned sixteen.

He backed up to the bed and let himself fall onto the mattress, his body bouncing a few times before he melted into the comfy bed. He took in the sights, happy that he could see the ocean stretching on forever from where he lay, the shimmering crystal water of the pool dissolving into the deep blue of the sea. It was a helluva view, and it puzzled him how he'd snagged such an amazing house at such a dirt-cheap price.

But maybe his luck had started to change.

CHAPTER TWO
TIED TO THIS PLACE

LIFE AS Myles knew it was over, his brain supplied just before everything went topsy-turvy and faded to black. He didn't know what happened exactly, only that he had been enjoying a beautiful morning with his boyfriend, James, out on the water. The day itself didn't have any prior meaning, but the ring he had zipped away in his pocket made it feel special.

After four years together, he'd decided to ask James to marry him. They were both professional surfers, and Myles had planned the day months in advance. He had to with their busy schedules. It took days of coordinating with their agents to carve out some time for a romantic getaway between booked commitments.

They woke up to a wonderful swell just outside the house they rented for the three-day weekend—nothing fancy or ostentatious, just a modest little beach house overlooking Tranquil Bay. The sunrise painted the sky in pinks and oranges, and the warm breeze blowing in the open doors felt like heaven, the ends of the white curtains that framed them dancing on the dark wood floor.

"Good morning, beautiful," Myles said, nuzzling his face into the warm, tanned neck of the body next to him.

James yawned as he stretched, one arm moving to drape over Myles. "How's it looking out there?" he asked at the end of another yawn.

"I'm more interested in how it looks in here."

"You know the rules, babe… surfing and then sex," James said with a chuckle.

Myles groaned but agreed. He wanted to pop the question out on the ocean anyway and had a feeling that if they didn't get out of bed right then, they'd stay there for the rest of the day. Not a bad plan in and of itself, just not the one he'd envisioned for the past three months.

They started pulling on their board shorts, both pairs red with a black stripe running down the sides, when James's phone rang. The harsh ringtone grated against his eardrums and drowned out the sound of the waves crashing in the distance.

"Don't answer," Myles pleaded, past ready to dive into the warm, salty water calling to him.

"It's Logan. I have to."

Myles shook his head, but James picked up his phone from the side table and slid his finger over the screen. He shrugged his indifference at Myles before answering and walking out of the room, a cheerful lift to his voice when he said, "Hey."

That kind of thing had become more and more troublesome over the past few months. James's agent had assured him he could handle everything while they were away, but apparently not. Myles tried to shake off the nagging thought that they had something on the side. He had no proof, other than the increasing frequency at which the two of them spoke.

He had confronted James about it a few times, expressed his fears, but his soon-to-be fiancé brushed off his insecurities, insisting the pair only discussed business. After a few months of reassurance, Myles convinced himself he'd imagined it all, that he was "just stirring up drama," as James had put it, but it didn't stop the pang of *wrong* that ran through him whenever Logan called.

With James in the other room, he took the opportunity to dig the engagement ring out of the box it had come in for one last inspection. He'd buried it in the bottom of his bag for safekeeping, so it took him a minute of rooting around before his fingers hit pay dirt. James liked the pop and sizzle of shiny and expensive things, but Myles had gone with something a little less flashy, a white gold band with a wave design encircling it. Myles had it sized for him and inscribed it with their initials.

He took a moment to admire the shine of it. James would have gone with platinum, but if he didn't like it, Myles could have it resized for himself. When he heard footsteps growing near, he took the ring from the velvety interior of the box and stuffed it into the pocket of his board shorts, then shoved the box back into the depths of his bag. He stood and hurried over to the door, leaning a shoulder against the frame as he watched the waves roll in. Once James rejoined him, they grabbed their boards and headed for the ocean.

His hands shook as they paddled out. He had practiced his speech, but he hoped he remembered all the words through his nerves when the time came. They caught a few good waves before a break had them sitting on their boards, happy to drift for a bit as they enjoyed the water. Myles never felt more at peace than he did on his surfboard. He considered the ocean his home, and he'd gladly spend all day in it if allowed.

He had no family to speak of, other than the deceased uncle who raised him. His uncle Joe had bought him his first surfboard and gave him his first lesson on his thirteenth birthday. After Joe passed away of cancer a few days shy of Myles's twentieth birthday, all he had left were his friends, and only a few of them close.

Thrill seeking became his way of coping, and while not the deadliest vice in the world, after Joe passed, he spent a few years putting himself in harm's way and making dumb, impulsive choices. Surfing had been enough once, but he tried to fill the hole left in his heart by Joe's death with anything that pumped his system full of adrenaline.

Finding James had felt like being thrown a life preserver just as he started to slip under the waves. James gave him something to live for and had pulled him out of a pretty self-destructive place. He wanted to make that permanent, that safety net, but after living together for three years he'd grown tired of waiting for James to take the initiative.

Instead he found himself on a surfboard in Tranquil Bay about to ask James to marry him. He had doubts about doing it out on the ocean. If his shaky hands dropped the ring, they might never find it again, but at least the salt water offered cover for his sweaty palms. He reached for the ring, but before he could get the zipper of his board shorts open, he felt the telltale signs of a riptide forming under them.

And that was the last thing he remembered.

MYLES WOKE on the beach, struggling to open his heavy eyelids. He felt dizzy and disoriented as he tried to piece together what had happened. Nothing good, he assumed, but he knew he had to check on James. He sat up to look for him, but a chill ran up his spine when his eyes landed on the only other person on the beach. He shook his head and blinked a few times to clear his vision, because that just wasn't possible.

Coming face-to-face with a dead relative would've thrown anyone for a loop, so Myles decided to call the very Joe-like figure walking toward him a hallucination. He didn't look dressed for the beach in white, flowing clothes that Myles had never seen on him before.

"What the hell happened?" he asked when Joe's look-alike came within hearing distance. Maybe he didn't want to know the truth, not when his gut told him something wasn't right. Perhaps he had some sort of head wound.

Joe laughed, and Myles hadn't realized how much he missed the sound of it. "I think you know what happened, kiddo." Joe stopped in front of him and stood over him, blocking the sun from his face.

"I...."

"Can't even stand to give your favorite uncle a hug?" Joe asked, holding out his hands as a big grin broke across his face.

"B-but you're dead. Is this a dream? I'm dreaming, right? This has to be a dream. Am I... I.... Shit, Joe, please don't tell me I died. I was... but James?"

Joe chuckled again. "Eloquent as always."

Myles got to his feet and threw his arms around Joe, overwhelmed that he could feel him hugging back. It was the only thing he'd wanted for the past eight years and he finally got it, but at what price?

"Will you please tell me what the hell happened? Am I hallucinating?" Myles asked as he pulled back. He kept his grip on the loose fabric at Joe's sides to ground himself, to prove it wasn't just a dream. The heat of Joe's body and the expansion of his chest felt real. But how?

"I don't know what happened to you. Only you can answer that.... But maybe we should take a walk. Down the beach? You always loved evening strolls."

Myles looked to the setting sun in the distance and had to wonder how long he'd been unconscious. "Can you at least tell me if James is okay? We were... when did it get so late? I just woke up an hour ago."

Joe started to walk toward the water's edge, and Myles followed close behind. "Time is nonexistent here."

"I knew it. I'm... holy shit, I'm dead, aren't I? I fucking died. I'm dead. And I didn't even get the chance to propose, did I? Why can't I remember? I can't believe you're here!"

Joe looked like the Joe he remembered, not the one who died in the hospital as mostly skin and bones, but the one before the chemo and the cancer ate away at his body, before his hair fell out and his skin became riddled with holes from IVs and tubes. His golden hair glittered in the sun, green eyes as bright as a four-leaf clover. And his smile brought Myles a peace he thought he'd never know again.

"I'm not here, not really. And neither are you," Joe said.

"Are you a ghost, then, a spirit? Why can I see you?"

"Well, I suppose 'ghost' would work. I am dead after all. You were there."

Yes, he had been there, and it was the worst day of his life, one he did his best to forget. "So this is the Beyond, then? I was picturing… more, but it's got a beach. That's something, right?"

"Finally a question I can answer. You always had a knack for asking the tough ones first. No, kiddo, this isn't the Beyond. It's much too… it's hard to explain, but take it from me," Joe said, putting his hand on Myles's shoulder, a gentle squeeze leaching the tension right out of him. "Everything's going to be just fine."

"You're going to take me there, then, like an angel or something?"

"It's not your time yet," Joe replied, turning to look out over the ocean. Myles followed his gaze and tried to steady the stream of questions that ran through his head at light speed. "For whatever reason, you're tied to this place. For how long, I can't say."

"What do you mean 'tied to this place'?"

Joe gave him a sideways smirk. "If you stray too far, you'll end up back where you started. That's about all I know. I'd really love to stay, Myles, but I have to be getting back."

"Wha'? What? You're going to leave me here?"

"I'll be around when you need me, but consider this lesson one."

"What do you mean 'lesson one'?" Myles asked, but Joe left him with more questions than he knew what to do with when he vaporized before his eyes.

"Joe!"

He dropped to his knees in the sand, letting his momentum drag him down on all fours. "Please," he begged, eyes welling up, "don't leave me, not again." He didn't bother holding back the tears when they started streaming down his cheeks.

He sat back on his haunches and howled out the warring emotions coursing through him. It was all too much. He couldn't be dead, could he? But he soon realized he couldn't feel the sunlight dancing on his skin or the ocean breeze rippling through his clothes—the ones he'd died in—

and neither could he smell the ocean, the salt of it, the earthy fragrance of fish and birds and crabs he knew all mingled in a stew of the sea.

He ran a hand through his hair as he looked around him, taking a moment to orient himself. In the distance, he spotted a few people on the beach, and without even thinking, he took off toward them, his feet moving before he had a chance to think. A hundred yards from them, he started to wave his arms and yell for help. Maybe that's where James had gone, to get him some medical help.

The gap closed to fifty yards, but then he felt his body shake. In an instant, he arrived back where he started from, in front of the blue house he'd rented for the weekend, just like Joe had said. He knew that wasn't humanly possible, so he took off again, screaming this time, and once again he found himself in the same place. He decided he'd gone insane after the fifth time, because that was one of the definitions of the word: doing the same thing over and over again and expecting different results. The only good thing was he hadn't gotten winded, but that didn't make sense either.

Once he realized the uselessness of his current plan of literally running in circles, he decided to try his luck inside the house—assuming he could get that far. He knew James would be able to see him no matter what. They shared a bed, a home, a future. What was he supposed to do without him?

Myles climbed the stairs to the house, only to discover he couldn't open the door. Every time he reached for the handle, his hand went right through it. When he went to bang his head on the door in frustration, he ended up falling into the house and landing pain-free on his face.

"If you'd been paying attention to ghost stories, you might've known that was going to happen," he berated himself as he got to his feet. He could almost hear Joe laughing at him from somewhere and lecturing him about lesson number two being how to walk through walls.

"James?" he called as he went into the bedroom. No answer. Their suitcases were gone, so he tried to open the drawers to double-check for their things, but he couldn't grip the knobs. The car wasn't in the driveway when he looked out front, and the house had been cleaned. His stomach sank at the thought that James had left him there. Myles had died, and James had gone. His whole world, everything he had, everything he was, disappeared in the blink of an eye.

How could he be a ghost, and why was he tied to a place he'd only been once, to a house he'd only slept one night in? Nothing made sense other than severe brain trauma. Nothing made sense but death. He was dead. He just knew it. That was it; he died. He didn't even get into the Beyond. Instead he'd somehow gotten himself stuck in the Between. It was, without a doubt, the worst day of his life.

CHAPTER THREE
HALF TO DEATH

IT TOOK Casey two days to call Rachel and explain his "late arrival." To spare himself a lecture, he lied and told her he'd gotten in earlier that day. She had insisted on coming over as soon as she could, but she had to wait until she picked up her eldest son from preschool. That left him with a few hours to kill, so he decided to head down to the beach.

The overcast sky made for a dreary day, but the sun did its best to peek through the clouds. He almost needed his jacket, the early spring weather being chillier than he remembered. After changing into his swim trunks—which were snugger than he wanted to admit—he grabbed a towel and the sunscreen before setting out to confront the cold water.

He had to traverse some rickety wood steps to get to the private beach of Tranquil Bay. The neighborhood sat on a ridge overlooking the ocean, negating the need for stilts, but he dreaded the trek back up the nearly two flights of stairs.

There weren't many people out that he could see, but he didn't know how many of the houses around had renters in them. He didn't intend to get chummy with the neighbors anyway, nor did he want anyone staring at the pudgy belly he sported courtesy of pizza and an overabundance of Chinese food. And maybe a little too much beer.

But he thought he deserved to drink his sorrows away. He'd suffered a lot in the past year. He didn't want to feel sorry for himself, but it was hard not to when he couldn't even stand to look at himself in the mirror. He didn't recognize himself anymore. Everything he was had burned away with his restaurant, and instead of a phoenix rising from the ashes, it was his waistline and self-doubt that grew out of them.

He dropped his towel on the sand and popped the top on the sunscreen. He had an olive complexion, but it had been ages since he spent any time in the sun. Late nights and heating lamps did little to tan his skin. The cool lotion soothed him, and after a few minutes to let it soak into his pores, he kicked off his flip-flops and made a beeline for the water. He'd mentally prepared himself for the lower water temperature in comparison to Los Angeles, but he feared his balls might fall off the farther he waded out. At least the sand felt silky underfoot.

When he got waist-deep, he dove under a breaking wave. He ran his hands through his thick hair as he broke the surface and blinked the salt water from his lashes. There was something freeing about splashing around and frolicking in the surf. He had spent so much of the past ten years working to build a career that he oftentimes forgot to have fun along the way.

In truth, he missed the water. Growing up, his parents toted him and Rachel to the beach every weekend and many evenings in between. They didn't always swim, but he enjoyed walking along the shore, collecting shells and various other beach treasures, just as much.

He had loved the days when his father had an afternoon off to take him fishing at the pier. He remembered the feeling of accomplishment when his dad pulled that first halibut off his line. His old man patted him on the back and gave him a proud grin. When they got home, they fired up the grill, and his dad taught him how to clean and cook it. The seafood dishes he made with fish he'd caught himself nurtured his love for cooking, and after that, they couldn't keep him out of the kitchen.

Casey swam around for a while before he tired himself out and bodysurfed on a wave back to the beach. He cursed himself for not bringing something down to drink when he reached his things. The exertion had made him thirsty. He picked up the sunscreen and the towel, draping the latter over his shoulders. After slipping on his shoes, he started back to the house, glaring at the stairs when he reached them, but at least there wasn't a soul around to watch him huffing and puffing on the ascent.

Jasper greeted him at the door when he finally made it up. "Hey, buddy. I told you I'd be back." Jasper meowed and rubbed against his wet leg. "Oh, come on. You're gonna get hair all over me," he chided, giving him a gentle nudge to stop. The cat replied with a deep growl before taking off toward the bed. Casey watched his strawberry blond tail disappear underneath it. "Okay, whatever."

He figured Jasper needed a little time to adjust to his surroundings. The sensitive cat would oftentimes run away and growl when new people came into his territory, but he'd never acted that way when it was just the two of them. Casey shook off the thought. They both had to adjust to the new environment, and he had no way of knowing how Jasper handled that sort of thing. Maybe getting his fur wet upset his delicate sensibilities.

"All right, scaredy-cat. I'll leave you alone." He tossed the sunscreen on the dresser and went to the kitchen for some water, making a mental note to go for a beer run and to the store for a few groceries later. He hit the shower after quenching his thirst and had just finished getting dressed when he heard a knock on the door.

AFTER AN hour with three rambunctious kids, Casey was glad to see them go. "How do you do this all day?" he asked Rachel as he helped to wrangle them into the slate-gray minivan they had arrived in.

"It's just nap time. I swear they're normally better behaved," she replied as she buckled in the youngest, who had just turned six months old. The poor thing had no hair, but his lungs had developed nicely. Casey's ears could attest to that. All the money in the world couldn't have persuaded him to get in the van with those squawking things.

"I would hate to see them at their worst," Casey muttered to himself. He struggled for several minutes to get Tony, the three-year-old, strapped into his booster seat before he gave up. "How the hell do you buckle this thing?"

"Case! Language please," she admonished, pushing him out of the way. "Tony likes his drama, but Will's usually a very happy baby and hardly cries.... I just wonder if it has anything to do with the house." She'd whispered the last part.

He looked at her, puzzled at what she'd meant by that. "What about the house?"

"Uncle Casey, can you come to my birthday?" little Ethan asked. "I'm gonna be this many." He held up four fingers, successfully confusing Casey.

"No, Ethan. That's how old you are now," Rachel corrected. "In two weeks you'll be this many," she said, holding up her opened hand.

"This many!" Ethan screeched, opening his hand with all five fingers spread wide. "And Tony is this... many," he continued, holding up two fingers.

Rachel shook her head at the mistake as Casey smiled at the kid and moved back so she could shut the door. "Two kids weren't enough?" he asked as he shook his head in disbelief.

She sighed. "It's just a bad day. It happens. Besides, I thought you liked kids."

"I do, I just...."

She wrapped her arms around him and pulled him in for a tighter hug than he'd expected, considering her small frame. Her black hair smelled like jasmine, and he let himself get lost in the first real contact he'd had since Isabel left him over two months ago. He could hear the children yelling and crying in the van, which put a damper on the mood, but he'd been in need of a hug for months.

He was reluctant to let go when she pulled back, and he didn't care for the look of pity she had etched on her face when she did so. "I'm sorry I have to go. We'll get together again, maybe sometime without the kids. Gary's good at helping out when I need a night to myself."

"Yeah, that'd be great."

"And we would love to have you at Ethan's party. I'll text you the details," she said before kissing him on the cheek.

He nodded and let go of her hand, following her around to the driver's side to open her door. It had been far too long since they'd seen each other, and he hadn't realized how much he'd missed her until that moment. She had three children now. She was a wife and a mother, while he had nothing but a failed career and a pissed-off cat.

"Hey, what did you mean about the house?"

"Just some rumors going around is all." She glanced back at the house, a strange look on her face as she pursed her lips.

"What?"

"It's probably nothing. You know how rumors are."

"Rach, just tell me," he groaned, tossing his head back. All three children had decided on throwing a group tantrum, and he wasn't above joining in.

"A surfer drowned in the bay a month ago, and since then people have been gossiping about it. You know how these things go around here. Unless you've forgotten."

"No, I haven't forgotten," he snapped, sensing her judgmental tone creeping in.

"It's really nothing, just that the surfer had been staying here. With all the freaking out going on about his death.... Just ignore me. I'm sleep deprived. And besides, you don't believe in ghost stories."

Casey let out a dry laugh. "No, I don't. People are so gullible."

"Exactly. See, nothing to worry about. I really should get these kids home, but we'll see you soon, okay? And if you need anything, please call me. I'm here for you. I know I have my own boring life now, but we're family. You've been through a lot, and I just want you to be happy."

"I'm good," he lied. "Really, I just needed a change of scenery."

She nodded, and he tried not to squirm under her scrutinizing eyes. "I'll call you later, Case."

"Yeah, see ya later."

"Bye, Uncle Casey!" Ethan yelled from the backseat.

"Bye, little monkey," he said as he waved back. He smiled at Rachel and stepped away so she could shut the door.

After he watched the van pull away, he went back inside, but not before rolling his eyes at Mrs. Walton, the most unsubtle snoop on the planet. He laughed to himself, thinking that she'd been the spook the whole town was talking about. That led to thoughts of the old lady on a surfboard, which had him cracking up by the time he got into the house.

Once inside he opened a few windows to air the place out. Will, being the inconsiderate baby that he was, had decided to take a dump as soon as they arrived, and he could still smell the remnants of baby shit in the air. After his epic ordeal, he decided to take a little nap before going to the store. He liked kids, he really did, but he found it hard to find the joy in life the past few months.

His psychiatrist said a little depression wasn't uncommon following a string of catastrophic events like he'd encountered with his mother and then his restaurant. The doctor gave him some prescriptions for anxiety and depression, which he knew he needed, and charged him way too much to talk about his feelings, or lack thereof.

He had his pills sitting on the island next to his glass and thought he should take one to combat the stressful afternoon he'd had. After filling his glass with ice and water, he took a good swig to swallow one down.

He reflected on his visit with his sister and her kids as he stood there in the kitchen, sipping his water. Rachel had looked a little tired but still the same. Her kids, on the other hand, had gotten so big since he'd seen them last. Tony had just turned one when their mother died. Now he walked and talked and was almost unrecognizable with hair and teeth.

Casey tried to think about how different his life would be if he'd had a kid Ethan's age. They never talked about it, but he suspected Isabel hadn't wanted any. But then again, maybe she hadn't really wanted him. He didn't know if he missed her or just the idea of her. There were times when he convinced himself she only wanted him because of his success. The fact she left so quickly when everything fell apart only gave a little more credence to the idea, but they'd had some good times too.

He finished his water then put the glass back in its place on the counter. The screaming children had drained him, and he thought the naptime Rachel kept mentioning sounded just about perfect. He was an adult; he was allowed naps if he liked.

Jasper followed him into the bedroom and jumped up beside him when he sat down. The fluffy cat never passed up a chance to curl into a ball on his chest. The purring tickled him, but they eventually settled in for a nice nap.

He gave Jasper a good scratch behind the ears as he tried to think up ideas of what he could do going forward. He didn't think he could handle trying to do the whole restaurant thing again, not so soon, anyway. That meant he'd need something else to tide him over while he figured everything out. He had a bit in his savings, but he didn't want to deplete it if he could help it, at least not until the insurance company sent him his check.

Working fast food was out; so were other restaurants. That left something like catering, which he had a little experience in, or maybe he'd just give up on cooking altogether. It no longer liberated him the way it had before, and his passion for food had died along with his future. Maybe Rachel's husband could get him a job down at the marina, but the thought of being around so many people sounded daunting.

Trying to figure out his life left him mentally fatigued, but it took a good half hour before he shut his brain down enough to where he thought he could sleep. Just when he started to drift off, Jasper reared up with a dreadful hiss, claws digging into his skin like hot knives.

"Dammit, Jasper, what is with you?" he asked, full of fright from being on the edge of consciousness when roused. He jolted up, heart in his throat. The sudden movement sent Jasper tumbling to the floor. "You keep scaring me half to death, man. Not. Cool. But, heh, it's a good thing cats always land on their feet." Jasper didn't seem very interested in listening, instead choosing to run under the bed as he flicked the tip of his tail.

Casey let out a tired sigh and fell back. He tried very hard not to think about what Rachel had said about the house, but it proved difficult.

She'd planted the seed, and he had started to fixate on it. "Idiot." He was being ridiculous, he knew that, and he partially convinced himself that Rachel made the whole thing up so he would move in with her and her family. She'd offered, but he'd declined. "You're just projecting," he told himself.

But the loud crash that came from the other room had him close to rethinking that.

Chapter Four
More Sensitive Than Humans

MYLES SPENT the next few weeks shuffling around aimlessly. His best guess put him at three weeks PD—or past death, which he refused to dwell on—though he had no real concept of time. The days felt shorter, and he would often look up and realize the sun had "jumped" positions in the sky. He'd counted twenty-three sunrises and twenty-four sunsets, but who knew how many days had gone by before he woke up on the beach.

He still had no memory of how he got there, but he figured he drowned because he didn't remember anything other than the riptide forming under him before he woke up in the Between. He'd noticed a few other occurrences of them along the coastline since he spent most of his time walking the beach, but he had a limit on where he could go. By his calculations, he had a good half-mile radius from the house to explore. Even a few steps beyond that put him back at the spot where he woke up.

And by explore, he meant he mostly sulked around, yelling at people in hopes that someone might hear him. He punched several people, or tried to rather, but his fist went right through their heads. He ended up falling on his face a few times, which thankfully no one witnessed. At first he feared he might hurt someone, but once he realized that was impossible, he took out his frustrations on unsuspecting and blissfully unaware bystanders.

That got old quick.

He felt no pain, not even when one of the neighbors drove through him with a car, which came as the only good thing about his current "condition." Every time people or objects passed through him, he felt tingly, almost like a strong breeze had gusted by. After the car incident, he decided to test his immortality by sitting on the ocean floor for a while. As it turned out, he didn't have to worry about coming up for air—or sharks. He didn't get hunger pains either, so he didn't need food or water.

Myles spent his days contemplating life, the irony of which was not lost on him. He considered himself the luckiest man alive to have died so close to the thing he loved the most, but then there was the whole dead thing, so that kind of negated the "alive" part.

No one told him death would be so boring. It wasn't bad overall, but the isolation sucked. He missed James terribly, and he missed interacting with people. He snuck into the neighbors' houses whenever he wanted, not to spy but to just sit on the couch and watch television in an attempt to feel normal. Marco from next door liked soccer. Myles didn't care for it, but it helped cut down on his boredom.

He liked sitting around and listening to Marco and his wife, Janet, talk about their day. Mundane things like what they wanted for dinner and even little arguments about Janet leaving wet towels on the floor excited him. Not being able to participate in the conversations, especially the ones that held his interest, frustrated him, but he had no other option.

The only person he interacted with was Joe, and that only happened on random occasions that lasted from several minutes to what felt like a few hours. Myles never knew when he'd pop in either. Joe didn't have many answers to any of the questions he was desperate to ask, but at least he had someone to talk to, someone he loved and missed who could see and hear him and acknowledge his presence.

"Hey, kiddo," he said in greeting, usually appearing behind Myles and scaring him. He had a feeling his uncle did it on purpose, judging by the wicked smile he wore when Myles turned around.

"Okay, that is just not fair. I'm a ghost and I can't scare people, but you keep giving me terrible frights every time you stop by," Myles said with a pout when Joe caught him off guard one morning.

Joe grinned even wider as he laughed. "I'd say I was sorry, but neither of us would believe it."

"It's been a month, Joe... I think. I've been stuck in this boring hellhole for a whole month. When can I go with you?"

"Son, I assure you this is not a hellhole. That place is hot, from what I hear, but the rest I can't answer. It's not my place, and I really don't know."

Myles groaned as he dropped down to sit in the sand. "I don't know why I'm here, I don't know how long I'll be here, I can't leave, I can't follow you to—what—the Beyond? What's the point of all this? I was a good person, I…." He brought his knees up to his chest and wrapped his arms around his legs, hiding his head as he did his best to hold back the anguish bubbling up to the surface.

He felt Joe sit down beside him and loop his arm around his shoulder. "It happened for a reason, but that reason hasn't been made clear yet. It will. You just have to be patient."

"I'm all alone here. I'm frustrated, and I'm scared that I'll never be able to leave, and I have no one but you. I've never had anyone but you. But just like when I was alive, you left me. You leave me every time. You keep leaving me, and I'm… why? Why did this happen to me?"

"You know what they say about animals? They're more sensitive than humans," Joe said. And with that, he disappeared.

Myles let out a tortured roar steeped in anger and bitterness, then sat there for a while staring out into the ocean. Why did Joe have to be so damn cryptic all the time?

IT TOOK days before Myles realized what Joe had meant. Mini, the Pomeranian from next door, came running up to him one morning barking her little heart out, and it scared the shit out of him. The yappy little thing must have spotted him walking down the beach and broke loose from her leash. On instinct, Myles went running into the ocean to get away from the bitch, but she kept barking at him until the old lady came and dragged her away.

One time he could dismiss as a fluke, but the next day he'd been out front heckling Eli the mailman when it happened again. Myles made a habit of following Eli around on his route after he thought Eli had heard him yelling at him one day. The old woman—Jean Walton, he deduced from reading her mail—took her dog out for a walk just as they started up her walkway, and as soon as Mini saw him, she went into hysterics. Mrs. Walton and Eli both thought Mini was barking at him, but Myles knew the truth.

He had always liked dogs, but boredom led to desperation, and he took any opportunity that presented itself to interact with the living, no matter what form. Antagonizing a poor little thing might have been a dick move, but he really didn't care at the moment. It wasn't like he kicked the dog, just barked and growled back at her. After he realized Mini could see him, he sought out other dogs, though for whatever reason, Mini seemed the most sensitive to him.

But this newfound ability didn't stop with dogs. One evening as he sat on the beach, he noticed a crab meandering around his foot. He stood up and moved to put his foot in the crustacean's intended path, and the crab moved around him again. He repeated the experiment several more times until the crab had enough and snapped a claw at him. It tickled.

Next came an incident involving a seagull. He had leaned against the railing on the deck to watch the sunset one night when the gull flew down and landed beside him. Myles cooed at it for a few seconds, but he must've scared it, because it took off, leaving a nice pile of poop behind. He even swam in the ocean for a bit with a green sea turtle that seemed to like him. Then he got too far out and ended up on the beach. That had upset him.

On the upside, slipping in and out of people's houses, listening in on conversations, kept him entertained. Then one night, as he sat at Marco and Janet's kitchen counter while they ate dinner, the topic of his death came up.

"I can't believe they cleared the boyfriend," Janet said before stuffing a forkful of lettuce into her mouth.

Marco finished chewing his bite before replying. "What boyfriend?"

"The boyfriend of that surfer, the one who drowned," she scoffed, shaking her head like it couldn't have been more obvious.

That had Myles perking up. He kind of figured he'd drowned, but he didn't understand how. He'd always felt at home in the water. For it to take him out like that had him confused.

"I was sure foul play was involved," Janet continued.

"Babe, let it go."

"How can I let it go? I know what I saw, and there were three people out there that day, not two," she said, her stern tone making her husband roll his eyes.

"You said it yourself. You were just confused. The boyfriend said he got caught in a riptide. Those happen a lot around here this time of year," Marco reasoned as he cut into a piece of meat.

"He was a surfer, which means he was a strong swimmer. All I am saying is that it's possible the boyfriend had something to do with it."

Janet's words felt like a punch to the gut. Was she implying James had something to do with his death? Because Myles didn't know how to process that kind of information. He shook his head at the absurdity of it all. They were in love; he was going to propose.

Marco sighed. "Stranger things have happened."

He couldn't listen to any more accusations, so he ran through the wall and took off toward the beach. The sun had started to set, the sky an angry red that directly reflected his mood. He spent the whole night under the stars as he tried to rationalize what he'd heard. Janet hadn't been there; she didn't know. The only problem was neither did he. James would, though; he'd clear everything up. All he had to do was find a way to get to him.

After that night, he overheard many different theories about what had happened to him. One had him dismembered by his ax-wielding murderous boyfriend, another had him faking his own death to collect the insurance money, and a father scared his son with a story about him getting eaten by a shark. His favorite story had him falling in love with a mermaid, and after having had enough of life on land, he'd decided to join her in the sea. He heard that one from a little girl who obviously watched too many Disney movies.

The town had never seen a tragedy of that magnitude, so everyone had an opinion on his death. That was another reason he followed Eli around. He could only go a few houses down, but everyone liked to stop and talk to the mailman. They didn't just talk about his death, though. It turned out the neighborhood was a hotbed of juicy gossip.

He had soon discovered that everyone referred to Mrs. Walton as Mrs. Grouch behind her back, and they all speculated as to the reason for her perpetually sour mood. Mr. Jones down the street had a younger woman on the side. The Jenkins family were having another baby, but they didn't know who the father was since Mrs. Jenkins got pregnant while they were separated, which was why they went back to couple's counseling.

Myles didn't like to pry into other people's business, but for lack of anything better to do, he took his entertainment where he could get it.

He spent most of his time on the beach, but when not outside or at someone else's house, he lounged around the empty beach house. There was an eerie quiet about it, which he found quite ironic since he was essentially haunting the place. He had trouble wrapping his head around being the haunter, but it wasn't until he came back from a stroll one afternoon and found a stranger lying on his bed that he realized he was probably going to be the antagonist of this guy's very own ghost story.

It took a moment for the shock to wear off, but once he got over his initial surprise, he asked, "Who the hell are you?" He knew he wouldn't get an answer, but then he saw the cat curled up on the invader's chest, ears perked up and his yellow eyes locked on Myles's. That was his in. "Hey, cat, tell your master to go take a flying leap off a short pier!"

Having never been a ghost before, he didn't know the procedure of how a specter went about haunting, but luckily the cat picked up on his presence. Myles started yelling nonsense and waving his arms around. When that didn't do much, he swatted at it, causing the cat to hiss its displeasure. The man on the bed didn't seem to pay much attention, though.

Frustrated at his ineffectiveness, he stormed out of the room. He knew the house was a rental, and he'd feared someone would show up someday, but after a month without any tenants, he grew used to being alone. He assumed the fact that he'd died while staying in it would scare off potential renters, but if he wanted the place to himself, he might have to do the scaring.

He went into the living room and yelled again as he tried to think of ways ghosts haunted houses in movies or television, though he had no idea if that kind of stuff would even work. Since the television was off and there wasn't a piano for him to attempt to play with, he decided to go into the kitchen. He remembered watching a show about ghost hunters late one night, and the poltergeist liked to bang the kitchen cabinets.

Either he didn't have enough strength or the program was a fake because every time he reached for the knobs, his hands went right through the doors. His anger and annoyance mounted the harder he tried. He had spent weeks alone in the house—he might as well have claimed it—and now some stranger thought they could roll up off the street and sleep in his bed. Well, he wasn't having it.

He did everything he could think of to make noise, but nothing worked. Eventually he gave up and went back to antagonizing the cat. He had a smidgen of success at that and spent a lot of time over the next few days teasing it. He felt bad about it, but he wanted them out of his house, dammit! He'd claimed it in death, and he didn't want strangers waltzing in uninvited and taking over his territory, the only sliver of existence he had.

When the sniveling kids arrived, it pushed his anger level through the roof. He liked kids, he really did, but if the cat could sense him, then maybe they could too.

He started making faces at the baby, sticking his tongue out and scrunching up his face, but that seemed to make him laugh. Then he started growling at him, trying to scare the tot with hissing and yelling. That worked better, and after a while he knew the baby had started to get upset. Which made Myles feel like a huge jerk when the crying began.

"Congratulations, Myles. You haunted a child," he chided himself. The good news was the kids left after that. The bad news, the man did not.

He learned a few things about his guest that day. The guy's name was Casey, which he imperceptibly mocked him about; his girlfriend had just dumped him, which Myles also mocked him about; and he had decided to stay indefinitely, which made Myles glare daggers at him that he wished more than anything Casey could see. It looked like he was stuck in a strange house with a roommate who couldn't even see him.

His death just kept getting worse, and Myles grew closer to the end of his metaphorical rope.

When the invader came back into the house after helping his sister put the kids in the car, Myles followed him to the bedroom. He paced for a while, thinking of what else he could do, but when nothing came to him, he teased Jasper some more. He must've gotten better at that because soon the cat jumped off the bed to hide under it. Unfortunately, Casey ignored him like usual.

He grew tired of that after a while and went into the kitchen to try to make some sort of racket. Anger welled up inside of him, and he did his best to channel it, everything that happened to him over the past month—his death, his reawakening in the afterlife, the fact he couldn't leave, the possibility James had murdered him, everything—and put all his energy into kicking the cabinet.

Lo and behold, his foot made a sound instead of going through like it normally did. He just hoped Casey had heard the loud thwack. Building on that momentum, he took a few deep breaths and then tried to pick up the glass on the island, the one Casey kept there all the time. The first attempt was unsuccessful, but he reared back and gave it everything he had as he swiped his hand forward over the marble countertop.

Not only did the glass move, but it also flew across the kitchen and hit a cabinet before breaking into shards on the cream-colored tiles. He did it! He moved a glass and kicked a cabinet. He made contact with objects in the real world, which meant he had officially graduated to a ghost haunting a house.

He did a little happy dance before leaning up against the cabinet to wait for Casey, because there was no way that crash went unheard. Myles crossed his arms and twisted his lips into an impish grin because things were about to get a whole lot more interesting.

CHAPTER FIVE
TALKING TO MYSELF

JASPER'S ANGRY growl rang out from under the bed when Casey got up to investigate the source of the crash. He padded across the wood floor and stuck his head into the living room. "Hello?" Why he asked that, he didn't know. The house sat empty save for him and Jasper, and a quick look around confirmed it. The only sign of movement came from the curtains in the living room as they rustled in the gentle breeze. "Just the wind," he told himself.

Casey initially thought a gust of wind had knocked something off the wall or one of the tables. He had several windows open to enjoy the beautiful trade winds, so it seemed like the most plausible explanation. After a quick scan of the living room, everything appeared in order. He checked the windows for signs of breakage, but they were all intact. Sighing, he looked toward the kitchen, and that's when he noticed the glass had disappeared from the island.

He swallowed and tried to calm his heartbeat as he inched his way into the kitchen. Once he rounded the island, he saw the glass lying on the floor in pieces. "There's a reasonable explanation," he told himself. There had to be. Maybe a rat had knocked it off. He hoped not, because he didn't have much faith in Jasper catching a rodent. He and Garfield shared too many traits in that regard.

But then he remembered what Rachel had said about the surfer dying in the bay. He didn't believe in ghosts, but he didn't see any harm in humoring himself. "Hello?" he asked again, his voice calm and quiet. "If you can hear me, give me a sign." He waited a moment, but when he heard nothing he scoffed at himself. "You're an idiot."

He went over to the pantry to get a broom and dustpan to sweep up the glass. Just as he turned his back, another thud came from behind him. He spun around as his heart leaped up into his throat, but there was no one there. Without thinking, he stormed over to the cabinet and yanked it open, only to discover a few canned goods that looked like they'd been around since the fifties.

He didn't realize he'd walked through the mess in his haste to investigate until he slammed the door. "Shit!" he grunted when the sharp pain from a shard of glass registered in his frazzled brain. He bent over and dug out the chunk, blood oozing from the wound but relieving most of the sting. He hobbled toward the counter to grab some paper towels and pressed them to his heel to stem the bleeding.

One minute he was standing there on one foot with his ankle crossed over his knee, and the next he'd fallen flat on his ass. "What the fuck was that?"

Okay, maybe he did believe in ghosts after all, because as sure as starfish regrew limbs, it felt like someone had tackled him to the ground. "I didn't do a damn thing to you, you invisible bastard. I'm going crazy, aren't I? Talking to myself? Hearing things?" He ran a hand over his face as he sat there with his back against the cabinet, trying to control his breathing.

He nursed his foot as he kept his eyes peeled for anything out of the ordinary. Psyching himself out wouldn't help him. He'd just lost his balance, nothing to worry about. His ankle rolled and he fell over. That sort of thing happened all the time. But why did the hairs on the back of his neck stand up as the feeling of being watched settled over him like a wet blanket?

"Okay, I'm losing my mind."

His body started to feel warm as his vision narrowed. He knew he'd slip into a panic attack soon if he didn't calm himself. He closed his eyes and began counting by eights, a trick his therapist taught him to use if he felt overwhelmed. By the time he got to two hundred, he felt a little better, but just as he went to stand, his medicine bottle flew off the counter and whacked him right on the forehead.

"Fine, you win, you lunatic. I'm just going to get my cat and go," he said, making sure to project his voice. He didn't know if ghosts— or figments of his imagination—could hear him or not. Damn, he had nowhere to go. He didn't want Rachel thinking he was crazy, even though he had no way of arguing that point at the moment. Maybe the fire had screwed up his head more than he originally thought.

Using the counter for assistance, he hauled himself up, then limped into the bedroom, all the while keeping a lookout for flying projectiles.

He had to coax Jasper out from under the bed but got him into his carrier with little effort. Casey wasn't sure if Jasper sensed the same weird feeling of being watched as he did, but the cat seemed just as ready to get the hell out of there.

He hurried to put on his shoes and headed for the front door, not even bothering to lock it on his way out. His heel still bled and stung with every step, but he made it to the car and slipped in, depositing Jasper in the passenger seat before struggling to jab the keys in the ignition. When he turned around, he nearly jumped five feet in the air.

Mrs. Walton had snuck up on him and now stood beside the car with her dog in her arms and a scowl on her wrinkled face.

"Christ!" Casey clutched his chest and forced himself to calm down all over again. This was just not his day. Or his year.

"Vacation over?" she asked, her voice a low grumble.

"Just, uh, going to see my sister for a while."

"With your cat?"

Before he could answer or tell her to mind her own business, Mini started barking at the house. "I would love to stay and chat, but my sister is expecting me," Casey said. He forced a smile and pulled the door shut, turning the engine on and putting it into reverse as quick as humanly possible. He just had to go. The string of unexplainable events had activated his fight-or-flight response, and he'd already made his choice.

He looked out the window and watched as Mrs. Walton set Mini down and let go of the leash. The dog ran up to the door and barked at it as she ran in circles, but he saw nothing. He faced forward and squealed his tires as he tore off down the street, his mind racing after having his first encounter with something he couldn't explain.

His hands shook when he pulled into the first gas station he came to. He needed a moment to compose himself after the ordeal, a chance to come down off the adrenaline high. Glad he had thought to grab his phone along with his wallet, he dug his cell out of his pocket and punched in his password so he could call his sister. He had to start over a few times, the tremors crippling his body too severe for him to press the right buttons.

"Hey, it's me," he said when Rachel picked up. It had rung four times, and he feared she wouldn't answer at all. "I was thinking that me and Jasper would come over for dinner tonight. I know it's kind of last-minute, but I thought I could maybe bring some pizza or something and we could watch movies." God, he hoped he didn't sound too desperate.

"Wow, Case. I figured you'd had enough of us for one day," Rachel replied.

Casey huffed out a dry laugh. "Gotta make up for lost time, I suppose."

Rachel sighed, and his heart dropped. He wouldn't blame her if she declined. She had three kids and a husband to consider. He was just the sixth wheel. "You know I'd love for you to spend more time with the kids, but tonight isn't really a good night." She took a long pause before she continued. "Is everything all right?"

"Yeah, just… maybe tomorrow, then."

"I'll let you know. It's hard planning around kids."

Casey heard yelling in the background and knew he needed to let her go, then devise a plan B. "I should let you get back to them."

"Thanks, yeah, maybe tomorrow. I know Gary would love to catch up."

He grunted at that. Gary was never a fan of his, nor he of Gary's. They butted heads more often than not. He said a quick good-bye, not wanting to drag out the awkward tension that had worked its way into the conversation, and then sat there for a few minutes wondering what to do next. His rumbling stomach decided for him.

A string of mom-and-pop restaurants littered the streets leading downtown, so he pointed the car in that direction and started driving. Without much thought, he pulled into the first drive-thru he came to— some hamburger joint—and ordered a cheeseburger with a large fry and a chocolate milk shake. Jasper meowed at him from the passenger seat like he was reciting his own order, so Casey added on a fish sandwich before pulling forward. They parked and ate, him breaking off pieces of fish for Jasper in between bites of his burger.

At least Casey had had the foresight to grab him on his way out the door. He hadn't wanted to leave Jasper in the house alone after their traumatic experience, and this way he had a legitimate excuse as to why he didn't go inside to eat. These days, him and the term "people person" didn't mesh well, and he tried not to think about what it meant that he'd rather eat in a car with a cat than inside with humans.

"I'm sorry, buddy. You tried to tell me there was something in the house with us and I just ignored you."

The restaurant had free Wi-Fi, so with a greasy hand, he did a search for the surfer Rachel had mentioned earlier that day. Several results popped up, and he went through them one at a time.

"Says the guy's name was Myles Taylor and he rented our house for the weekend," he said to Jasper. Or maybe he just liked talking to himself. At this point he couldn't rule out some sort of psychotic break. That happened sometimes after people's lives had fractured into pieces. "And they cleared the boyfriend of foul play. Looks like he just got caught in a riptide and was carried out to sea... poor bastard."

Why had he taken up residence in the house, though? Casey thought ghosts only appeared when the person died violently, when they got stuck between living and the afterlife. Although drowning in the ocean seemed like a pretty traumatic way to go. But he didn't believe in the afterlife or ghosts, so what did he know?

Nothing, which was why he continued his research.

The sun had set by the time his phone ran out of juice—he hadn't had the foresight to grab his charger as he fled the scene—but he didn't feel ready to go back yet. So he started the car and spent a good half hour driving around town as he got caught up in nostalgia, but he'd take anything to keep him out of that house.

He'd dreamed of leaving their sleepy little paradise all throughout high school. Eventually he did and made a name for himself out there in the real world, one he'd loved. He'd come back a broken-down man with his life in shambles and no idea how to fix it. The more he tried to get it back on track, the more he felt like he was sinking in quicksand.

Now a bizarre thing he couldn't quite comprehend had happened in his kitchen, and he didn't know how to proceed. But he couldn't worry about the big picture when he needed to figure out where he was going to stay for the night. He thought about a hotel, but he didn't want to waste money on one. He passed a church and thought about contacting a priest about doing an exorcism, but he decided to keep that as his trump card.

He also passed a sign advertising a fortune-teller. He wondered if she did readings. How exactly did one go about setting up a séance? Then he passed a psychiatrist's office. That sounded more appropriate. Maybe he needed some stronger medication. He'd had a panic attack in the kitchen, and his therapist had told him that hallucinations were possible with an episode. He just never thought it would happen to him.

Okay, he was being ridiculous. Ghosts didn't exist.

With a determined nod, he turned the car around and headed back toward the rental. He had no other option at that point but to suck it up. Jasper didn't appreciate being crammed in the cage again after the long trip they had taken two days before, and he didn't want the little guy to have to suffer any longer. Then again, the cat did appear to be more perceptive about whatever happened, unless he'd imagined that too.

He pulled up in the driveway and turned off the car. *If* a ghost was haunting the house, he had no way of knowing if the spirit belonged to the surfer or someone else. He also had no way of communicating with it… him… them… and didn't know if it would murder him in his sleep. The entity already had one injury to its name, so anything was possible.

He didn't need anything else to add to his misery. First thing in the morning, he'd call the owner and file a complaint.

It took several deep breaths and a long pep talk before he made it out of the car. He got Jasper out, making sure to close both doors quietly. He didn't want to alert the ghost to his presence any earlier than he had to. Of course it was possible the ghost had already heard him pull up. He really needed to do some more research on communicating with the dead to figure out how all of that worked.

Where exactly did this newfound interest in the dead come from, a freak kitchen accident? He was a chef—a former chef—who had trouble making toast without having a mental breakdown, so of course the incident happened in the one room he already had trouble setting foot in. Where the hell had his life gone so wrong?

He took slow, deliberate steps to the front door, now glad that he hadn't bothered locking it. He held his breath as he twisted the knob and pushed the door open, the pitch black only freaking him out a little. Why did he come back? If he ended up getting carved to pieces by something supernatural, he was going to be pissed.

"Hello?" he croaked, turning on the closest lamp and setting Jasper down. His fingers trembled at his sides, so he stuffed them in his pockets. "I'm not gonna hurt you, and uh, I'm just going to forget that you broke a glass and knocked me over… and for the record, I don't believe in ghosts."

Apparently he chose the wrong words, because a bang came from the kitchen.

"Okay, maybe I should believe in you. Maybe I should say 'I didn't,' but okay, look, man, I don't know what I'm doing here. I've had a very bad couple of months, and the last thing I need is some asshole ghost trying to kill me."

That got him another thud.

"I'm… what do you want? Should I call a priest? I don't know what to do." Casey was at a loss. He'd stumbled into unknown territory. "I have nowhere to go. Just leave me alone for the night and I'll go first thing in the morning. Can I sweep up the glass without you tackling me?"

He assumed the silence meant yes.

"Thanks."

Casey slinked toward the kitchen, turning on every light he passed, and went over to retrieve the broom. He drew out each cautious movement, like one would do if approaching a timid animal. He tried his best not to come off as threatening, although he didn't know how anyone could threaten a ghost. That wasn't true. He'd done it with talk of an exorcism a few minutes ago.

"Just going to sweep this up and I'll be out of your way. Is that okay?"

Silence.

"Okay, and since we're talking and all… have you been harassing my cat?"

CHAPTER SIX
THE CRAZY ONE

MYLES TRANSFORMED into a ball of fury when Casey came out of the bedroom. He wanted the man gone, and he vowed to do whatever he had to do to make that happen. When Casey had his back turned, he kicked the cabinet again. The man rushed over, stepping on some glass in the process. He might've been concerned under normal circumstances, but he was amped by the fact he made himself known to an actual human being for the first time.

When Casey bent over to stop his foot from bleeding, Myles took the opportunity to ram him in hopes of exorcising some of his frustrations. He honestly thought he'd go flying through him like he'd done to every other person he tried to ghost fight over the past few weeks, but for whatever reason, he made contact, their hips colliding and knocking them both on their asses.

After he got over his initial shock, Myles began to laugh. He felt exhilarated to have made some sort of contact, to be heard and acknowledged, and it prompted him to really look at his intruder for the first time, to acknowledge him as a person in return.

Myles was as gay as they came, and Casey was anything but his type. For starters, he had tons of facial hair, which Myles had a slight aversion to, but it looked good on him. Even through the ragged beard, his sharp features stood out. His full lips, a rosy hue, contrasted against the dark beard, as did his light brown eyes that reminded Myles of raw honey. Pale, olive skin appeared sunburned across a freckled nose.

Casey had a pudgy belly, and judging by his tight clothes, it must've been a recent development. Myles and James had washboard abs, but the extra pounds kind of suited Casey. In fact Myles found him quite attractive, all things considered. At six foot, Myles had a couple of inches on him, but he thought they were roughly the same age. And he knew Casey was single after having eavesdropped on his lamenting session with his sister.

An uptick in Casey's breathing put an end to Myles's observation. He'd had a few panic attacks of his own after Joe died, and he watched Casey go past scared into panic mode. He wanted to be helpful and give him his pill bottle, but when he tried, he couldn't make it budge. He heard Casey huffing behind him, so he closed his eyes and tried to concentrate. Before he knew it, he'd sent the bottle flying right into Casey's forehead.

"Shit, sorry!"

But that must've pushed Casey over the limit because he decided to leave. Myles watched as he stood and made his way into the bedroom. He followed but hung back as Casey collected his things. He'd accomplished his goal, but why did it make him feel like such a jerk? He'd haunted a baby and a defenseless cat, though he thought he had good reason, and now he'd frightened the only human he'd made contact with.

On the other hand, he was dead and couldn't leave the damn house, so as far as he was concerned, the house belonged to him. If he wanted to be alone in his misery, he felt entitled to it. Is that what made evil spirits so vengeful, anger over having died?

Just to make sure Casey left, he walked him out to his car. Nosy Mrs. Walton must have seen Casey packing up because she dragged her little yapper outside at the same time.

He waited for Casey to pull the car out of the driveway before going back inside. Mini had corralled him onto the porch, but he didn't pay much attention to her barking anymore. He'd had fun at first, winding her up, but now he felt ashamed of himself for teasing her and the cat. Believe it or not, he liked animals.

The house sat quiet after the living inhabitants left. He had a feeling of triumph over driving them out until the sun went down. Then he started to wonder if he'd made a mistake chasing Casey away. They had made contact; he'd touched him. Casey had heard the noise he made and helped him overcome his first hurdle. And what did he do in lieu of a thank-you? He sent him packing.

As if summoned by his brooding, Joe popped in for a visit. "Hey, kiddo."

His lips pursed as he let go a heavy sigh. "Hey, Joe," he said, and so what if he wore a pout?

Joe took a look around at the mess, then looked back at Myles. "What happened here?"

Myles furrowed his brow as he thought about how to reply. "I... I'm not sure, really. I got pissed off and ended up breaking a glass. Then I tackled the guy who moved in."

"Oh," Joe replied, and it confused Myles as to why he appeared so casual about the news.

"I touched another living being, Joe, for the first time in almost a month, and all you can say is 'Oh'? What about 'Wow, that's amazing' or 'Congratulations, what did it feel like?'"

"Why are you sulking?"

"I'm sulking because I don't know what I'm doing here and you won't help me," he whined. "Why can't I go with you? I'm ready. Take me to the Beyond. I hate it here. Someone took over the house I'm tied to, and I am all alone."

"Have you thought of the possibility that your purpose, the reason you're still here, might have nothing to do with you?"

Myles glowered at him for a moment, because he hadn't. He'd heard stories of ghosts hanging around to take care of unfinished business, but he couldn't think of anything he had to do other than contact James. He surveyed the damage—the broken glass, the blood trail Casey had left behind—and sighed again. Even if he had unfinished business, by the looks of things, he'd just make it worse.

"You do know that what you just said literally makes no sense?" When Joe didn't answer him, he looked back over to where he'd been standing. "And of course you disappeared." He shook his head and went on with his sulking.

MYLES NOTICED the headlights of a car about two hours later, according to the clock on the microwave. He felt relieved that Casey had come back. His guilt had started to eat away at his conscience. He didn't know how to apologize, though, or if he could still communicate with him, but he wanted to try. And he was willing to be a little nicer about it.

Casey asked him some questions, and he did the only thing he could think of to answer. He kicked the cabinet for no and stayed silent for a yes. He didn't know if Casey would pick up on it, but if he did, they'd have some sort of system sorted out. He never thought about how hard communicating without words or sight could be.

He watched Casey clean up the glass that he broke. He swept it up into a dustpan and threw it in the trash. Then he got a new glass out and filled it with water to take one of the pills from the bottle Myles had been nice enough to throw at him earlier. He'd never heard of lorazepam before, but he'd seen Casey take one when he hyperventilated the other day. Damn, he really was a jerk.

"I'm Casey, by the way. In case you didn't know."

"I'm Myles, but you can't hear me, so now who's the crazy one talking to himself?"

"That's Jasper," Casey said, nodding to the cat, who had perched on the back of the couch to watch them both. "I think you might be Myles? Knock if that's right."

"Way to mess up the system. A knock is supposed to mean no," Myles replied, rolling his eyes. But he obliged and kicked the cabinet.

Casey laughed, but it had no humor in it. He looked like he was in total disbelief, and Myles couldn't blame him. He remembered Casey saying he didn't believe in ghosts, but he hadn't either... until he'd woken up as one.

"Okay, do you know you're dead?" Casey asked.

"Well, yeah. It's kind of obvious." Another kick.

"Are you here to hurt me?"

"No," he scoffed. "I was just mad... and you can't hear me." He really wished he could write or something, because this thud/no thud system didn't lend itself well to meaningful conversations.

"Okay, I'm going to take that as a good sign. Do you want me to leave? I know this is your house, but I was just renting it while I figure out what to do with my life. Because I'm losing my mind just like I lost everything else."

Myles watched him slump against the counter. Casey looked worse off than he did, but he could only speculate on that because he had no idea how he looked. "You're preaching to the choir. I lost my life."

"Maybe that was too much. I'm sure you don't give a fuck about the guy who you think is squatting in your house—" *Thud.* "—but can I just stay the night?"

"I haven't tackled you yet," Myles said as he kicked the cabinet.

"Thank you... sorry, this is kind of tripping me out... look, I don't know what happened to you or why you're here, but I just want to get some sleep. I've had a long day, I'm tired, but my cat is freaking me out because he's following you with his eyes, I'm assuming, and I just need to lay down…. Maybe we can 'talk' in the morning?"

It was probably best to let Casey sleep. For the first time since he'd woken up on the beach, Myles felt a little tired himself. He didn't really sleep anymore—his sleep state felt more like a resting trance. He had some awareness of everything happening around him, but it was hazy.

"Is that a yes?"

Myles kicked the cabinet, which had already gotten to the point of annoying. That night he slept in the guest room. And he wasn't too happy about it either; he missed his ocean view.

THE NEXT day he and Casey did a little more "talking" over breakfast. The conversation consisted of yes or no questions about breakfast food, and he hated that he couldn't ask anything back. He did have some fun with Casey when he bumped him while he poured his morning coffee. He spilled it on his foot, the uninjured one. Myles hadn't intended to scald him. He just wanted to see if he could still make contact with him.

"I'm going to take a shower, and then if you want me to go, I'll go, but I'll need to figure out where I'm going to stay first. Is that okay?"

Myles rapped his knuckles on the table, and that's when it hit him: Morse code. He couldn't remember if it went long, long, long, short, short, short, long, long, long, or the other way around, but he just started tapping out the rhythm and hoped Casey could figure it out. He didn't know anything other than SOS, but he'd learn it if he had to.

"Is that… Morse code?"

Thud.

"I don't know it. Do you?"

Silence.

"Hold on!"

Casey ran to the office and grabbed his laptop before returning to the kitchen table. A minute later they had the alphabet in Morse code pulled up on the screen. And the first thing Myles spelled out was *thank fuck*.

Next came a series of disjointed words: *dead, stuck, can't leave, alone.*

It took a while for Casey to decode and jot down each letter, but Myles considered it progress. They could make it work. It had him elated that Casey could understand him, even if they had to go a letter at a time.

"Do you know what happened to you?" Casey asked.

No remember

Casey's face fell. "I read about that…. I'm sorry you died."

Me too Myles slowly replied. He had to wait until Casey decoded each letter before moving on, but he had nowhere else he had to be.

"You were with your boyfriend, right?"

Yes

"That must be rough on you. My girlfriend left me, and I thought that I hit rock bottom, thought I was done, but here I am sitting in a strange kitchen communing with a ghost."

Call James

"You want me to call him? And, I mean, do you think he would believe me? Hell, I don't even believe this is happening," Casey said, running his hands through his dark hair. "I just need some time to process this, maybe call my shrink."

Myles reared back his head and groaned when Casey got up from the table. He paced awhile, then went into the bedroom. Myles followed him but decided to give him some privacy when he went into the bathroom. The loud "Don't follow me" was kind of a deterrent. Jasper had followed them as well and sat down to meow at the bathroom door.

"Look, I think we got off to a rough start. I said some things. You hissed some things. Why don't we just forget about the whole thing and call it a truce," Myles said to the cat.

Jasper flicked his tail in what Myles thought was annoyance, but he figured he deserved that.

Casey came out of the bathroom ten minutes later dressed in a pair of too-tight jeans and a T-shirt that framed his shoulders rather well but highlighted the rolls around his belly. "I'm going to the store and maybe to see my sister. Can I trust you not to hurt my cat while I'm gone?" His tone sounded almost teasing, but they weren't quite there yet.

Myles rolled his eyes as he knocked *yes* on the dresser. "You know you really don't have to yell."

CHAPTER SEVEN
FAULTY WIRING

CASEY GRABBED his keys and fully charged phone, then headed to the car. He had reservations about leaving Jasper in the house with Myles's spirit, but he couldn't take him along just to leave him in the car while he ran around town. Jasper would have to fend for himself for a few hours. He had no reason to believe Myles wouldn't keep his word. He'd just have to have a little faith.

He waved to Mrs. Walton as he got in the car. She'd come out to spy on him no doubt and glowered back. Why had he decided to stay in this hellhole?

As his first act of business, he pulled out his phone to call his psychiatrist back home. Dr. Patel began treating him when Cinder burned and had given him his private cell phone number to use in case of emergencies. He had almost called last night, but he thought the doc would've referred him to a hospital, and he wasn't ready to commit himself just yet.

Dr. Patel sounded concerned when he told him about the strange occurrences he'd witnessed and his "conversations" with the ghost in his rental house. He reminded Casey that one of the side effects of his medicine was hallucinations, and if they persisted, they might have to change his meds. The conversation made him feel better. Maybe he hadn't gone completely crazy.

Casey pointed his car in the direction of the closest McDonald's to get a cup of coffee while Dr. Patel made some calls. He had tried to talk him out of making a fuss over him, but the doctor insisted he see someone that morning. Casey relented. Seeing a shrink beat stress eating away his problems, though he had no qualms about doing both.

Twenty minutes later, Dr. Patel called back with the name of a colleague nearby and instructions for him to head there right away. He didn't like the idea of Dr. Patel using up favors on him, but at that point he felt like he was teetering on the edge of an abyss—one false move and he'd tumble down the rabbit hole.

Twenty minutes after that, he sat down on a comfortable couch and began to recount his last twenty-four hours. When he got to the part about the Morse code, he just knew the doctor would send him to the hospital, but she turned out to be more understanding than he thought.

"So this ghost, he told you his name was Myles? The surfer who drowned recently?"

"Yeah… I mean we used Morse code."

"You said you hadn't heard anything strange until your sister mentioned him?"

"Right, well, besides the cat acting weird. Do you think I made the whole thing up?" Because he was starting to think he had.

"No, I think you believe you communicated with something or you wouldn't be here. But—"

"There's always a but," he hissed under his breath.

"It's likely you heard about this death and projected your psychosis onto it. It's a common occurrence. What I would like to do is switch out your medication and see if that helps alleviate your… for now let us call them auditory hallucinations," she said as she clicked her pen and started scribbling on a notepad.

"I want you to start taking these immediately and schedule an appointment to come back next week, sooner if you feel it's necessary. Daniel Patel and I went to med school together, and I told him I'd take excellent care of you while you're here in Land's End." She handed over the prescription and started another note, which she handed over as well. "Here's my cell phone number if you need it."

"I appreciate you seeing me on such short notice, Dr. Roberts," he said as he stood. He shook her hand and then showed himself out. She had also told him to stop drinking, but he kind of tuned her out at that point. He didn't see the necessity of it, but he'd give it a try… maybe.

The prospect of new meds had him feeling optimistic, so the whole half hour hadn't felt like a complete waste of time. He felt better about the situation and convinced himself that whatever had happened with the spirit was all in his head… until he passed the sign for the fortune-teller five minutes later. He didn't know what compelled him to stop, but he didn't think it could hurt.

He pulled into the driveway of an older house with chipped paint and dark curtains hanging over all the windows. It wasn't the kind of place he thought he'd ever venture inside of willingly, but desperate times. At least it appeared more *Addams Family* and less *House on Haunted Hill*. He climbed the steps to the porch and rang the bell before he could change his mind.

A woman of about fifty, short with long curly brown hair and rheumatic fingers, pushed open the door. She had a deep purple shawl draped over her shoulders and a knowing smirk on her thin lips. The rest of her was clad in all black, and she wore a thick layer of makeup. Her dark beady eyes regarded him for a moment before she moved and made a motion for him to come inside.

When he just stood there weighing his options and the likelihood of him making it back out the door once he went in, she stomped her foot. "Are you just going to stand there? Joe told me you were coming."

"I don't know any Joes," he said as he ran the name over in his head only to come up blank.

"Yes, but a Joe knows you."

"I think you have me confused with somebody else. I should go."

"It has to be you," the woman said as she turned to venture back into the house.

He had no idea what that meant, but something drove him to step across the threshold. The parlor looked like a scene out of a madman's lair, with bottles of different colored liquids and herbs on shelves and various other knickknacks strewn about. A few skulls littered the checkout counter—some animal in appearance, some he hoped were only human replicas—and along every wall, bookshelves sat holding books that looked at least a hundred years old.

"I'm Bobbie," the woman said as she passed through a black beaded curtain into another room. "And you would be?"

The hairs on the back of his neck stood on end, and a bone-chilling yet calming feeling enveloped him. "Casey." He walked through the beads and rolled his eyes at the crystal ball in the center of a round table covered by a black lace tablecloth. He scoffed at the thought of being lured in by all the pomp and circumstance.

"That ball is just for show," Bobbie said. "Some people prefer the spectacle, but not you."

Casey nodded and looked around some more. The room was darker than the first, and the whole place looked like it was copied and pasted right out of a cheap horror movie. "So this 'Joe' person? How exactly does he know me?"

Bobbie was running her fingers along the spines of books on a small shelf behind an ornate chair. "He doesn't, but you have a mutual acquaintance it seems… ahh." She pulled out a small hunter green book and turned to face him. "You might find this useful."

He took the book as she held it out and read the title out loud. "*Communing with the Dead and the Almost*? You can't be serious."

"There's a spirit in your house."

"It's not my house."

"No, but he is your problem."

"Listen, lady—"

"Bobbie."

"Listen, *Bobbie*. The only problem I have is the faulty wiring in my brain that has me on medication, which is making me see and hear things that can't be there. Now I don't know what kind of con you're running here, or why I even bothered entertaining the idea, but I don't need your book and I don't know anyone named Joe. So if you'll excuse me, I need to run by the pharmacy," he said, dropping the book on the table, its lightness not making the dramatic sound he had aimed for.

"He needs your help," she singsonged as he turned to storm back through the house.

"I'm the one who needs help," he shot back over his shoulder. "You're just trying to sell me a book."

"Consider it a loan."

He stopped a few feet shy of the door. She said that now, but she'd probably end up trying to sell him something eventually.

Things hadn't gone as expected after he'd left the house. He'd hoped a nice morning out would clear his head so he could work through his issues. He'd moved back home for that reason, to get away from the demons, his failures, haunting him in Los Angeles. Now a whole new set replaced them, none of which made him feel any better about the life he had in LA….

The trip to the doctor had done him wonders, but in the span of ten minutes, he had regressed and found himself in the strange house he'd noticed on his way into town. He'd visited two different places and met two different women who told him two different things, one of whom tossed out names of people he didn't know. And to top it all off, he was actually considering the offer.

"He likes the water. A bit ironic, maybe fortuitous, but he's the most at peace there," Bobbie said.

"Am I supposed to help him cross to the other side? Go to the light, find that big wave in the sky?"

"I don't know. He might have unfinished business trapping him between the two planes. This is usually the case, and it's possible he may remain stuck until he has completed it. Or he could be a guardian spirit to you or the house. These things are hard to understand from the living realm."

Casey huffed out a long, exaggerated breath. "Give me the damn book."

HE PULLED back up to the house just before lunch. His errands had taken over two hours, and all the while his anxiety had grown in regard to how Jasper fared alone. He spotted the tabby stretched out on the back of the couch as he opened the door, but Jasper jumped down to greet him, rubbing his body on Casey's legs while he took the groceries to the kitchen. He'd done his shopping while he waited for his prescription to be filled and picked up some more beer despite the advice of Dr. Roberts.

He popped a bottle open and took a long pull. The warmth of it did nothing to quench his thirst, but he was desperate for some kind of buzz. After putting away a few frozen pizzas and various other junk food items—and changing into more comfortable clothes that weren't threatening to cut off his circulation—he made himself a sandwich and grabbed a bag of chips. It was a nice day, so he decided to eat out on the deck.

He hadn't used the pool yet, or the barbecue grill in the corner, but the table next to it had gotten a lot of use. Despite having to contend with the annoying seagulls, he liked to eat on the deck. Maybe he'd gain the confidence to use the grill someday, but for now he was content to live on sandwiches, pizza, and beer.

"Myles? You around?" He shook his head at asking such a question. He didn't think it wise to entertain his hallucinations. Or to commune with the dead without much experience.

When he received no response, he felt relieved. He knew the medicine couldn't have had an effect so quickly since he'd only taken the first pill moments ago, but maybe there was something to be said for the placebo effect.

He returned his plate to the kitchen and grabbed another beer before retrieving the book off the couch, where he'd tossed it on the way in. A nap on the couch sounded tempting, but he decided to head back outside and check out the book, Jasper following on his heels. He made himself comfortable in one of the deck chairs and got two pages in before he fell asleep.

When he woke up, he could tell Myles was near. Jasper's ears flicked at the tips, his eyes fixed on the chair next to them. But more than that, Casey could *feel* him. "You shouldn't sneak up on people like that." That got him a few thuds that he scoffed at. "I don't have my cheat codes. Give me a sec." He went inside—presumably Myles followed—and sat down at the kitchen table to open his laptop.

Book

"Yeah, I...." Should he lie to a ghost? What if Myles had stowed away in his backseat all morning? "On the way to the store, I saw a sign for a fortune-teller and stopped in. She kind of threw this at me," he said as he held up the book. "It was really weird, though. She said someone named Joe said I was—"

Before he could finish, he heard the name Joe repeated several times. *Out loud.* It was almost like a low hum, and if he hadn't known what the word was, he might not have picked up on it.

"You know a Joe?"

Uncle, dead, Myles tapped out.

Casey leaned back in his chair and ran both hands through his hair, his nails scraping over his scalp. "Holy shit... this, I don't even... I heard you. I heard you say 'Joe.'" He sat back up and started flipping through the book. "Here... it says spirits can communicate more effectively when emotions are running high... which explains last night."

You help

"I don't know how. I can't even help myself right now," he said as he frowned.

James

Casey pressed the heel of his palm into one of his eyes. "As far as I know, you're still a hallucination." He flinched at the angry sounding thuds that came after. "But I got some new medicine now, and I'm going to give it a few days, and if I still hear you after that, I'll see what I can do about this James guy. Though it'll probably just get me committed. Do we have a deal?"

Fine

Good God, what kind of lunatic made deals with their imagination?

CHAPTER EIGHT
BREAKING THROUGH

CASEY HAD heard him, his voice, when he yelled Joe's name. He hadn't expected that, but the new development thrilled him. Maybe he had gotten stronger or learned how to harness his energy into communicating better, even though he had no idea how. He hoped the book the fortune-teller gave Casey would help him in some way. They spent the evening reading it. Some parts Casey would read out loud—his deep voice a welcome sound compared to the near silence Myles spent most of his time surrounded by—and some he read over Casey's shoulder.

They devoted the next couple of days to testing out some of the techniques the book suggested. They tried communicating at different times of the day. Casey heard him more clearly in the evenings and midmornings, so they did the most talking during those times. Casey heard him say Joe's name several times and also James's on occasion. He even said "Jasper" once, after Myles and the cat had made up from their rocky start.

As the week went on, Casey learned how to pick up on his presence. When Myles asked him about it, he shrugged and said he felt eyes on him when Myles came around. Casey also picked up on clues from Jasper: a flick of the tail, ears lying down, him tracking something that "wasn't there."

Oddly, he had a feeling Mrs. Walton could sense him too. Mini gave him away a lot of the time, but the times when the dog didn't try to nip at his heels, he thought he felt beady old eyes watching him. It gave him an eerie feeling, but it made him understand how Casey felt. He tried to stay away from her all the same. He also made sure to give Casey privacy when appropriate. A reputation as a perverted ghost sounded less than appealing.

Myles and Casey's conversations remained superficial at first. They stuck to topics Casey had researched. Unfortunately, they didn't find much help in the book, other than the suggestion to communicate at different times of day. They both had a good laugh when it suggested a Ouija board, but they already had a good system with the Morse code. Both had become pretty good at it over the last several days and relied on the list Casey printed out less and less.

He loved when Joe visited him. Myles hadn't believed in the afterlife, so getting to see Joe again warmed his heart more than he could've ever anticipated. He didn't offer much help, though. Myles asked him for tips when he showed up one evening during one of his and Casey's "talks," but Joe told him he was a spirit, not a ghost. Myles failed to see the difference.

Even so, he tried to introduce the two of them. The brief conversation didn't go anywhere, but at that point, they were the only two people who knew about Myles's existence—unless you counted the animals and Mrs. Walton, which he did not.

After a few days, they settled into a routine. Casey slept until nine or ten, then got up and made himself toast or toaster pastries for breakfast to go along with his morning coffee. They sat outside on the deck and talked while he ate. Myles always got a little weak afterward, for lack of a better word, and needed rest, which gave Casey time to surf the Internet. Sometimes he looked up things about the paranormal, but most of his research centered on food. Even though Myles hadn't had any hunger since he woke up on the beach, some of the pictures gave him cravings.

Once Casey woke from an afternoon nap, they'd head down to the beach. Casey sometimes talked to him because he knew Myles followed him around, but he kept that to a minimum when out of the house. He knew Casey didn't want to appear completely off his rocker, even if he still believed that himself. On occasion Myles overheard him muttering things about hallucinations and how they should've stopped by now.

Not to mention the one time he eavesdropped on Casey talking on the phone to his psychiatrist. He admitted that he still talked to his delusions, which discouraged Myles, but he knew Casey wasn't crazy, even if no one else did.

Casey drank a lot of beer, Myles observed, and some days he took longer naps instead of going down to the beach. Myles knew a thing or two about depression and certainly recognized the classic signs in Casey. He'd seen some dark days after Joe died and knew the struggles that came along with a life-altering event and the accompanying feeling of your life being over. But now that he knew death, he almost longed for those dark days.

Casey began to open up as the days went by. The more Myles learned about him, the more he sympathized with him. He knew about Casey's sister, a little about his restaurant—mostly that he didn't like to talk about it—and that he got panicky at the idea of doing any cooking. Myles understood why he thought he was losing his sanity.

As a ghost, Myles had plenty of time to think and ponder things he otherwise wouldn't have cared about, more specifically what Joe had said about his reasons for sticking around the beach house. Casey lingered in the back of his mind as a potential reason for his inability to move on, and the more he learned about how fucked-up his life had gotten, the more prominent the thought. What if he had to help Casey pull his life back together? He hoped not, because what the hell could he do in his current state?

Myles assumed he needed to get closure with James or to give James closure before he could leave, and he really hoped Casey would help with that. They'd agreed to wait a week for Casey to come to terms with his presence before contacting James, but he had all the time in the world. If closure didn't get him moving into the Beyond, then he'd have to give some more thought to the idea of helping Casey.

The possibility existed that Myles's unfinished business had no relation to either of the men. What if he had to wait for Mrs. Walton to die so he could escort her to the other side? What if his job was to watch over the house and its inhabitants indefinitely? What if he had no purpose at all and was stuck because of a clerical error? The endless list of possibilities had his head spinning, and he hated not knowing where to start. He'd been stranded in the Between without a road map, and that frustrated him more than anything else.

The uncertainty led Myles to come up with two goals for himself: to get better at communicating verbally and interacting with objects. The book said he needed to manipulate the energy around him but conveniently left out the "how to" chapter. And Casey failed to find anything written on the subject from a ghost's perspective, no *How To Haunt for Beginners* they could pick up for him.

Manipulating objects didn't come easy. He had trouble understanding how he could kick things and tap on tables one minute then travel through walls the next. He knew he swiped the glass off the table the first night he and Casey made contact as well as threw the bottle of pills at him, but anger and rage had fueled those encounters.

He tried to use anger as a way to channel his focus on objects. Every day he attempted to pick up the glass Casey left out on the table as he thought of things that pissed him off. Casey might change his mind about an exorcism if he started breaking glasses, but since he'd already had success with it once, he figured it was as good of a place to start as any.

He practiced with Casey's pill bottles too, and while his inability to pick them up left him furious, he had no success save for making contact a few times. As his frustrations mounted, he did his best to harness them, objects growing more solid against his palm with each swipe of his hand. But no matter what he did, he couldn't replicate the results of the first night.

Another goal he set for himself involved petting Jasper. The cat had become more and more comfortable and at ease around him after Myles stopped harassing him. Anytime Jasper walked by, he would reach for him, but his hand went right through every time. Jasper didn't seem to mind, though. The first few times, his orange hair stood up, but the more Myles tried, the less he reacted to it.

In complete contrast, he went out of his way to keep from touching Casey. He didn't want to push his luck with the only person he'd connected with. Sure, he could've gone next door and asked—haunted— Mrs. Walton to see if she'd take an interest in helping him out, but she seemed like the kind who would brush him off and say she didn't want to get involved.

Whether he wanted to admit it or not, he was stuck with Casey, and Casey was stuck with him for the foreseeable future. Despite their own rocky start, it pleased him that Casey hadn't decided to leave after their first encounter. Myles inadvertently injured him, but the man came back with his cat and willingly communicated with him. He wondered if the result would've differed if Casey hadn't been on medication, but it didn't matter in the end.

WILL YOU help, Myles asked after the agreed upon waiting period had ended. He didn't know if Casey would honor their informal agreement or not, but from what he knew of his living houseguest, Casey seemed like an upstanding guy. He'd had a rough time of late, but who didn't from time to time?

"I really don't know what I can do." Casey sighed as he bit into a piece of the pizza he had just removed from the oven. "H-hot."

Need help

Casey took a swig of beer after burning his tongue and thought for a moment before he replied. "How am I supposed to do that? Do you have his number? Am I just supposed to call him up and tell him I can talk to dead people? Will he even believe me? Will anyone believe me? Because if it were me, I'd hang up in my face."

Honestly, Myles didn't know. James wasn't exactly spiritual. The water and the waves had always been their place of worship. Talk of the afterlife never came up much. Myles wanted to believe something existed after death, especially after Joe died, but he sure as shit didn't believe in ghosts. He couldn't blame Casey's skepticism, nor would he blame James's, but he needed Casey to try at least.

Please

"I'll see what I can do." Casey sighed before taking another bite of his pizza. He must've burned his mouth again, and Myles couldn't help but laugh at him as he shook his head. "Don't laugh, you ass," Casey snickered. It took a moment for them both to realize he'd been heard. "Wait... I heard you laugh!"

"Can you hear me now?" Myles asked, but after a few moments, he had to revert to tapping out his reply. *Getting better*

"Yeah, maybe someday we won't need to use the code anymore."

"I'm counting on it."

MYLES BUGGED Casey every evening to help him contact James, and every evening Casey made excuses. On one hand, Myles understood that maybe he didn't want to come off as one of those phonies who came out of the woodwork after a loved one died. It was one thing to admit to a therapist that you were hearing things, but it was something else to go from not believing in the supernatural to campaigning on one's behalf.

But that didn't stop Myles from pestering him about it.

Myles needed to gain strength if he wanted to prove to Casey he hadn't made him up. He hoped manipulating something light might work better than a glass or Casey's pill bottle, so one evening, after Casey made up another lame reason why he couldn't contact James, he tried and succeeded in sweeping the Morse code paper off the table.

Casey picked it up, obviously not having realized Myles had done it. It took three more attempts before Casey caught on. "Is that you?"

Myles replied with a thud, and Casey rolled his eyes.

"Well, cut it out."

As if it was a direct challenge, Myles flung the paper off the table again, but he raised the stakes by knocking over an empty beer bottle as well. "I should have expected that. And I think you might be getting stronger."

"You think?"

"Yeah, you just knocked my bottle over—wait, did you just say 'You think?' Because I swear I heard that."

"Yes," Myles hollered as he stood up.

"You moved the chair too," Casey pointed out. "Say something else… like what's your favorite food?" Myles answered with "chicken parmesan," but Casey must not have heard him. "Nothing?"

Myles deflated. Baby steps. *Chicken parmesan*

Casey let out a sigh and slumped in his chair. "I thought we were getting somewhere. You know, one of the reasons I've been stalling is because I thought it'd be better if James could hear you when I called."

Myles conceded the point, but he wondered if he could communicate better in James's presence. James might give him more strength and determination, but the possibility remained that he wouldn't be able to communicate with him at all. Myles could end up blowing his only chance. Maybe they should wait until he had a little more control over himself, which made him want to try even harder.

Moving the paper and the beer opened the floodgates for experimenting with different objects. As his ability to interact with the real world increased, he began moving things around. He started with a watch on the dresser that Casey never wore. He also moved a few things in the bathroom, like a toothbrush to the other side of the sink, but Casey didn't seem to notice any of it. In fact, Casey remained mostly oblivious to his new game until Myles started messing with the sheets with him still in them.

After he'd realized Myles's game, Casey told him to cut it out, but Myles laughed and found something new to move out of place.

But one morning he scared them both when he reached for the sheet and grabbed Casey's ankle by mistake. Casey jolted straight up from a dead sleep, eyes going wide as he looked to Jasper, who lay stretched out on the pillow beside him. "M-Myles? Did you just do that?"

"Yeah, sorry."

"You scared the crap out of me."

He chuckled to himself. "I was reaching for the sheet."

"And grabbed my ankle?" Casey asked as he rubbed the sleep from his eyes.

"It was an accident." Myles knew Casey liked to sleep past ten, which wouldn't roll around for another three hours, but he wanted to take advantage of the fact they could communicate verbally. "Guess I'm feeling especially strong today."

"I'll say… but at least you didn't tackle me this time," Casey said with a smirk.

"Maybe next time."

"It's a nice morning."

Myles followed Casey's gaze out the door. It reminded him of the morning he died, the morning he'd planned on proposing to James. The ocean looked perfect, crisp and clear. The sun had just come up, the brightening sky still mottled in oranges and pinks. But he didn't want to think about that day, about dying. He couldn't tell for sure, but he guessed it had been about six weeks since he woke up on the beach, and he still couldn't remember the events leading up to it.

Casey sat up and stretched, the white sheet falling down his bare chest and displaying a heavy dusting of dark hair. "I could really go for some bacon."

"So could I, but—you know—*dead*."

"Yeah, sorry. Do you ever get hungry, though?"

"No. I watch you eat and wish I could have a taste from time to time. But I didn't really eat a lot of junk food. I was an athlete, and I know a lot of people don't really see surfers as athletes, but it takes a high physical fitness to ride the waves I rode. I kind of miss that too."

"I never got into surfing. I preferred sailing. The wind blowing through my hair, the feel of the boat breaking through the waves, being so far out you didn't know which direction land was. Maybe I can take my nephews one day." Casey sighed and pulled the sheet up over him. He still looked tired, and Myles decided to leave him alone.

"I'll let you go back to sleep."

"Thanks," he said before he let out a yawn and lay back down on the bed. "I think our conversations are getting longer."

Myles smiled. "Yeah, I've noticed."

God, it felt good to be heard.

CHAPTER NINE
SOMETHING SWEET

TWO WEEKS in the house and Casey finally gave in to the idea that he wasn't hallucinating. The realization came with a boost to his mood, and he went out and bought himself some bacon and eggs to cook, baby steps back into the kitchen. Unfortunately it didn't go as well as he'd hoped.

He burned the bacon, which he usually didn't mind. He liked it extra crispy, but he'd let it go too far past edible. He'd singed it, turned it to ash like he'd done to Cinder, and that set off a wave of memories flooding back in. The smell eventually got to him, and it soon reached a tipping point between the wonderful aroma of bacon and that of charred dreams. It overwhelmed him, invaded his senses like a dust cloud blocking out the light, suffocating everything under it. In an instant, it transported him back to the night when everything had fallen apart.

He managed to kill the heat on the eggs before he slumped to the ground, chest heaving as his vision blurred. His stomach lurched and the room started to spin, and he knew he should have grabbed his pills on the way down. They sat above him on the counter, but the thought of getting to his feet didn't compute. So he sat there, curling in on himself as he tried his best to get his breathing under control.

All of a sudden, something brushed his leg. He looked down to see Jasper rubbing against him, and he reached blindly to pet him, the soft fur under his fingertips anchoring him to reality. But he also felt something to his right, against his shoulder, like someone had sat down beside him. When he looked over, he saw his medicine sitting there. He took the bottle, fished out a few pills, and swallowed them dry.

"Meds," he thought he heard someone say, but his brain had shut down too much to process it.

He curled into a ball, hugging his knees to his chest as he forced himself to relax, trying his best to do the breathing and counting exercises Dr. Patel had taught him. Running his fingers through Jasper's hair worked wonders, but a sense of comfort came from what he eventually realized was Myles sitting next to him. He helped him, put the pills within his reach, and sat there beside him as he fell apart.

Casey decided then and there that he had to do something to help him.

Myles deserved to move on. The Beyond beat hanging around a house with a colossal failure. All he did these days was sleep as he gave himself over to the bottle bit by bit, just like his father had done in the end. He always feared he'd follow in his footsteps, but at least he didn't have a family to abandon along the way.

"Myles?" he asked. He never knew when he'd get an audible response, but it made him feel better when he did.

"Yeah?"

The sound of Myles's voice comforted him even more. "I'll help you with James."

"Yeah?"

Casey nodded and took a few more cleansing breaths. "Yeah. We're stuck with each other for now.... I guess I could just leave. No one would blame me for fleeing a haunted house, but I don't think you're here to hurt me. Except maybe that one time you knocked me over," he said, trying for a chuckle that sounded much too strained to be believed.

He heard Myles laugh along with him. "You deserved it."

"Maybe, but if I help you get to the other side, it might help me somehow. I don't know, that's probably selfish of me, but it couldn't hurt."

"Thank you. I appreciate you trying."

Casey felt the change in pressure when Myles got up. And he thought he saw him walk out the kitchen door onto the deck. The distortion lasted for a fraction of a second, but the door appeared to have shiny, wavy lines on it in the shape of a person, like you would see in the road on a hot day. He couldn't make out any features, only an outline, though he knew deep down it belonged to Myles.

That made him curious.

When the room stopped its pitch and roll, he got to his feet. He knew he couldn't deal with his ruined breakfast at that point, so he went to fetch his laptop from the bedroom. Dr. Roberts had suggested he not look up things about the dead surfer, and up until that moment he had obliged, but now he knew Myles's ghost haunted his kitchen. And after seeing his outline, he itched to know what he looked like.

He ran a quick Internet search and found hundreds of pictures of him, most of which were taken while he surfed. In some he looked deep in concentration, his eyes narrowed as he focused on the wave underneath him. In others he had a wide grin plastered on his rather gorgeous face that exuded happiness. It made Casey contemplate whether or not he'd ever known that kind of happiness.

Myles had bright blue eyes, he'd noticed in a few close-ups, and a chiseled jaw that looked as sharp as a blade framing plump watermelon-pink lips. His light brown hair had streaks of golden highlights from a life spent under the sun, and his body looked as ripped as they came, all six-pack abs and rolling muscles, his tan skin glistening with salt water in most of the photographs.

He looked like a damn model, picture-perfect, and to offset the near-foreign warmth creeping into his bones, Casey reminded himself the poor man had died. He didn't deny his attraction to men; it happened from time to time. He'd even dated a few back when he lived in New York. The deceased part unnerved him a little, though, but he remembered all the people still fawning over a long-since-gone Elvis and other departed actors and musicians, and it made him feel less like a perv.

Nonetheless, he moved his focus onto James. Myles had given him his phone number, but he didn't have the courage to call. What exactly would he say? "I'm not crazy, but I'm living with your dead boyfriend." He didn't think that would go over too well. He hunted around until he found an e-mail address instead. With that, he and Myles could sit down and plan out exactly what they wanted to say.

MYLES DIDN'T come back around until later that evening. Casey thought he needed some space after he'd agreed to help him reach out to James. He recognized how much of an asshole it made him to refuse in the beginning, but in his defense, he'd thought he had a few screws loose because of the whole ghost thing. He felt better now. His head had cleared, and he felt more invigorated than he had in a long time. He had a goal; he had purpose.

Dinner consisted of a sandwich and beer, one of his staple meals. It took him all day to gain the courage to go back into the kitchen to clean the dishes, but he managed. Now they sat outside enjoying the sunset while they tried to pen the e-mail to James.

It started simple enough, just a usual salutation followed by "I know this is going to sound crazy, but...." There was really no way around it. No matter what he did, he'd come off as a lunatic. To offset that, Myles came up with some very personal details to include in the e-mail in the hopes it would help to convince James.

Casey tried to think about how he'd react if Isabel died and tried to contact him. Two weeks ago he would've laughed it off, but he couldn't say the same now. He'd given in to curiosity, which convinced him to follow through with e-mailing James, even if he had to write more than one e-mail. He just hoped he wouldn't get hit with a restraining order or something to that effect.

"Is there anything else you want to add?"

No

"Okay, I'm hitting Send," Casey said, the cursor hovering over the button on the screen. Myles had worn himself out speaking. Casey knew it took a lot out of him to communicate verbally, but Casey looked forward to hearing him talk more and more.

Casey had looked up interviews of him on the web during his research and discovered Myles had a pretty sexy voice when he'd been alive: smooth and deep and not what he'd expected. But he quickly learned Myles wasn't the typical surfer dude. He went to college and got a business degree, graduating with honors. His surfing career fell into his lap when he befriended his agent in the surf shop he worked at to pay for his education. In one interview, he joked that a big sponsor only signed him because he looked kind of good in a swimsuit.

When Myles spoke to him, his voice sounded airy and raspy, but he realized that as their communication improved, more of his natural voice came through. He knew Myles had died several weeks ago and had to learn through trial and error how to communicate with him, but Casey could see his progress.

As a skeptic, ghost stories never appealed to him, but since meeting Myles, they fascinated him because he was living one.

Once he pressed the Send button on the e-mail, he leaned back in his chair to enjoy the view. The sun had started to sink into the water, and the sky burned red. Beauty abounded, and he couldn't think of anywhere else he'd rather be in the moment. Back in LA, he would've taken the view for granted. A sunset hadn't interested him in a long time, but out here he had time to appreciate the little things.

But his ringtone tore him out of the moment. He'd put his phone number in the e-mail he sent to James, but he didn't think he would've called that fast. He picked his phone up from the table and checked the

ID. "My sister," he said out loud. He couldn't always tell when Myles hung around, but better safe than sorry.

"Hey, Rach, what's up?"

"Can you be a doll and pick up the cake for Ethan's party tomorrow?" Rachel asked.

He could hear his nephews carrying on in the background and rolled his eyes. His nerves might not hold up against an afternoon with a bunch of obnoxious kids, but he did promise he'd attend. After he'd missed four prior birthdays, Rachel had insisted he show his face.

"Sure, where's it at?" he asked with a reluctant sigh.

"Are you going to be a blowhole about this?"

He laughed at that. "Blowhole?"

"When you have three children, you learn to curse creatively. So get your crab cakes in gear or I'll kick you in your starfish, understand?"

"No, not really," he said with another chuckle. "But I said I'll get the cake." He knew he could've made one better. He hadn't trained as a pastry chef, but he liked to dabble in baking from time to time to keep his skills rounded. Of course after the breakfast debacle, he didn't dare.

"Thank you. I appreciate it, Case. It'll really help me out. I'll send you the address of the bakery. And could you try to arrive thirty minutes early so we can set it up?"

"All right, ten thirty it is. I'll see you tomorrow."

"Thanks again. Have a good night."

"Night, Rachel."

He hung up the phone and decided to go inside for the night. "Come on, Jasper, let's see what's on television. Probably nothing on a Friday night, but we'll see." Casey heard a thud after that and smiled to himself. He knew Myles liked to feel included. "Fine, Myles. You can come too... but I get the final say."

Just as he thought, nothing but reruns and bad sitcoms littered the channels. They settled on some cartoon program Myles made a thud for. Casey hadn't had time to watch much television and didn't really care what they watched. The show entertained him enough to keep his interest, but he found himself nodding off after a while.

"I think I'm turning in."

He turned off the television a little after ten and went to bed, but he had trouble falling asleep. Different scenarios kept running through his head about how things with James would pan out. He didn't have much hope of being believed, but on the off chance James did come to commune with Myles, he wondered if his spirit would disappear.

Truth be told, he kind of liked having Myles all to himself like an imaginary friend. He wouldn't admit it, but he felt a little jealous at the idea of someone else communicating with his ghost. On the other hand, he hated the idea of Myles stuck in between realms when he had the power to help. Maybe next week he'd go back to Bobbie and see if she had any other books he could borrow.

After an hour or so of tossing and turning, he fell into a fitful sleep. That left him sluggish the next morning. He gave serious thought to calling his sister with an excuse, but he knew she would see right through him and call him on it. Besides, he kind of hated himself for screwing things up with her so many times and wanted to do better.

He managed to pull himself out of bed and jump in the shower after his alarm went off a second time. Myles told him he steered clear of the bathroom for privacy reasons, a fact Casey appreciated if true. But he was especially thankful that morning because he woke up with a hard-on begging for attention. He didn't know what to think about that. He hadn't had sex in several months, so he shrugged it off as a normal physiological response to his current drought.

With things taken care of in the bathroom, he got dressed and grabbed a Pop-Tart. He thought about sucking down an early morning beer, but he knew Rachel would have a fit if she even so much as smelled alcohol on his breath.

"All right, you two. I have to go to that party. Can I trust you guys to behave?"

As if to answer, Jasper let out a meow and hopped up on the couch, his favorite place to take a nap. Casey didn't know if Myles was around, but he told them both good-bye and headed out the door.

Minutes later he pulled up to the bakery where the directions had led him. It looked upscale, with a pastel color scheme and a huge display case housing all sorts of delectable creations. The place looked packed as well, but that didn't surprise him with it being a Saturday morning.

He waited in line for his number to be called and scurried up to the counter. "How can I help you this beautiful morning?" the man behind the counter asked with a warm, infectious smile. Casey couldn't help but smile back.

"Yeah, I'm here to pick up a birthday cake for Rachel Dorey. I hear it has dinosaurs on it."

"Ah yes, I decorated that one myself," the man replied.

Casey glanced down at the name tag that read *Matt*. "I'm sure it's great, then."

Matt laughed. "I don't like to brag, but I make a mean dinosaur cake. Let me just grab it from the back."

Casey watched as the baker walked toward the back, tossing a smile over his shoulder before he disappeared. As he stood there, Casey tried to decide if Matt was flirting or just doing his job. He didn't have much success. He couldn't remember the last time he'd flirted with anyone, let alone a man.

After recalling the way Matt had smiled at the other customers, he decided the too-attractive-for-him baker liked to smile. Matt's biceps protruded out of his one-size-too-small shirt, and his jeans fit him in all the right places, skintight on his thighs and highlighting a plump ass. He had green eyes, which popped out against his almost overtanned complexion, and Casey figured most of the customers came in to see him, as opposed to getting breakfast.

Casey, on the other hand, didn't feel attractive in his current state. He'd thrown on a pair of ratty jeans and an old T-shirt, something he didn't mind getting dirty. He couldn't see how anyone would take an interest in him anyway, with the way his belly spilled out of his jeans. Besides that, he didn't think he should jump into another relationship, all things considered. Then again, maybe bakery therapy could help.

Soon Matt walked back out with a big box in his hands. He opened it up when he got to the counter so Casey could inspect the cake to make sure everything looked satisfactory.

"Looks great," Casey said once he double-checked the spelling.

Matt smirked. "Tastes great too."

Casey reached around to pull his wallet out. "Thanks, how much do I owe you?"

"Your wife already paid."

"Rachel's my sister, actually."

"Oh, sorry about that. Anyway, it's already taken care of, but in that case…." Matt reached into the display and pulled out a bear claw, slid the pastry in a bag, and put it on top of the box as he winked. "Have one on the house."

Casey blushed. "That's not necessary."

"I insist," Matt said, tilting his head as he looked into Casey's eyes. "You look like you could use a little something sweet."

Matt's voice sounded like a soft purr, and Casey tried to keep his cheeks from giving him away. His awkwardness showed enough on its own. "Who turns down free sweets? I'm Casey, by the way."

"Matt, if you didn't know by the name tag."

"I did notice that," he said, smiling back. "Uh, well, I should get going. Otherwise my sister might send out a search party."

"We wouldn't want that."

"No, probably not."

"Let me know how you like that bear claw," Matt said, nodding to the pastry with a syrupy sweet smile.

Casey quirked a brow. "I suppose that implies I'll be coming back?"

"I sure hope so."

Wow, okay. Yes, definitely flirting. He thanked his lucky stars he'd taken care of things in the shower that morning, or else the walk to the car might've been rather embarrassing. But who in their right mind would want a guy like him?

CHAPTER TEN
WORST-CASE SCENARIO

MYLES'S NERVES eroded with each passing minute as they waited for a reply from James. They'd sent it twelve hours ago, but he made Casey leave the laptop on and open while he went to his nephew's birthday party. He wished he could've gone. Getting out of the house would've done him some good. He loved the beach, but having such a small area of existence made him feel imprisoned. A little variety would've gone a long way.

He took a relaxing walk on the beach at noon. The crowd thinned around lunchtime. Not that he cared—no one could see him anyway—but sometimes the occasional dog would come running up to him. And sometimes the seagulls hovered around expecting food. One of those avian bastards even dive-bombed him, tickling him as it passed through.

The gorgeous day had him risking it. The low tide allowed him to walk all the way out to the sandbar with his head still out of the water. He tried not to think about the underwater structure being the reason he died. He knew how riptides formed, when sandbars broke apart, leading to a surging of water out to sea. He knew how to escape them, swimming parallel to the shore. He'd gotten caught in and successfully escaped a few in his lifetime, but how did he get swept out to sea that day? Why hadn't James rescued him? Had he even tried?

Every morning he hoped he'd remember what happened to him, but the memory never surfaced. And maybe it never would.

When the tide started to rise, he decided to make his way back to the beach house to see if Casey had returned. He'd had enough solitude for one day. The Between was a lonely place, and over the past few weeks, he'd grown to welcome Casey's presence. Casey made it bearable. What would Myles do when he decided to move out?

He found Casey sitting on the couch with a beer in hand, petting Jasper. He flopped down next to him and plopped his feet up on the coffee table. Casey must've heard him because he turned to look his way. The bags under his eyes looked more pronounced than usual. He'd just gotten back from a child's birthday party, so Myles understood his fatigue.

"How'd it go?" Myles asked, testing to see whether or not Casey could hear him.

"It was a madhouse," Casey said before taking a long pull from the bottle. It looked half-empty. Myles wished he could've had a beer. The condensation rolling down the bottle almost had his mouth watering. He missed chilling out after a long day and settling down with a nice lager.

Casey put his feet up on the coffee table, his body slumping down as he crossed his arms. "I like kids, and it was nice hanging out with my nephews, who I don't even know, but not the ten other kids running around. They were loud. And annoying. Just popped a few aspirin."

Myles sympathized. "I don't envy you."

"I guess it could've been worse. And I did talk to a hot baker this morning…. I think we flirted, but I'm pretty rusty."

Myles didn't know how to take the news. He felt a pang of jealousy at the fact Casey could interact with people. The only person he could talk to was Casey, if you didn't count Joe, who came around less and less the more he communicated with Casey. He'd ask his uncle about it the next time he saw him, but Myles knew he wouldn't get a satisfying answer.

His craving for beer only intensified when Casey started in on his second. He wished for a small taste, even though he didn't like the brand. More than beer, he missed coffee. Casey had a pot going most mornings and sometimes alternated with beer throughout the day, but it sucked that he couldn't even smell it. If he had to choose between touch and smell, the weakest sense, he'd go with touch, but he really missed his coffee.

THE NEXT several days went by uneventfully. He waited around the laptop, hoping for a reply from James, but one never came. He begged Casey to pen another, but it took days before he reluctantly agreed. When the next weekend came and went without a reply, he convinced Casey to call.

"Do you really think he'll answer?" Casey asked, holding his phone. They sat around the kitchen table, and Casey had just popped the last pork dumpling from his Chinese takeout into his mouth.

"I have no idea. He might think you're someone wanting an interview or something," Myles said, shrugging before he remembered that Casey couldn't see him.

"Do you think he'll be able to hear you through the phone?"

Myles groaned; he hadn't even thought of that. "I hope so."

"Okay, but if this goes bad, I'm not sure what else we can do."

Myles gave him a hopeful look. "You promised we'd try. I've been getting stronger every day, so maybe he'll hear me."

"All right, you win. Worst-case scenario is he blocks my number." Casey took a deep breath and made the call.

"Hello?" a voice said over the speakerphone. Myles knew it wasn't James right away, even through the choppy reception.

Casey cleared his throat and replied, "Uh, hi. Is this James Caputo?"

"May I ask who's calling?"

"Yeah, my name's Casey. I'm calling to follow up on an e-mail I sent—"

They heard a shuffle, followed by the man's muffled voice as he called out, "Hey, babe? Some guy named Casey's on the phone for you."

Then it hit him, his heart sinking once the lightbulb went off in his head. Myles recognized the voice. It was Logan, James's agent. And he called James "babe"? He'd been dead less than two months and James had already moved on? Had their relationship meant nothing to him?

"Yeah, my name's Casey. I'm uh, I'm a friend, was a friend, of Myles Taylor."

"Are you the sick fuck who keeps e-mailing me?" James yelled into the phone.

"I know I sound a little crazy, but—"

"But nothing! I lost my boyfriend, and you keep e-mailing me telling me you can talk to his spirit? How fucked-up is that? Do you get off on hurting people who are in mourning?"

"Mourning? How long did you wait before you jumped in bed with Logan?" Myles asked, but he didn't know if James heard him through his own ranting, or if he could hear him at all.

"You're one sick fuck! Do not call me again!" James shouted before hanging up the phone.

Myles drooped in his chair. He didn't know what to say. He felt numb and sick to his stomach. How did everything get so turned upside down? He honestly thought James would still be in mourning, would still be missing him. The revelation did nothing but reinforce all the suspicions he'd had about James and Logan, about them having some kind of relationship behind his back. He hadn't wanted to look at it before, didn't want to believe James would do that to him, but he'd run out of excuses for him.

"I'm sorry," Casey said, breaking the festering silence that blanketed the house. "I wish he would've been more reasonable."

"It's...." Myles wanted to say "fine," that things would be okay, but James had made it clear he didn't need any closure at all. He'd already moved on. So where did that leave him? To continue to walk around aimlessly with no bright lights opening up for him? Joe didn't come to walk him through the pearly gates. No angels appeared on their golden chariots. He remained stuck in limbo.

"Did you know the guy who answered?" Casey asked.

"Yeah, his agent, Logan."

"Do you think they were...?"

"Together?" Myles scoffed. "I had my suspicions, but I didn't listen. Hell, I had a ring in my pocket when I die—when it happened. I had planned to propose that day." He dropped his head to the table and buried his face in his arms. "I thought it'd go away, that nagging in my head, but I wanted... I wanted to be happy, you know? I wanted... I had no one in my life before him. After Joe died, I had no one. Then... he was all I had."

"I'm sorry you had to find out this way, but maybe it was a rebound thing. Some people seek out others for comfort after a loved one dies."

"Yeah, maybe," he conceded, but he didn't really believe that. James had cheated on him. He knew it just like he knew the tide had started coming in. He could just feel it.

"Damn, I'd offer you a beer, but...."

"It'd go right through me," Myles said with a mirthless laugh.

"Yeah."

Myles stood, pushing out his chair when he did so. "I think I'm gonna go take a walk."

"Did you want some company?"

"No, I think I just want to be alone for a while. A bit ironic since I'm usually alone, but I just need to think."

Casey got up as well and stretched in place. "I think I might head to bed, then. It's getting late." With a yawn, he turned and started for the bedroom.

Myles went to the door and walked through it. The sun had set a while ago, and the breeze nipped at his cheeks. He could feel things like that better at night, the change in air temperature. He took the stairs down to the beach and made for the ocean. The moon sat low on the horizon and reflected off the water. It was a beautiful night.

He could see remarkably well. The moon shone bright in the dark sky and illuminated the crabs scurrying along in front of him. He sat down to watch a few leaving tracks in the sand. Just as he opened his mouth to call for Joe, he felt a presence beside him. He never had to call, though. Joe always seemed to show up when Myles needed him most.

"Was he cheating the whole time?"

"What do you think, kiddo?"

Myles dug his fingers into the sand, the cool grains gliding under his fingertips. It felt real, so real, and so did the betrayal in his heart that sent it withering into heartbreak. He'd wanted his suspicions to be wrong. For a long time he didn't want to know the truth, but now it had slapped him in the face. The whole time he'd tried to ignore it, to make it go away with rings and romantic trips, suggestions of couple's counseling, all the while ignoring the signs lit up as plain as day.

"I was too blind or too stubborn to see it," Myles admitted. He tried to think back to when he first had the feeling they had something going on behind his back, but he couldn't pinpoint it. Maybe it had always been there.

"I think you're stronger than you give yourself credit for. You always have been, but sometimes people can't see what's right in front of them."

"Only because I didn't *want* to see." Myles blamed himself. He'd let it go on, let himself believe the lies James spun so beautifully from loose lips.

"Because you didn't want to look."

"What am I supposed to do now? I thought if I could talk to him that he would… we would have closure, that I could go with you and get out of this purgatory or whatever the hell this place is, the Between."

"Is that why you wanted to talk to him, or was it something else?" Joe asked as he bumped his shoulder into Myles's.

"I don't know. It's not like I could've asked him to come and be with me. What was he supposed to do, kill himself? What if he ended up somewhere else? I'm not even sure if anyone else can hear me but Casey, anyway."

"Perhaps you're meant to be here for some other reason, Myles. Maybe you should test some boundaries, stretch your limits."

"What does that even mean? I thought that's what I've been doing. Every time I run, I get zapped back to this place." He turned to look at Joe, but just as he thought, he'd already disappeared.

Boundaries. He'd spent two months testing boundaries. He could touch Jasper now. One time he even felt the downy softness of his fur, and he knew the cat felt him too. Casey had told him he saw his outline once. He didn't know how he managed that, but he'd tried to work on becoming visible ever since. Plus, he could talk for longer periods at a time. What more could he do?

After sitting on the beach for a while wallowing in self-pity, he went back inside. He heard Casey snoring in the dark bedroom. He always tried to give him his space, even though Myles still saw it as his house. But tonight he didn't want to be alone. He made his way through the bedroom door and lay down on the floor by the bed, where he soon drifted off into what he called his hibernation state. He didn't dream, but he could tune out the world around him. It reminded him of deep meditation, and he enjoyed the peace it brought him. He only wished it brought answers as well.

THE NEXT morning, he "woke" to a light pressure on his chest. Jasper sat on top of him, and he looked up to see Casey peering down at them both, brown eyes wide with wonder. Casey seemed to meet his eyes as he let out a laugh. Myles hoped he didn't think of him as some sort of weirdo for sneaking into his room.

"What?"

"Jasper's floating," Casey replied, his tone that of awe mixed with humor.

"You should take a picture. No one will believe you otherwise," Myles spat out with heavy sarcasm. The whole thing with James and Logan still upset him, and he figured he had every right to his anger.

Casey swung his legs off the side of the bed and frowned down at him. "I'm pretty sure no one would believe me anyway."

Myles sat up, the movement causing a startled Jasper to go sputtering across the floor. "Sorry, Jaspy."

Casey climbed out of bed, yawning as he stretched his limbs. His shirt rode up just a little, exposing his pudgy belly to the world before he quickly covered it. A random thought of blowing raspberries on his fuzzy stomach wandered through Myles's mind. He coughed to cover up the laugh that it brought with it, but it had him wondering if Casey was ticklish.

"I'm going to attempt breakfast again," Casey said, refocusing his attention. "I would offer you some, but…."

"I'd oblige, but…."

Myles got up off the floor and went out into the kitchen while Casey broke off for the bathroom. He didn't miss bodily functions, except maybe the whole drinking part, especially when Casey started brewing the coffee and he only had his memories to remind him what it smelled like.

Except sex. He had started to miss that a little. He hadn't had any sort of sexual urges up to that point, probably because he'd focused all his attention on James and getting into contact with him. Now that he'd failed at that, he needed something else to focus on. Perhaps the recent strengthening of his senses amped up his sex drive.

Or maybe it had more to do with the fact that he'd started to find Casey attractive.

CHAPTER ELEVEN
PICKING ME UP

"SO... IF I start to have a panic attack, you're going to stay with me, right? Like last time?" Casey asked as he started getting the pans ready to make breakfast. He had already pulled out the bacon and eggs and a few pieces of bread to make toast. By accident he almost got out enough food to feed the both of them but readjusted it so as not to make Myles uncomfortable.

He hadn't minded Myles sleeping in his room. James had dealt his specter buddy a huge blow the night before, and he knew it took a toll on him. In the event of a role reversal, he knew he wouldn't have wanted to sleep alone wherever Myles usually slept—or hibernated, as he liked to call it. Casey didn't know how much help he could offer, but he decided to try to keep Myles engaged for a while in hopes of lifting his spirits.

"What are you smirking at?" Myles asked.

Casey could sense Myles perched on the island. He'd had to swat him off a few times in the past when he'd gotten in the way. Of course, he could've worked through him, but the thought of doing so felt disconcerting and maybe a bit rude.

"What have I told you about sitting on the counter?" Casey chided.

"How did you know I was sitting here?" Myles asked, a hint of bewilderment in his tone. He chuckled at the look Casey cast in his general direction. "Ugh, fine.... Better?" he soon asked from somewhere behind him.

Casey smiled to himself. "Much."

"I think you're getting better at picking me up."

"Yep."

"Man, I wish I could surf. The swell is killer out there today."

Casey looked through the window to see for himself. The waves looked picturesque, but he didn't know much about surfing. He turned back to the eggs and cracked them into a bowl, then tossed the eggshells into the sink, where Jasper waited to lick them clean. "Death sounds pretty boring."

"Says the guy who hardly leaves the house. If I didn't know better, I'd think you were the one tied here."

Casey's shoulders stiffened at that. He couldn't argue with him. He'd holed up in the house for too long, but the thought of interacting with people sent tendrils of anxiety slinking around him like spike-covered vines pricking his skin. He'd always preferred working in the back of restaurants to the front where customer service came into play. He didn't hate people, but now with his self-esteem at an all-time low, he didn't want to bother.

"Sorry, Case, I didn't mean—"

"No, you're right. You're dead and can't leave, and I'm alive and won't. I get it… kind of messed up," he said as he began to beat the eggs, taking out his frustrations on them. "After Cinder burned—"

"What's Cinder?"

"That was the name of my restaurant."

"Wait. You're telling me the name of your restaurant, the one that burned to the ground, was Cinder? As in 'a small piece of partly burned wood'? That kind of cinder?"

"Oh, the irony," Casey said as he rolled his eyes. "Seems to be the topic of the day."

Once his pan preheated, he tossed in the bacon while he started cutting up a few peppers for his eggs. Despite his usual preferences, he found himself comfortable with having Myles around to talk to while he cooked. It did wonders to keep him out of his own head, and despite the painful topic of discussion, it felt oddly therapeutic.

"Why'd you want to be a chef?" Myles asked, his voice coming from beside him now. Casey could almost feel him peering over his shoulder.

"Uh… well, I guess it was when my father left. I was only ten or so, but I thought I had to be the man of the house. My father did most of the cooking, and I thought it meant I had to take over that role. It's weird to think about, but him leaving was one of the best things that could've happened to me because it opened the floodgates to my passion.

"I just fell in love with the whole process. It soon became my way out of this town, a skill I had that no one could take away instead of the thing that had tied me to my family. It was an escape, you know? I resented my mother for a long time after my father left. I blamed her when I should've been blaming him, but I didn't really know any better. I was a broken teenager."

"I know all about being a broken teen. My parents died when I was eight, plane crash, and my uncle Joe took care of me until he died of cancer a while back."

"Damn, that sucks. My mom passed a little over a year ago. So it's just me and my sister, her kids. Her husband's a good man, but we've never really gotten along."

"What about your father?"

"We haven't heard from him since he left, almost twenty years ago. Last I heard, he drank himself to death," Casey said. He flipped the bacon this time before it could burn and started to heat the skillet for the eggs. "I left as soon as I was able, heading to New York. After getting some experience under my belt, I decided to try and strike out on my own in LA. I wanted to make something of myself, showcase my skills. Kind of egotistical, I know, but I felt like that was my calling."

"Why did you move back?"

"To Land's End? After Cinder, I felt like all my dreams died too. I came back hoping to find something, to get my life on track. Sounds kind of lame out loud. And don't ask me why 'home' felt like the place to escape to instead of running away to New York again, to the city that welcomed me with open arms after I thought I left this place for good. That probably would've been wiser, huh? But you saw me the other day. I froze, burned the bacon, and had a panic attack. It's just… the idea of working in a kitchen right now is… it's too much…. Maybe someday."

A few moments of silence set in while he juggled the scrambled eggs and removed the bacon from the stove. He thought Myles had run out of steam, but then he spoke again once Casey had sat down at the table.

"Are you afraid to cook now?"

Casey blew out a loud sigh. "I don't know. It's not what I'm afraid of exactly, but just being in the kitchen again after seeing the restaurant, what used to be Cinder, smoldering, it's seared onto my brain. It was a traumatic event. That's what my therapist called it. And now it's gone.

"Maybe I shouldn't be so messed up over a damn building. I got a nice chunk of money back from the insurance, but it's like a piece of me burned that day, and I don't know if I can go back to that. My sister said I was being a baby about it, but Isabel used to say I was in mourning." Casey shoved a piece of bacon into his mouth and relished the salty taste. Food had a way of settling his nerves, but Myles kind of did too.

"Who's Isabel?"

"Oh, my ex. She promised she'd stay by me, but then she ran off with all my shit and left me. I don't think that helped my issues."

He heard Myles sigh in the seat beside him and swore he felt a gentle pressure on his arm. "I'm sorry. She obviously didn't deserve you if that's how she acted."

"I suppose," he said, reaching for the salt and pepper to season his eggs. "I don't think James deserved you either."

"Thanks."

Casey started to feel a little weird eating in front of Myles. At first he'd only thought of him as some sort of invisible voice or a fog or something, a hallucination, but the more they talked and got to know each other, the more he started to see him as a person. He could envision Myles sitting next to him, elbows on the table as he watched him stuff his face. Was it rude to eat in front of a ghost?

"I hope that tastes good," Myles said, "because it looks so delicious."

"Are you sure you don't get hungry?" Casey mumbled around a mouthful of eggs. Okay, *that* was rude.

"I hadn't before I saw all that! I feel like I'm watching a cooking show where I can see the yummy food but I can't eat or smell it. Hey, maybe you should do one of those cooking competitions we watch on TV sometimes."

Casey downed some beer as he mulled over the idea. "With my luck, I'd probably freeze midshow and have to be carted off in a straightjacket."

They both had a good laugh at that.

"Oh God, watching you eat is worse than when you show me those food blogs you're always looking up," Myles teased.

"You don't like food blogs?" Casey asked.

"Nah, my time on the Internet was spent wisely on gay porn. That might be one thing I miss more than beer."

"Right, I assumed you were gay from the whole James thing." Casey berated himself for mentioning the guy's name. Myles probably didn't want to talk about him, but he did open up about Isabel and cooking, two things *he* had no interest in talking about.

"I'm Myles Taylor. I'm dead and I'm gay."

"I'm Casey North, and I'm a depressed chef and pansexual… and probably an alcoholic," he added as he washed down some eggs with a swig of beer.

"They say admitting it is the first step."

"Yeah, well...."

"So pansexual, then? Does that extend to apparitions?" Myles teased.

Casey laughed for a solid minute at that because the thought had never crossed his mind. But once he calmed himself, he took a minute to think it over. "I've always been a firm believer in 'the heart wants what it wants,' and while I am attracted to and have dated both men and women, I think what's on the inside is a helluva lot more important than the outside."

"Doesn't really answer my question, though," Myles pressed.

"Can you blame me? I'm still not a hundred percent convinced you're real."

"Yeah, that makes two of us."

They didn't talk for the rest of the meal, which left Casey wondering if Myles had worn himself out. Their conversations lengthened every day, but he regretted not asking Myles more about himself. He knew Joe served in the Army and they moved around a lot, but he hadn't thought to ask more about his parents, or even how he was holding up after talking to James the day before.

Fear kept him from asking about that last one. He wouldn't have known how to comfort Myles or even what to say other than sorry, and that didn't seem like enough, considering the circumstances. Maybe he'd try later once Myles had regained some of his strength. In the meantime, he planned to go back to Bobbie the fortune-teller for some more books that might help them.

He took a nice long shower after breakfast and decided to go to the store. Mrs. Walton stood out in her front yard with Mini, and both turned to look at him when he unlocked the car. He waved in an attempt to be neighborly, but that now-infamous scowl of hers made him question why he even bothered. He seriously considered the possibility that her face had gotten stuck that way.

The drive through town made him realize how much had changed since he left over a decade ago. They had converted the pizza place he worked at in high school to a coffee shop, and the deli his sister had worked at had a Now Open sign under "Bettie's Boutique." More chain restaurants littered the streets, but they hadn't replaced all the mom-and-pop shops on Shoreline Drive. He figured the Land's End tourism committee had made sure of that.

When he'd come home to visit, he never stayed long. A few days for his mother's funeral had been the lengthiest stay he'd had in years, but only because he and Isabel had gotten into a fight and she'd taken off with his car. He didn't know what he'd been running from all these years, some repulsive force keeping him away, but he found himself more at ease as he drove along the streets that morning.

Before he knew it, he had pulled the car into the bakery parking lot without a thought. It was midmorning, and the place looked a little busy. Regardless of his yummy breakfast, his stomach rumbled at the memory of the bear claw he had the other morning—which tasted every bit as scrumptious as it looked—and his mouth salivated for another bite, even though his palate usually leaned toward the savory side of things.

Nonetheless he pushed the bakery door open, the bell overhead jingling as he moved into the store. He tried not to look too conspicuous as he surveyed the staff, searching for familiar green eyes, but he sighed when he saw no sign of Matt. It wasn't until he got up to the counter that he noticed him coming out of the back with a stack of boxes that looked like cupcakes, judging from the different colors in the cellophane window.

"Jenson?" Matt called out as he set the boxes on the counter before turning his attention to him. "Hey, it's Casey, right?" he asked with a smile. "Stopping by for another bear claw?"

Before Casey could reply, a young woman with two kids in tow sidled up to the counter. "Thanks, sweetheart. You have the best cupcakes in town... buns too," she cooed with a salacious smile, and Casey tried not to roll his eyes at her cloyingly sweet flirtations.

"Come back and see us, then." Matt waved before looking back to Casey. "Sorry about that. How can I help you this beautiful morning?"

Casey flashed a bashful smile and met Matt's emerald eyes. "I had an early breakfast," he lied, "but I have a craving for a little something sweet. Any suggestions?"

"I think I have some delicious espresso donut holes that might hit the spot. How about a free sample?"

Before Casey could agree, the baker had moved down the counter, where he reached for a bag. He gave Casey a little smirk that might have contained a wink as he slid the display case open and dropped a few donut holes into the bag, almost a half dozen by Casey's count. Matt held them out, their fingers brushing as Casey took the bag.

They stood there with eyes locked until Matt motioned with his head for Casey to try one of the confections. Obliging, he reached into the bag and pulled out one of the light-colored treats, biting into it with a delicate grace as he maintained eye contact. "Mmm, this is wonderful. I can really taste the coffee," he said, watching as Matt's eyes lit up.

"I'm glad you like them. They're my own recipe. It took me months to perfect it."

Casey knew the mixed feelings of frustration and accomplishment that went along with tinkering with a recipe. It had taken him quite a while to perfect his signature dishes at Cinder. Unfortunately, the memory of that started to kick off his panic, and he did his best to blink away the dizziness threatening to send him into a tizzy.

"Are you all right?" Matt asked, his face a mask of concern.

"Hmm? Oh yeah, it's just... it reminded me of my restaurant," Casey replied, shaking his head in a sorry excuse to clear the memory.

"You have a restaurant? In Land's End? How come I haven't seen you around town before?"

"I, uh, I used to have one in LA before it burned down."

"Wow, sorry to hear that. It sounds horrific."

Casey felt his palms starting to sweat, his clammy hands losing the grip on the bag. Why here? Why now? The morning had gone so well until then. He'd even left his pills at home, but now he had nothing to keep him from going into full panic mode. He needed to get out of there before the walls closed in on him. "More like a nightmare. Sorry, these were delicious, but I-I think I should be going."

Matt frowned and nodded. "Sorry if I upset you."

"No, it's fine," he panted, his breathing picking up, but he couldn't get enough oxygen into his lungs.

"Are you sure? You don't look too good."

"I just... need some air and I'll be fine. These are really good, though. I'll come back for more," Casey said, forcing a smile despite the fact that his heart felt like a stampede of racing thoroughbreds galloping inside his chest.

"We have other things too. The cream puffs are really good. Or the cannolis. I don't make the pies, but they're good for special occasions."

Casey clutched the bag tighter, hoping the conversation would soon be over. "I'll keep that in mind."

"Here, take one of our cards. That way you can give us a call for orders or… if you want to know when I'm not working so I don't stick my foot in my mouth again," Matt said, ducking his head a little, but Casey was too far gone to analyze the reason for it.

He took the card and slid it into his back pocket. "Thanks, I'll be back." If he didn't die on the way out.

Matt smiled. "I'll hold you to that."

Casey waved and hurried out of the store. When he got to his car, he started on his breathing exercises. He'd felt good up to that point, but maybe he should've listened to Dr. Roberts when she said for him to take his pills even on good days. The residual anxiety left over from cooking must've lingered.

Matt seemed like a nice guy, but Casey doubted his interest in a fat slob who hardly left the house. He'd smiled wide at the Jenson woman too, so Casey decided he just took customer service very seriously.

He shook off those thoughts as he tried to calm his nerves. He'd gotten better about talking to people—talking to ghosts—about what happened to his restaurant. Dr. Roberts said he should try to share his experience with others, but she probably hadn't meant to do it with hot bakers with nice eyes and delectable-looking buns who must've thought him damaged goods after his near meltdown.

Either way, he was glad to be out of the bakery and in his car where he could breathe. He rolled down the window so the sea breeze could waft in and started back down Shoreline Drive.

Chapter Twelve
The Superstitious Side

Myles fell into a bored stupor after Casey left. He'd started to enjoy the man's company more than he'd anticipated. They hadn't gotten off to the best start, but they had learned to live with each other. Even though Casey could leave at any time, Myles often wondered why he hadn't yet, why he'd bothered to come back that night after Myles attacked him in the kitchen.

Casey had said he didn't have anywhere else to go, but he could've found a hotel to stay at or another house to rent. He'd had plenty of time to look around for one the past few weeks. But if he didn't mind living with a spirit, then Myles decided not to question it. He liked having someone around to talk to. Casey even let him have a say in what they watched on television, something James never had the courtesy to do.

He noticed Casey becoming more comfortable with him as well. Casey often asked if he wanted a beer or something to eat when he made something for himself. At first Myles thought he did it as a joke, but somewhere along the line he realized Casey saw him more as a person than a spirit. Subconsciously or otherwise, he treated Myles like a real person, not just some entity stuck in the Between.

He didn't want to admit it, but Myles kind of missed him. After weeks spent alone in the house, he'd grown lonely, until Casey and Jasper arrived. Usually when Casey left the house, he'd go for walks. Sometimes he'd do the same while Casey took a nap, either to stroll on the beach or to check out the latest gossip with the neighbors. He didn't really think of it as spying but more like watching a television show, since no one picked up on his presence.

After his daily walk with Eli the mailman, he headed home, but before he made it inside, he noticed Mrs. Walton peeking out at him through the curtain. And not just her usual passing glance either. The nosy woman had both of her beady eyes trained right on him. Sometimes Casey would look at him like that, like he could see him, even though

Myles knew he couldn't. He tried to make himself more visible, but how exactly did one harness energy?

He narrowed his eyes at her but shuffled inside, frowning at the fact that Casey hadn't come home yet. The clock read noon, and he wondered when he'd be back. He sat on the couch and waited for thirty minutes, then decided to head down to the beach. He missed spending a whole afternoon surfing, offering himself up to the waves as time appeared to stop around him, but he didn't think he could control a board in his current state.

What a damn shame.

The choppy waves looked terrible, he noted, as he started down the stairs to the beach, but when he took the first step, he felt as if something pushed him from behind. He lost his balance and tumbled all the way down to the bottom, landing on his back on the packed sand. His head throbbed, and he had trouble catching his breath.

It took him a moment to get his bearings and shake the confusion that set in, because it didn't make sense. He didn't *feel* things; he hadn't before, anyway. How the hell had he fallen down the stairs?

By the time he got to his feet and dusted invisible sand from his clothes out of habit, the pain had evaporated. Only the memory remained, but it felt old, like it had happened ages ago, not seconds. The next time he talked to Joe, he'd ask about the possibility of other spirits hanging around. He hadn't seen any, but he couldn't rule it out.

He shook off the weird déjà vu and continued on, scoping out a place in the sand to sit for a while. A family splashed around in the surf, which had him trying to remember his childhood. Nothing specific came to mind, only fragments, pieces here and there mostly of his mother, but he enjoyed watching the children doing their best to stand up on their boogie boards.

They kept popping up too soon, the break just ahead of their starting positions. The girl would get her balance as she stood up, only to sink when the wave left her behind, but her brother had trouble getting his footing. Myles would've given just about anything to run out and give them a few pointers, but he didn't think it wise. Worst-case scenario, he'd scar them for life.

He missed surfing like he would a severed limb. Surfing gave him purpose, and while he wouldn't claim to be the best in the world, he'd surfed some nice waves in his day, made a little money from it along the way, and met some amazing people. They traveled a lot, he and James, chasing bigger waves—and James bigger paydays—but he liked immersing himself in different cultures, seeing parts of the world most people wouldn't dream of, riding waves only the elite would even dare.

But he missed the spiritualism of it the most. Everything fell away when he drove his board over the water: the horrible year he'd spent watching Joe wither away, the day he found out his parents died, the gut-wrenching suspicions he'd had about James and Logan, everything. He wondered if that's how Casey used to feel in the kitchen. If it was, Myles wanted to help him get it back. Maybe that's why he couldn't move on.

On his way back home, he found himself stopping in front of Mrs. Walton's house. He groaned at the prospect of climbing the stairs. Why couldn't he just float up there? Instead he had to trek up to her deck before slipping through the door. Myles didn't know what possessed him to do so, but the thought did make him wonder if he could actually possess someone. He would have to get Casey to look into that. He wouldn't do it unless he deemed it absolutely necessary, but he thought he should know his limitations. Joe did tell him to test his boundaries.

Once inside he tiptoed through the kitchen. He didn't know if she could hear him, but he proceeded with caution nonetheless. He held in a laugh as he slithered through the house 007 style, a spy on a top-secret mission. Wow, he was even more bored than he thought. When he got to the living room, he found Mrs. Walton sitting in a recliner with her eyes shut, but as if she had sensed his presence, her eyes shot open and zeroed in on him.

"I didn't invite you in," she grumbled, and little Mini in her lap stirred at her words. The Pomeranian turned and started to growl at him.

Myles could feel his jaw drop. "Y-you can see me?"

"I got one foot in the After as it is. 'Course I can see you."

"But how? Casey can't even…." He didn't know what to say about that. He and Casey started communicating weeks ago, but Casey had only seen him once, and just a glimmer of him.

"Winfred pointed you out," she said, nodding to something behind him.

Myles turned and saw an old man lying on his side on the couch. He looked just as old as Mrs. Walton, but unlike her, he wore a smile on his wrinkled face, two dark chocolate-brown eyes twinkling up at him.

Myles saw right through him, an obvious apparition, but he looked rather solid as well.

"Who are you?" Myles asked as the old man pushed himself up into a sitting position.

"Name's Winfred Walton, but you can call me Fred," he replied, extending a hand. "Was wondering when you'd stop by, but I figured the ol' ball and chain here did a good job of keeping you away."

Myles stared down at the outstretched hand like he didn't know what to do with it. "H-how long, how long have you been…?" He had another ghost living next door this whole time and he didn't even know it. He'd only ever seen Joe, and only at random intervals. "Wait, did you push me down the stairs?" he asked, brow furrowing in both confusion and curiosity.

"No, can't say I did…. And I've been here a few years now, to answer your first question."

"Four," Mrs. Walton corrected, her sour expression not letting up.

"Hush now, Jeanie. The kid's only been here, what, two months now?"

They both looked at him, but Myles couldn't remember exactly. He nodded in lieu of an answer and then flopped down on the couch next to Fred. "Do you go to the Beyond like Joe? Or are you stuck like me?"

Fred sat back and let out a contemplative hum. "Is Joe that older fella?"

Myles ran a hand over his face as he leaned forward to place his elbows on his knees. He had so many questions that maybe Fred could answer, but he didn't want to set the bar too high since Joe hadn't helped much. "Yeah, he's my uncle."

"Ah, yes. I take it he comes from the Beyond? Our grandson does that from time to time," Fred said, his slight smile faltering as he looked toward his wife. "But our daughter isn't able to."

"Oh… sorry. I just have Joe, but now I'm stuck here, and I don't know why."

"Think I'm stuck here till Jean decides to come with me," he said with a chuckle, his smile returning in full force. Mrs. Walton scoffed across at them as she shook her head. "She's always been stubborn."

"If you can see me, Jean, how come you didn't say anything?"

"It's Mrs. Walton to you. And I don't know you," she snapped, her thin lips pursing to a straight line, the skin around her eyes creasing as they narrowed in at him.

"Oh, Jeanie, be nice to our guest. It's good to have someone else around from time to time," Fred said. He met Myles's gaze. "Don't mind her. She hasn't been the same since the accident."

Myles hoped to break up the awkward silence that moved in after that. He turned his attention back to Mrs. Walton. Maybe she could give Casey pointers. "How come you can see me and Casey can't? We've talked, but he only saw my outline once. Every time I see you, it's like you're looking right at me."

"Mini."

Myles waited for her to continue, but she remained silent. "That's it?"

"Jean," Fred said with a stern voice.

She shot daggers at her husband but then sighed and answered. "I've been living with a ghost for four years. I know what to look for. Mini pointed you out, and after that, I knew. And as for not saying anything, unlike your friend Casey, I'm not one to make myself look crazy talking to thin air when I'm out of the house." With that she turned up her nose and looked away.

Fred hummed as if in apology. "She also didn't know whether Casey knew or not, or even if your spirit could communicate with the living. They label you crazy if ya go around telling people they have spirits in their house."

Myles had to give him that. "So she can see you? Can Casey see you? Or other people? And how come I haven't seen you before?"

"If I want them to, they can, but Jeanie doesn't like me leaving the house just in case. We don't know what other spirits are out there, and she's a little on the superstitious side. She doesn't want any evil spirits following me home."

Myles was horrified at the thought. What if he brought an evil spirit into his house? "That can happen?"

Fred shrugged his crooked shoulders. "Who knows how these things work."

Myles needed to be more careful, then. He didn't want anything happening to Casey or Jasper. "So if I wanted Casey to see me, how can I do that?"

"Can you move things? Talk?"

"Yes, the first time I moved something I was angry. I ended up throwing a glass and a bottle of pills at Casey, but I've gotten better at controlling things. Like I can pet Jasper, our cat. And we've been talking for longer intervals. That's a good sign, right?"

"Hmm, yes, I suppose." Fred let out a sigh and paused for a moment. "I'm gonna be honest with you. I don't know how I do it. It started with a deep longing to comfort my Jeanie after I died. I wanted to hug her one day, so I did. The sight came after, but it was a similar thing. I wanted her to see me, concentrated on it, and voila. It took time, but I got there. Keep at it."

That didn't offer Myles much help, but he felt grateful for the tips. Fred had more experience than he did, and he trusted what he said. "I appreciate it. Joe hasn't exactly offered as much guidance."

"'Course not, he's from the Beyond. Things are different there. The rules probably are too. But we'll all find out someday."

By the look on his face, Myles had to wonder if he believed that. What would happen if they didn't move on, if they hadn't by the time the sun burned out or the earth disintegrated under their feet?

"Are there any more of us around here?"

"Ms. Miller down the street," Mrs. Walton answered. "She's been dead awhile. Drowned out there a few decades ago. Don't see her much, but she's up on the hill, last house before the overlook."

Another drowning victim. Tranquil Bay was anything but.

Myles talked with the couple for an hour after that. They told him about their grandchildren and their children. He didn't have the guts to ask about the accident they mentioned a few times, but he did tell Fred he couldn't remember how he died. The old spirit told him not to fret about it. "Nothing you can do about it now."

They also told him not to bother with the fortune-teller in town. She wasn't a medium any more than Mrs. Walton was, just someone who had her own guardian spirit helping her communicate with others. Mrs. Walton said she had gone to see her in the beginning but that her advice didn't help any more than simple trial and error. He and Casey had already figured that out.

He did owe the quack for convincing Casey he was real and not some hallucination brought on by a chemical imbalance, or faulty wiring as Casey called it. If Casey hadn't visited her shop that day to get confirmation, Myles wondered if he would've left. He didn't want to think about that, though. It had all worked out… so far.

As soon as he heard Casey's car pull up next door, he excused himself. Fred told him to stop by anytime amid Mrs. Walton's glowering but silent protest. He thanked them both and started home, choosing the front door so he didn't have to take all those stairs. Dead people didn't need the cardio, but it did have him wishing he could fly or float or transport from one place to another. Maybe he could trial and error that too.

CHAPTER THIRTEEN
WORSE OFF NOW

TURNING ONTO a side street, Casey found himself in front of the fortune-teller's place again. The near panic attack he'd suffered at the bakery was unfortunate. Thankfully, he managed to get his breathing back under control by the time he turned off the engine. He thought about going straight home, but he needed to return the book before Bobbie charged him a late fee or something extortionate like that.

Bobbie's place felt just as creepy on the inside as he remembered, and the strange feeling that they weren't alone crept up his spine like a mallet over the ribs of a xylophone. But he did his best to ignore that.

"Has the book aided you and your friend?" Bobbie asked when he handed it over.

Casey hadn't thought about Myles as his friend, but he supposed that was an accurate description. Myles had helped him through a panic attack, and they'd spent lots of time together over the past few weeks. "He's getting better at communicating verbally. I think I saw his body—is that what you would call it?—once when he walked through a door, but that's all…. Oh, and I think Jasper feels him when he pets him. That's our cat."

She led the way into the back room. "Animals, cats in particular, are more sensitive to the spirit world. It's very probable that this Jasper has been aware of his presence since you entered the house."

"Yeah, I kind of figured that out," Casey said as he moved over to one of the bookcases, reading over the names of the old books on the shelves. "Even before me and, uh, my friend could communicate, Jasper acted odd… but I'm not sure how much the book has helped him."

"The book was meant to help you. There is no help for him. Not from here, and most likely not from the other side either."

"What the hell does that mean? He's stuck? In the Between forever?" Stuck to that house? What would happen to Myles when he left and someone new moved in? What if they didn't like him and tried to exorcise him or something?

"I can't know for how long or to what purpose he's here, and as I'm sure you are aware, he doesn't know either."

Casey massaged the ridge of his brow with his thumb and middle finger. "What about exorcism? Would that help him? Get him to the Beyond?"

"I don't meddle in religious practices. A priest might better answer those questions, but of what I have seen, if the spirit isn't causing harm or possessing a person, there's no need to bother with something that might not work. You may invite something even worse in. The spirit will eventually be able to find their reason for being trapped in the Between."

"We contacted his boyfriend, hoping that it would bring them some closure, but it turned out the boyfriend didn't need any and had moved on to someone else. We don't know what else to do. He wants to figure out a way to move on. That's his main concern… and I promised I'd help him."

Bobbie had started moving around the bookcases reading the different titles, but that made her turn to face him, her dark eyes meeting his. "Hmm, most interesting. Are you sure foul play wasn't involved? This is a common reason why they don't cross over, the desire for their soul to get justice for what happened to them."

"I don't know. He said he doesn't remember what happened when he died. The news reports said he got carried out to sea and his body was never found."

"Another reason is to protect a loved one. Is there a family member, perhaps?"

"His only family member is already in the Beyond. And his boyfriend doesn't want anything to do with him," Casey said, furrowing his brow out of annoyance. He wasn't getting anywhere with her.

"Well, this might change things."

"Change what things?"

"Perhaps it's not his issues that are keeping him here," she said as she turned away. "Maybe it's you who needs him?"

Casey scoffed and moved around to examine another bookcase, this one with several knickknacks that reminded him of voodoo trinkets he'd seen in a movie once. "Why would I need him? I'm… well, I mean I have issues, but who doesn't? I have never met anyone who needed a spirit from another realm to 'heal' them."

"What brings you to Land's End?" she asked, sitting down in her ornamental chair. Her crystal ball lit up, and he shook his head at the spectacle of it all.

"I had some problems, and I'm working through them with a—why am I telling you this? It's not relevant to his problem. I just need a way to help him find his reason for staying behind instead of moving on."

"I read palms. Perhaps by reading yours I could help you figure it out." She knocked on the table, indicating for him to have a seat.

He eyed her incredulously. He knew it was a stupid idea, but he decided to indulge her since she had kind of helped when she offered him the book. He found parts of it interesting, but in the end, the lack of relevant information didn't surprise him. No one but the dead could answer their questions, and apparently they didn't know anything either.

"Don't mind the smoke. It's just to set the mood," she said, smirking as a billowing cloud of fake fog bubbled up from under the table. Casey frowned but sat down.

AFTER WASTING thirty minutes of his life, Casey slid back into his car. Bobbie's reading didn't impress him and consisted of the usual generic lines he'd heard in movies: *I see danger in your future. You will be faced with a tough choice ahead. Someone has come into or will come into your life who will change it forever.*

He could've gotten a more detailed fortune from a cookie.

On his way home, he stopped at the grocery store. He needed to restock his beer supply, and he also wanted to pick a few more things to try to cook. As he perused the aisles, he wondered what kinds of things Myles had liked, back when he could eat, of course. He grabbed some ingredients for pancakes. Maybe Myles preferred waffles, or even french toast. He frowned at the thought that it didn't matter anyway.

Isabel had liked grapefruit and english muffins for breakfast, things that didn't have to be cooked. She'd liked his cooking in the beginning, but he'd had concerns they'd started to grow apart over the last year or so. Her interest in things they used to do as a couple waned, and maybe his did too, but at least he showed a willingness to try. He did his best to keep her happy, taking her out to fancy restaurants as he told himself lies about checking out the competition.

He hadn't thought about the part he played in their failed relationship. After Cinder burned down, he gave up trying, gave up the pretense of it, of doing his damnedest to keep them afloat. Sometimes relationships faded, and there wasn't anything that could be done to salvage them. Maybe he should've fought harder for her, but he was in no shape to do so when she left.

By the time he got to the checkout counter, he'd started contemplating whether or not to give her a call. The whole business with Myles and James got him thinking about closure and what would happen to him if he died with things left hanging between them. They hadn't spoken since she moved out and had only exchanged a few texts. It couldn't hurt any worse than the actual breakup.

Once he'd loaded the groceries into the backseat, he got in the car and pulled out his phone. If he had too much time to think about it, he knew he wouldn't call, so he hurried to pull up her number and hit the Call button. She picked up on the third ring, and for a split second he felt paralyzed. He wanted to hang up, but he soldiered on.

"Casey? Is that you? Hello?"

"Hey, Izzie, yeah it's me." A hefty silence settled in, broken only by her loud sighs before he found his voice again. "Look… I just called to, uh… I was thinking about you, about us, about how we left things, or rather how you left things, and I guess… I just want to know why."

"Casey, I… things between us had been wrong for a long time. You had to know that, right? I know what I did was all kinds of messed up, but you checked out on me. What was I supposed to do?"

"I checked out on you? I was hurting. I was reeling after everything that happened. You said you'd be there by my side, and you bailed. And on top of that, you took all my stuff!"

"And you didn't come looking for it, Casey! Did you even want to? Want me? You didn't call, you didn't come looking, and you didn't fight for it, for us. You just gave up on everything. What was I supposed to do? Sit there and watch you spiral?"

"You were supposed to be there for me! I lost everything when you left, literally everything. You were all that I had after Cinder, and you walked out on me. How do you think that made me feel? Why would I fight for someone who abandoned me? Who clearly didn't want anything more to do with me?"

Another long silence gave him time to absorb what they had both said. She had some good points, but so did he. Maybe he should've gone after her, fought for their relationship, but it was too much for him to deal with at the time. He had thought of being on his own as a curse, but in all honesty, it felt like relief from a heavy burden.

Cinder burning down had given him time to breathe, to think about things without having to worry about taking care of her needs, about nurturing a floundering relationship, about running his restaurant, even. When it came down to it, his happiness had vanished a long time ago, and not just because of Isabel. So maybe it was a good thing that she had walked away when she did, that his whole world fell down around him. Maybe the time had come for him to start rebuilding it.

Or maybe he was fooling himself with the idea that he had any pieces left worth salvaging. He ran a hand through the scruff of his thick beard. If nothing else, he could grow out his beard and become a bum.

"Izzie, I didn't call to fight. I really didn't. And this might have been the most civil breakup I've ever had, but I just wanted to know why you left…. Were you unhappy with me?" He steeled himself for the answer, because he already knew it.

"I was unhappy with us, but I still love you…. I'm sorry, Casey. I am. Part of me hoped you'd called to work things out. I've been waiting for you."

"You thought I called because I wanted you back?"

"Don't you? Because I'm willing to give it a try, if you've gotten your life back together."

Casey scoffed, banging his head against the headrest. He hadn't even thought of that as an option. In fact, he felt strangely content to bury the hatchet and move on, or try to, anyway. Their problems didn't rest solely on him—maybe most of them but not all—and he couldn't pretend that him getting his life back together would magically fix things between them.

"For your information, I haven't gotten my life back together. In fact, I'm worse off now than I was when you left. I had to get another shrink, because one wasn't enough when I started seeing ghosts."

"Casey?"

"Yeah, that's right, I live with one, talk to him too. My closest friends right now are Jasper and a dead guy! You still want me back?"

"Jesus, Casey, what is wrong with you? We were having a civil conversation and you go psychotic on me? What the hell are you talking about?"

At that point, he knew damn well how crazy he sounded, but in for a penny, as the saying went. "I see dead people, or one in particular, and he's kind of hot. Or was, back when he was alive. Jasper sees him too. I can hear him. We talk all the time. He even helped me make breakfast this morning. I cooked, in a kitchen, for the first time in months, and I didn't freak out."

"Well, you're starting to freak me out. Maybe you should call Dr. Patel," she suggested, only the slightest hint of concern in her tone.

"You know, I can understand you leaving me at my lowest. I was in a bad place and you couldn't handle that, but taking all my shit with you was just pathetic. But I was willing to overlook that because I felt guilty about not being able to give you the life I thought you deserved, but for you to sit there and imply that all our problems were my fault and that you're willing to take me back as some kind of favor to me is utter bullshit.

"So no, the reason I called was not to grovel at your feet for another chance. I only called because I wanted some goddamn closure. But now that you pissed me off, I want my stuff back, all of it, undamaged. Text me the address, and I'll send a truck to pick it up. Other than that, I don't think we have anything left to say."

He hung up before she had a chance to respond. He hadn't stood up to her in a long time, and he felt like an asshole about it, an idiot for even trying. The closure felt nice, though. Maybe he would've been more impressed with his palm reading if Bobbie had mentioned how relieved he'd feel after biting the bullet and calling Isabel.

The conversation didn't go exactly the way he had hoped, but he felt lighter now that he'd aired out all their dirty laundry. He got to say his piece, and he might even get some of his stuff back. Not that he cared about any of it but his appliances, specifically his bread and pasta makers, but his sous-chef had those anyway.

He tossed his phone on the passenger seat and started the car. He looked forward to getting home and sharing his catharsis with Myles. He hadn't lied to her about his only friend being the spirit he shared a dwelling with. And if that made him crazy, he could live with it.

CHAPTER FOURTEEN
A CRUEL FATE

MYLES FOLLOWED Casey into the house as he carried in his groceries. Jasper greeted them both with a meow as he scent marked their legs. Myles smiled down at him, happy to be included, but his expression fell when thoughts of helplessness set in. He watched Casey move around the kitchen as he put everything away, and Myles wished he could've done something useful for a change.

"Hey, Myles? Are you around? Thought I'd tell you about my day," Casey said once he finished with the groceries. The contagiousness of his jovial mood did wonders to chase off the gloominess of Myles's.

He watched Casey grab himself a beer and settle on the couch, his hand rubbing over his potbelly. Myles had followed him into the living room and flopped down in his usual chair, leaning back with his feet propped up on the coffee table. He tracked the movement of the beer bottle to Casey's lips. He didn't know which one he craved more: a taste of the brew or the way Casey's lips pursed around the rim of the bottle.

Myles answered with a "Yeah, I'm here" that must have gone unheard. He figured he'd spent too much effort talking with the Waltons, but he'd enjoyed the conversation, and Fred had given him hope that Casey might see him someday. After Casey called for him again, he had to fall back on kicking the coffee table to communicate.

"Tired? That's all right. I can still tell you about my day if you want."

Thud.

"Okay, so you know that bakery I went to for the cake? With the hot baker?"

Myles groaned as Casey recounted his tale. It explained his chipper mood, flirting with the stupid baker again. He supposed he should've been happy for his friend, but he couldn't help turning green with envy. He couldn't leave his mile of paradise, but Casey had no problem going off to flirt with hot bakers while he sulked alone. He hadn't fared well in life, but he didn't expect things to suck in the afterlife too.

"But then I started to have an attack. It was horrible. I felt like a freak and ran out of there as fast as I could. He probably thinks I'm some sort of weirdo now." Casey paused to take a swig of beer, his shoulders relaxing as he went on to talk about Bobbie the fortune-teller, but Myles couldn't get his brain off the baker.

And maybe the way Casey's Adam's apple bobbed when he swallowed.

He perked up when Casey started in on his conversation with his ex-girlfriend. "I have to thank you for giving me the courage to pick up the phone to call her. I know it might not seem like much, but it was a big deal to me. I've just been thinking about what happened between you and James, and I guess I wanted a little closure...."

Closure. He wished his went a different way too, but at least he felt useful for a change. If his purpose didn't involve himself, then he wanted to try his best to help Casey get back on his feet, like some sort of guardian angel or something. He hadn't sprouted wings or anything, but who knew how those things worked. If Casey ended up as his charge, he vowed to do his best to keep him safe and happy.

He didn't really think of Casey like that, like someone who needed protection, but maybe he needed a little guiding. Myles had no idea how something like that worked, though. Damn, he really wished the whole dying and getting stuck in the Between had come with a manual or a course on how to actually do it.

"Then I told her I wanted all my stuff back. It was like I was possessed. Did you possess me? Ha, just kidding! Do you know how to do that, though? Never mind. I don't want to know. But man, Myles, I wish you could've seen me. I was on fire. It felt so satisfying to be able to speak my mind after having all that guilt inside me. I feel... liberated. If I was anywhere other than this tiny ghost town, no pun intended, I'd go out and celebrate."

He tried to find a glimmer of happiness for Casey within him, but Myles's mood started slipping back into brooding self-pity. He wanted Casey to see him. He wanted to feel normal again. He wanted to be alive, instead of having to live vicariously through Casey.

He got so wrapped up in negative thoughts of how much being dead sucked major ass that he hadn't noticed Casey going quiet across from him. When he looked up, Casey's brown eyes fixated on him with more focus than usual. He didn't think anything of it at first—Casey knew he liked that chair—but on closer inspection, Myles noticed his stunned expression.

"What?" Myles sighed, not expecting Casey to hear him.

"I… can see you."

"What?" he shrieked.

"I-I can see you."

"And hear me too?"

"Well yeah, but Myles, I can see you!"

Okay, that was what he thought Casey said. He wondered how he looked to him. To himself, he seemed the same as the day he died. They had watched some shows about hauntings, and the spirits usually appeared as clouds of mist or orbs of light, sometimes as dark shadows, but very rarely did people claim to see the spirits clearly.

"What do I look like?"

Casey rubbed his eyes and blinked a few times. "Like, uh, well, I can see through you, but you aren't just an outline like you were the first time. You have substance? I don't really know how to describe it. You look like the pictures I have seen of you… kind of like I imagined you to be."

Casey's eyes took him in, and Myles turned self-conscious under the scrutiny of his gaze. "So basically I look like the ghost of my former self?"

They both chuckled at that, but Casey nodded. "You look good, you know, for a ghost and all."

"And you can hear me now," Myles added, hoping to steer the focus off his physical form. Moments ago he'd been desperate for Casey to see him, but now that he could, Myles wanted to disappear. He didn't want Casey to see him as a ghost, even though that's what he was.

"Whoa, what happened?" Casey asked, his eyes now darting around. "You disappeared."

He wanted Casey to see him and he could, and then he wanted to disappear and he disappeared? This ghost business made absolutely no sense.

"I don't know how I did it."

"Maybe you just need to get a little stronger."

"And how exactly am I supposed to do that? It's not like I can lift weights," he teased.

Casey rolled his eyes, taking another drink before he replied, "I don't know. I've never been dead before. But you haven't either. Too bad Joe isn't much help. Maybe you should find another ghost guru."

"I think I just did."

AFTER MYLES told Casey about Fred, he spent the rest of the afternoon popping in and out of the house while Casey snoozed on the couch. He followed Eli on his mail route for a while—the gossip came as a nice distraction and gave him a chance to get out of his head—but his thoughts kept circling back to Casey.

He had seen him. They had established a new kind of contact, and it sent him reeling. He'd wanted it, or thought he had, but it didn't satisfy him as much as he'd hoped. Casey had seemed pretty excited about it, which was how he had expected to feel, but instead he felt self-conscious… and dead. Very, very dead.

Of course he already knew that, but the cold reality of it had smacked him in the face.

He'd spent the last three months or so trying to make himself visible, trying to get anyone to take notice of him, to acknowledge his existence, but when someone finally had, all of a sudden it became too real. He could no longer dismiss it as a weird dream or some sort of strange experience. Someone had seen his ghost form, and no matter what happened from then on, he couldn't deny his death. He had to accept it, but that kind of finality felt like a sucker punch.

And Casey, the one person who believed in him, who he could talk to and who he'd started to grow a little attached to, had seen him, seen his true form: the hollow shell of the man he used to be. What really bothered him, what he tried to push down into the abyss, manifested itself in the form of jealousy. He envied that damn baker.

What did he hope could come of the developing feelings he had for Casey, someone who would remain very much alive for the next fifty years or so?

Nothing.

He sat down in the sand at the edge of the beach to sulk, burying his feet in the bits of broken shell and eroded earth as the sun began to set. Just as he'd thought, he felt Joe appear to his right. "I want to go with you."

Joe draped his arm over his shoulder and sighed. "Oh, kiddo, it's not your time."

"I have nothing here, no reason to stay. I'm ready to go."

"Living wasn't easy. What makes you think death is?"

"Can you stop being philosophical for one second?" Myles yelled, scoffing when he scared a group of seagulls off. "I know why I'm here now. I'm supposed to help him, right? Get his life back on track, go back to cooking, and find someone to love. Well, I can't do it, okay. I can't. Tell whoever's in charge up there to find someone else."

Joe removed his arm but pressed his shoulder into Myles's. "I've never known you to be a quitter, son. What makes you think you can't?"

"Because it's too hard. He mentioned the baker a few times, and already I hate the guy. That means something. That means I'm not objective. I can't help him. I can't watch him fall in love with someone else." Myles twisted his fingers into the soft sand as he tried to zero in on the roar of waves crashing in the distance to calm him. "I like him. I don't know why, but I do. And maybe it's just circumstances, because he's the only person I interact with, but what if it's more than that?"

"What if he's your soul mate?"

Myles scoffed again and shook his head. "I don't believe in that sort of thing. And even if I did, what a cruel fate to meet them after I died."

"So you have a crush on your roommate. If you have feelings for him, wouldn't the right thing to do be to help him find someone worthy of him, someone who would treat him well and who could make him happy? Don't you want him to be happy?"

"Dammit, Joe! I told you to stop being philosophical."

Before he could admit that he had a point, Joe vanished. He felt like an asshole for yelling at him, for chasing him off.

The surge from the tide started to creep up the beach, the surf lapping at his bare feet. He wanted to sit there and let the ocean wash over him, wash him out to sea so he could drown properly this time. Maybe he'd get to go to the Beyond with Joe and the rest of the dead where he belonged. He lay back and stared up at the clouds rushing by overhead, hoping he might ascend right into them.

Soon the salty water began to beat against his calves. Only he wished he could've felt it. He'd made a determined decision to stay there until his sour mood passed. It couldn't do him any harm, and he didn't know if staying in the house with Casey was wise. He thought about going to the Waltons', but he didn't want to burden them. He could've slipped into the Camarillos' house; they wouldn't have noticed him.

When the surge had come up to his thighs, he decided to get up and drag himself to the house. He'd just stay in the guest room. Casey never went in there. He'd remain close but out of the way. Limiting his contact with his housemate felt like a safe compromise. It'd help keep the ridiculous attraction blossoming inside him at bay.

Why did he have to overreact about every little thing? Casey wouldn't waste time on an apparition when he had a hot baker out there waiting for him. Myles couldn't cook, couldn't bake, and couldn't even touch him. What kind of relationship could they have under the circumstances? An unsatisfying one, to say the least.

Forcing one foot in front of the other, he trudged up the steps. He looked around the kitchen and saw a few takeout containers on the island. Casey must not've felt brave enough to cook. That didn't surprise him. He knew breakfast had taken a lot out of him from an emotional standpoint. He moved into the empty living room, which did surprise him. Casey never missed *Wheel of Fortune*.

"Casey?" he called against his better judgment.

"Bathroom," Casey hollered from the other room.

"Just checking."

Jasper rubbed against his leg and let out a soft meow. He reached down and stroked his fur for a few moments before proceeding into the guest room, the shut door keeping Jasper from following him. He felt bad when the tabby cried for a minute, but he hadn't figured out how to work doorknobs yet, not that he needed to.

He did a belly flop onto the bed, groaning when he rebounded a few times. In the beginning, he assumed nothing would beat the horrible reality that he'd died. Now he knew a fate worse than death: falling for someone alive while trapped in the Between.

But having no control over either really took the cake.

CHAPTER FIFTEEN
A LITTLE SOMETHING EXTRA

CASEY HATED that he couldn't see Myles. He questioned his sanity quite often, because what kind of grown man had an imaginary friend? But when he saw Myles sitting in that chair, his essence, his spirit, his ghost, he wanted to believe. Myles didn't stay visible for long, but Casey knew he'd have his strength built up in no time. And after a chat with Mrs. Walton, he had confirmation of his sanity.

Myles looked like the pictures Casey had seen of him. His chiseled jaw and piercing blue eyes had Casey close to swooning, and his hair looked so perfect—light brown at the roots with golden hues—that it had Casey white-knuckling his beer bottle to keep from jumping over the coffee table and running his hands through it. Not that he could.

And that's when he knew he was in trouble.

He chided himself for his inappropriate thoughts, but his unexpected attraction to Myles caught him off guard. He'd admit that he generally felt more attraction to men than women, but a ghost seemed like a whole other level. Yes, he identified as pansexual, but he didn't know where ghosts and otherworldly entities fell in the grand scheme of things.

Myles had died; they couldn't change that. But now he found his fingers itching to look up every picture of him he could find on the Internet. Having an attraction to a dead person didn't seem too out of the ordinary, but he doubted it fell within the realm of healthy relationships to actually date one. His therapists would have a field day if he admitted it. They would institutionalize him for sure.

Perhaps he just felt a little lonely. A few months had passed since he and Isabel broke up—and years since he'd slept with a man. Maybe he needed to get laid. He should probably go back to the bakery and ask Matt for his number. Dating an actual person would help get his mind back on the world of the living. He chalked up his weird interest in Myles to the fact that the spirit was the only friend he had in Land's

End. Now that he'd gotten some semblance of closure from Isabel, he felt ready to start putting himself out there.

CARS FILLED the bakery parking lot and overflowed into the street when Casey pulled up a few days later. Why hadn't he left sooner? He thought the early morning rush would've wound down by ten, but the midmorning rush must've taken its place. He had to wait in line for a few minutes behind a woman with her two wailing children, but when he got up to the counter to find Matt smiling at him, he knew he would've waited twice as long.

"Good morning, sunshine," Matt said, and Casey might have flushed a little at the flattering greeting.

"Hey, how is it going?"

"Excellent! What can I get for you today? Would you like to try one of the turnovers? I have some peach ones that just came out of the oven."

He nodded and tried to remind himself not to grin like an idiot. But he didn't have high hopes he'd succeed. "Yeah, that sounds good." His stomach started to protest his lack of breakfast, but he thought it best to try to cut down on the amount of junk he stuffed himself with. His jeans all felt too tight, and he didn't want to have to buy an all-new wardrobe, not when he had no revenue coming in.

Matt leaned over the counter and whispered, "How about I throw in a little something extra in exchange for your number?"

Casey couldn't say no to that win-win situation. "I think that's an even trade." He watched as Matt walked down to the end of the display case and picked up a sack. He slid in a turnover and dropped an éclair into the bag. Casey didn't care for them much, but he couldn't argue with free.

Without a word, Matt dug around in the pocket of his apron for a pen and handed it to Casey along with an empty bag. He wrote his number down on it and slid it back across the counter in exchange for his pastries.

"Can I call you tonight?" Matt asked, a hopeful smirk on his face.

"I look forward to it," Casey said, smiling back. He paid for his peach turnover and the coffee he added to his order and took a seat by the window. He thought about going home, but he liked the scenery, and he liked the peaceful music playing overhead. Well, up until the mom with the obnoxious kids sat down at the table right next to his and drowned it out. He tried to ignore their cries for sugary confections but gave up when he finished his very delectable turnover.

On his way out to the car, his sister called and invited him over for Sunday dinner. He didn't want to go, but he'd promised his therapist he'd try to reconnect with her. Dr. Patel seemed to think it might help his mental health if he put some effort into bettering the few relationships he still had. He'd try; that's all he could do.

He found Myles sitting on the deck when he returned home. Jasper meowed from where he'd stretched himself out across Myles's lap, and Casey bent down to scratch him behind his ears. Their fingers brushed in the process, and Casey let out a little laugh. "What?" Myles asked.

"I think I felt you," Casey explained as he pulled an empty deck chair closer to the one Myles and Jasper currently occupied. "It felt like an electric shock."

"I'm not visible, am I? I really can't tell, you know."

"No, but I definitely felt something."

Casey sat down and lay back on the lounge chair. The day had turned cloudy, the forecast calling for light showers. He hated storms, but he'd be okay as long as the thunder and lightning kept its distance. "So... I gave Matt my number this morning." He tried not to turn pink at the admission, but he had a feeling he failed.

"You mean the baker?"

"Yeah, he gave me a free éclair. Do you think that means he's interested? I mean, obviously he is if he asked me for my number, and he gives me free food every time I go in, but...."

"You're really bad at the whole dating thing, aren't you?" Myles asked, his tone a little clipped, but Casey assumed he felt off-kilter.

Myles hadn't seemed comfortable talking about the real world as of late. He understood, but Myles was the only *person* he really had to talk to, and he wanted to share his excitement with him. "We can talk about something else if you want."

"No, it's fine. I mean, I'm pretty bad at it too... was pretty bad, so I'm not one to judge."

"If you aren't comfortable—"

"I said it's fine... really."

Casey sighed and leaned his head back on the chair. The whole ghost thing had started to frustrate him too. Myles seemed really cool, the kind of person he would've loved to go out and have a beer with, but that was impossible now. Maybe he should keep the baker stuff to himself. He didn't want Myles to feel left out, and besides, they had other things they could talk about.

MATT CALLED around five that night, and they made plans to meet up at seven for dinner. Casey usually preferred staying in for dates, but he put on his best—and loosest—pair of jeans and his favorite shirt. Myles gave him a hum of approval on his attire, although reluctantly, and he headed out the door.

After he pulled up to the restaurant Matt had chosen, Casey met him at the front door. They had to go two towns over to find a Mexican restaurant, but they shared a love for the cuisine. Casey had stayed away from restaurants since the fire claimed his own, and the thought of going inside made it hard to swallow. Somehow he managed to hold it together in the beginning.

But after they placed their order, the smell of fajitas wafting over from the table behind him triggered an attack. His breathing shortened and his palms began to sweat. "Will you excuse me?" Casey asked, but he'd already stood up and started toward the restroom before his date could reply. Thank God Myles had insisted he bring his medication.

The restroom sat empty. He barely noticed between the narrowing of his vision and the sweat pouring down his forehead. He cupped his hands under the faucet and took a drink of tap water, splashing his face a few times before heading into the closest stall. Getting his head between his legs sometimes helped, so he sat on the toilet as he fiddled with his bottle of pills.

God, he ached for Myles's comforting presence. He couldn't even call him for a little pep talk.

After struggling with the stupid childproof cap, he twisted it off and fished out a few pills with shaky fingers. He didn't bother counting them, just threw his head back and swallowed. His counting-by-eights trick helped a little, as did the whole head-between-his-legs thing, but it must've taken longer than he thought because he soon heard the door open and Matt calling his name.

"Y-yeah, I'm all right, just uh…." He looked down at his shirt soaked through with sweat and knew he had to get home.

"Did you need me to call an ambulance?"

"No, I'm… I just need a minute," he replied, but the little voice in his head said he needed Myles.

He had already ruined the date and figured Matt wouldn't give him another chance, so he decided to suck it up and face him. He wiped his brow the best he could with a little bit of toilet paper and stood. When Casey opened the door, Matt straightened from where he'd leaned against the sink as he waited. Casey didn't bother looking in the mirror; he knew he looked like shit.

"Sorry, I just…." He couldn't think of another way to spin what had happened, so he went with the truth. "I had a panic attack. It's been a long time since I've set foot in a restaurant, not since mine burned down, and I wanted to be ready, but I'm just… not." He didn't realize he'd said everything to the floor instead of Matt until a gentle finger lifted his chin.

"It's really fine. We can always go back to my place. Most people think I'm just a baker, but I did go to culinary school," Matt said with a warm chuckle.

"Are you sure? I mean, you still want to?" he asked, a bit surprised that someone as cute as Matt would want him in his current state of disarray.

"Yeah, why not? You're cute, and you can probably cook better than me, and maybe we have some other things in common. More importantly, I'd like to find out. I'll go have the kitchen make our orders to go and we can go to my place."

Casey tried to ignore the look of hope on Matt's face, but he'd take it over pity. "As nice as that sounds, I think I should probably just call it a night."

"Are you sure?"

He nodded, and they went back to their table. Or Casey tried to go back to the table, but he ended up taking a detour and heading right out the door. Matt came out of the restaurant a few minutes later with two bags. He handed one to Casey. "I believe this one is your enchiladas."

"I'm sorry about this."

"Hey, don't worry about it. Just call me when you get home so I know you made it." Casey got in the car and looked up at him with apologetic eyes. "Really, it's fine. I get it."

"Thanks, I appreciate it," Casey said, reaching for the door handle. Matt helped him shut the door, and Casey gave a short wave before pulling out of the parking spot. Well, that had turned into a complete catastrophe. At least the food smelled good.

He sulked up the walkway once he got home, then made his way to the kitchen for a fork, not bothering to reheat the cold food.

"You're home early," Myles said from behind him.

"I…." He paused, not really sure what to say. He could've lied, said the guy turned into a jerk or that he got stood up, but he didn't see the point in it. He felt a hand on his shoulder, or the ghostly equivalent, that same shock he'd felt before. "I had a panic attack in the restaurant."

"Are you okay?" Myles asked with a gentle squeeze of his shoulder that he absolutely felt.

"Yeah, he said we could reschedule, and he seemed to understand."

Myles removed his hand, and Casey soon heard feet banging against the island. Without turning around, he knew he'd find Myles sitting on the counter in what had become his favorite spot in the kitchen. He didn't acknowledge how long the phantom feeling of Myles's hand lingered on his shoulder because it was inconsequential.

He sent Matt a text after he sat down, and then dove into his dinner. Myles had joined him at the table. The awkwardness of someone watching him eat had dissipated in the last few weeks. He'd grown to expect Myles to join him for meals to the point that he'd feel lonely without him. They watched some reruns of an old sitcom before bed, but he couldn't wait to climb in and attempt to forget about his crappy date.

Maybe next time he'd invite Matt over. That would entail him taking his chances in the kitchen, but if he had Myles around, he might be more comfortable with it. He hoped he would, anyway. But the next time they made plans, he should probably let Matt do the cooking.

MATT SURPRISED Casey when he called the next day while on his break at the bakery. He wanted to check in on him. To be honest, Casey felt weird about someone showing an interest in him. He didn't feel his most attractive as of late, and he obviously had things he needed to work through. Then again, he'd started to itch for a little *physical* companionship. He did have needs after all.

So when he found himself on his back on Matt's couch the next night, with a hand up his shirt and the guy's tongue down his throat, he ignored the voice telling him to slow down. Matt was a good kisser, and the finger-licking chicken and rice dish he'd made had him sated. He hadn't made out with anyone but Isabel in years, and he missed how it felt to kiss someone breathless, but when Matt tried to slip his shirt off, he sat up and pushed him away.

"Sorry, I just think we should take things slow." He felt like a tease, a virgin teenager afraid to go all the way, but it just didn't feel right, despite what the chubby in his jeans said.

Matt sat up and adjusted himself. "Yeah, I get it."

He sat up as well and fixed his shirt, which had hiked up a little, thankful that Matt seemed understanding. "Sorry."

"Hey no, it's okay. I can do slow."

"Maybe next time I can cook you dinner at my place, as an apology?"

Matt smiled and ran a hand over his cheek. "I'd like that, but you don't need to apologize."

"I'm really glad you understand." He ran a hand over his kiss-swollen lips as a cloud of awkwardness rolled in. "I should probably head out, then."

"Are you sure?"

"Yeah, but I'll text you." Casey stood up, and Matt walked him to his car, giving him a peck on the cheek when they got there. "How's Friday at seven?"

"Sounds great."

"Great, I'll text you the address."

"It's a date." Matt smiled as he helped Casey shut the door.

On the drive home, he wondered what had possessed him to offer up dinner. He knew deep down it would backfire on him; he just knew it. But even if it did, at least Myles and Jasper would be there to guide him through it. He wondered what Matt would say about him living with a ghost.

Chapter Sixteen
Dumbo's Feather

CASEY HAD spent the last few days buzzing around the house, and it had started to get on Myles's nerves. Sure, he might've resented his recent happiness and the stupid baker at the root of it all, but it had more to do with the fact that, over the past week or so, his little crush on Casey had become more and more obvious. He hated it, he hated himself for it, and he hated Casey for ever moving in.

"God, you're such an idiot," he chided himself. He didn't think of himself as a jealous person. Not once did he get jealous when James flirted with reporters or photographers or anyone else. He didn't even mind when he flirted with Logan, even after he had his suspicions about the two of them, so he didn't get the whole Casey and the baker thing.

"I'm not sure I can do this," Casey said from the kitchen. Myles could sense him going into panic mode. He got up from his spot on the couch and joined him.

He felt torn between helping him overcome his anxiety and letting him suffer, because if the latter happened, then maybe he'd cancel his little date. Myles had to overcome his jealousy. It wasn't fair for him to intervene in Casey's life, nor was it his place to get in the way. And he certainly had no business falling for someone still very much alive.

"Order takeout and pretend you made it," Myles suggested, half teasing and half serious.

"He's a chef too. He'll know," Casey replied.

Myles quirked a brow in confusion. "I thought he was a baker."

"He is, but he's also a classically trained chef."

"Well, in that case," Myles said as he rolled his eyes, "maybe he'll know, maybe he won't…. If he likes you, he won't care. Either way you'll be fine. I'll be your assistant, or whatever you call it."

"Sous-chef," Casey corrected.

"Yeah, that."

Casey pulled out the steaks he'd marinated all night and set the bag in the sink. "It's probably a good idea that I'll be grilling these. Maybe it won't be so bad," he said as he shrugged. He went back to the refrigerator and gathered his ingredients for the side dishes.

Myles watched as he got to work mixing and chopping different herbs and spices. After deliberating for days, Casey decided on roasted potatoes and mixed vegetables to accompany the meat. Only once did he get a little shaky, his breathing picking up, but Myles swooped in and distracted him because he wanted to be a good wingman, dammit. It had nothing to do with the fact that he wanted an excuse to stand so close to him.

When the doorbell rang, Myles went into stealth mode. "Good luck."

Casey sighed and wiped his hands on a nearby dishrag. "Thanks."

He'd told Casey he'd spend the evening on the beach and maybe stay with the Waltons to give them some privacy. He lied. He wanted to stick around and check the guy out. He also wanted to keep an eye on Casey just in case he needed him. Jasper might give him away, but he had to take the risk.

Matt kissed Casey when he opened the door, and Myles held back a groan. The guy didn't look *that* attractive, but maybe Casey liked the preppy frat boy type. Myles followed as he led Matt out to the deck. They had a few beers while Casey grilled their steaks. It made Myles proud that he didn't have any trouble manning the flames, but he didn't like the way Matt hovered around him, hand on the small of his back. That was his issue, he knew, so he did his best to ignore it.

Jasper didn't like the guy either. Every time Matt tried to pet him, he let out a low growl and moved away. Myles took that as a good sign, but he wanted to give Matt a chance for Casey's sake… or so he kept telling himself. Because maybe the bitterness that he couldn't nose into the thick carpet of Casey's hair while he cooked had started to get to him.

Matt and Casey made small talk, which, if you asked Myles, felt stilted and awkward. Then they went down to the beach for a walk before sunset. Everything went great—for Casey—and when they got back to the house, they settled in to watch a movie. Myles made sure to stand so he wouldn't tempt Jasper to sit in his lap.

The date seemed picture-perfect, and they agreed on a second movie, this time a romcom, and Myles just knew it would lead to some making out. He wanted to leave because he really didn't want to have to watch that, but when Casey excused himself to go to the bathroom, Matt pulled out his phone and shot off a few texts.

Myles moved behind him so he could read over his shoulder, and what he saw made him livid. The dick bag had made plans to meet up with someone else after his date with Casey. He knew a hookup when he saw one, and no one could mistake *Gonna make u ride my dick so good when I get there* for anything else.

He couldn't help himself. Slapping the guy upside his head had been an instinctual response. Anybody would've done the same, living or dead. His anger had boiled over at the thought of someone disrespecting Casey like that, to such an amazing person, and Matt's head obviously needed some sense knocked into it.

"What the hell?" Matt yelped, rubbing the back of his head. He swiveled around, but Myles made sure not to show himself yet.

He wanted to march into the bathroom to tell Casey what Matt had done, but before he could, Casey walked back into the living room. He sat down on the couch next to Matt and snuggled close. The sight turned Myles's stomach. He had to get that guy out of their house. He'd assumed the position of Casey's guardian spirit, and he would save Casey from the douche bag as his first act of duty.

Once the next movie had started, Myles flicked the guy's ear. To his credit, Matt did his best to shrug him off, but Myles persisted. He had nothing else to do but to stay there and pester him until he left Casey alone. He tried for a wet willy, but that didn't work since his hand went right through Matt's head. Then he tried to tug on his hair a little, but he had the most success with slapping him upside the head a few more times.

Matt squirmed and twitched so badly that Casey ended up pausing the movie. "Are you okay?"

"Yeah, I think there might be a bug flying around in here or something," Matt said, smiling sweetly, but Myles heard the buzz from another text going off in his jeans.

Myles leaned down and whispered in Matt's ear, "Lying cheater."

"What the hell was that?" Matt asked, batting the air beside him. "Did you hear that?"

"Hear what?"

"I thought I heard something.… Sorry, it's probably nothing. I don't usually watch scary movies, so the one we just watched must have me a little on edge."

Myles waited for them to get comfortable enough for Casey to start the movie again before whispering in Matt's ear again. "Cheating asshole."

"Okay, this is… did you hear *that*?"

"Maybe it was the wind," Casey reasoned, but he didn't looked convinced. "It can get pretty windy up here on the bluff. At least I *hope* that's all it is."

Myles knew that last bit was directed at him, so he didn't bother whispering the next time he spoke. He wanted Casey to hear him too. "Are you going to tell him about Tommy?"

"Please tell me you heard that!" Matt hollered, his voice shaky as he jumped off the couch. Myles smirked to himself. The guy deserved a lot worse, but he did the best he could.

"Who's Tommy?" Casey asked, brow furrowing. He suddenly looked sad and small, and Myles felt like a huge jerk for ruining his evening, but he knew what it felt like to get cheated on, and he didn't want Casey to go through that if he could help it.

"I don't know a Tommy."

Myles scoffed. "Maybe the booty call you set up after this date might ring a bell."

"Who the hell is that?" Matt shrieked, his face paling as he looked around at thin air.

"I don't hear anything," Casey said.

"He was sending some guy texts while you were in the bathroom, Casey."

"I was… how did…. What the hell is going on here?" Matt asked. "Is this some kind of prank or something? Because if it is, I'm not amused."

"Who were you texting, then?" Casey asked, and Myles turned his anger inward for causing the frown that had Casey's features all contorted. But it was Matt's fault, wasn't it?

Myles took a swipe at the guy again, and that got him moving toward the door. "We aren't exclusive or anything. Fuck, we only had two dates. A date and a half, since you bailed on the first one."

"You said you understood," Casey said in a quiet voice.

"I made you dinner, paid at the restaurant, and gave you free pastries. The least you could do was blow me," Matt huffed as he yanked the door open. "I don't know what the hell's going on here, but you can find yourself a new bakery."

"It's not like your food was that great anyway," Casey shouted, slamming the door behind him when he exited.

He leaned his back against the door and buried his face in his hands. Myles didn't know what to say. Maybe he shouldn't have haunted Matt, but he saw no other option. Casey deserved better than that creep anyway, so maybe it was best things ended before they got more serious. But why did it make him feel like such a jerk?

"I'm sorry it didn't work out," he offered, shrugging as he sat down on the arm of the couch.

"You're sorry?" Casey sneered, fire building in his amber eyes. "You spied on us, attacked my date, drove him away, and all you can say is 'sorry'?"

"He made plans with another guy behind your back!" Myles countered, his sympathy morphing into defensiveness. He'd done Casey a favor by getting rid of that asshole, and now Casey wanted to lecture him for it?

"Is that what ghosts do when they're bored? Screw with other people's relationships?" Casey continued. He pushed himself away from the door, and Myles stood too as he approached. "You had no right to interfere like that!"

They stood nose to nose, and Myles figured he could see him, thanks to his seething anger and the fact that Casey looked right into his eyes. Myles thought about thumping him between the eyes right where he'd hit him with the pill bottle during their first encounter, but he resisted. He'd just wanted to save Casey the heartbreak of falling for Matt. Why was Casey giving him shit for it?

"In case you didn't notice, I did you a favor. And I have *every* right. I'm your goddamn guardian angel."

"I didn't ask for any favors, and I didn't ask for you!"

"Well, then maybe you should pack up your shit and leave," Myles said.

"Maybe I will."

"Good!"

Myles stomped toward the back door, but Casey hadn't finished. "In case you forgot, you're the one who needs to move on!"

"I didn't forget," Myles yelled back. "Because if I were still alive, I could slam this damn door in your stupid face!" Walking through the door out onto the deck muffled Casey's reply, but he knew he wouldn't want to hear it anyway.

He stormed down to the beach. Things had deteriorated between him and Casey at breakneck speed. He thought he'd done a good thing by exposing Matt's true colors, and maybe someday Casey would understand, but he also had a point. Perhaps Myles had crossed the line by terrifying his guest. Waiting till Matt left might've worked out better, but he couldn't take it back now.

Moping was the only thing he wanted to do, so he sat down and shouted at seagulls for a while. One would land nearby, and he'd holler and curse until the poor thing flew away. The sun had set a while ago and the beach sat deserted, but he still had little control over when and where people heard him. The yelling felt therapeutic, but he didn't think he should chase anyone else away.

He didn't head back to the house until early morning. He figured Casey had probably gone to bed hours ago, so he thought it best if he spent the night outside on the deck. He wouldn't have made any noise unless he wanted to, but he didn't want to chance waking or running into him, if Casey hadn't already left. Sadness replaced Myles's anger, and he feared going inside would confirm that he'd driven Casey away. He couldn't face it, not yet.

MYLES WOKE up when the kitchen door slid open. It gave him a few seconds to prepare for Jasper when he charged out and pounced on him— he swore he could almost feel his claws digging into his thigh. Myles sat up and started to scratch the base of his tail, eyeing Casey as he stepped out with a mug of coffee. He felt relieved that they hadn't left yet, but that didn't mean they wouldn't.

Casey sat down on what had become his deck chair. A beat of silence followed. Myles didn't know what to say. Thankfully Casey broke the ice. "I'm sorry I got so mad last night."

"I'm sorry I ruined your date," Myles replied. Honestly, he hated upsetting Casey more than ruining the date.

"You were just trying to do the right thing, and I appreciate that, I really do, but that wasn't the right way to do it."

"I know, Case, and I'm sorry, but I just couldn't let him play you like that. Not after what James did to me. You deserve so much better than an asshole like him." And he sure as shit deserved better than a ghost. Myles needed to get over his little obsession, because he had nothing to offer Casey but phantom caresses and a touch-starved future. That was no way to live.

"Maybe next time just talk to me first before you go all poltergeist and haunt my dates, would ya?"

"Yeah, I think I can do that."

"Good… so we're good?"

"Yeah, we're good."

Casey smirked at him over the rim of his coffee mug. "Good, because I need you to help me make breakfast."

"Why do I suddenly feel like Dumbo's feather?"

At that they settled into easy laughter, Myles thankful at having narrowly escaped driving Casey away a second time. He had expected to feel Casey's wrath, but it turned out that he understood. He and Jasper would remain, and Myles could—metaphorically—breathe a little easier. The downside, when he sat at the table to watch Casey eat the bacon he made for breakfast, all Myles could think about were memories of how it tasted.

The longer it dragged on, the more Myles hated being dead.

CHAPTER SEVENTEEN
RIDING OUT A STORM

CASEY NOTICED the storm clouds pushing in from the west around noon as they started to filter out the bright sunlight. Myles had said something about storms rolling in that evening, and it looked like they had arrived ahead of schedule. When Casey asked how he knew that, Myles told him he could tell by the change in wave pattern. He also felt the electricity building in the air and expressed how much he loved thunderstorms.

Casey, on the other hand, didn't care for them. Every crash of thunder scared him, and even with his eyes closed, he would see each strike of lightning as it lit up the dark sky. If he didn't have such a stubborn streak, he would've asked his sister if he could crash on her couch for the night. But although a ghost had assaulted and haunted him, either his stupidity or his pride had kept him from seeking emotional support, so he'd be damned if a thunderstorm would be the thing to send him cowering for comfort.

He hoped Myles stayed close by, at least for the worst of it. His spirit always did wonders for keeping Casey's mind off things, and not just while he made breakfast. The same might be true during the storm, but he didn't want to think about it. It'd only up his anxiety, and he had enough of that already.

Things had gone back to normal pretty quickly after their fight. A week had passed, and he hadn't gone back to the bakery since. If nothing else, his waistline would fare better for it. Unfortunately, he woke up that morning with a craving for a bear claw. Myles suggested that he make his own, but the storm pushed in quicker than he expected.

He put his plans for running to the store on hold because he didn't want to risk getting caught out in it. Instead he ordered Chinese food. Thank God they delivered. When it arrived, he grabbed the last beer and ate dinner over the sink. He watched out the window as the clouds hanging heavy over the water moved closer and closer by the minute.

He called out to Myles, but he went unanswered. He didn't want to go through the storm alone.

After he finished dinner, he made his way into the bathroom. He needed a shower, but he didn't think he had enough time. Needing something to do, he picked up his electric razor and eyed it for a moment. He didn't feel particularly attached to his beard. It was more a testament to his depression. One day he woke up and didn't have the energy or drive to shave anymore, and before he knew it, he looked like Sasquatch.

But he had started to feel better as of late, better than he'd felt in months. Hell, he'd cooked in the kitchen that morning without Myles and without panicking. He scratched his chin and turned his face from side to side as he contemplated whether or not to take the plunge. With a deep breath, he switched on the razor, the mechanical buzzing egging him on.

It took him a while, but soon his sink filled with a dusting of black hair and he could once again see the lower half of his face in the mirror. He switched off the razor and ran his hand over his chin, the stubble grating on the pads of his fingertips. Before he could go over it with a blade, Myles called from the living room. He gave a short answer before he picked up the shaving cream and covered his face.

He didn't really need a close shave since he planned on spending the rest of the night at home, but he'd already started, so he figured he should go all the way. He washed the residue off his face when he finished and reached for the aftershave. The whole thing felt cathartic and helped to keep his mind off the terror brewing outside, but as soon as he heard the first crack of thunder, he hightailed it out of the bathroom in search of Myles.

"Where are you?" he asked when he got to the living room. Jasper rubbed against his leg, and he bent down to scratch him under the chin. "Myles?" he tried again. He frowned when he didn't get an answer, suspecting that Myles didn't have enough energy to respond. Casey wasn't prepared to deal with the storm on his own.

He went to the kitchen island and took one of his pills, anticipating the rise in his anxiety levels. When he walked back into the living room, he noticed Jasper hovering around the door of the guest room. He knew before he opened the door that Myles was in there. He had to be. Jasper gravitated toward him like a piece of metal to a magnet.

Casey pushed the door open and whispered into the dark, "Myles?"

"Yeah, I'm here," he replied with a sigh.

"I know this is kind of like your room, but I was wondering if I could maybe crash with you tonight?" He really didn't want to sleep in his room, with all the glass from the doors and windows. He didn't think they would break, but the lightning would no doubt light up the whole room with every strike, and he wanted to forget the storm—not have a constant reminder of it every few seconds.

He took a few steps into the room. "I'll sleep on the floor if you like. I just don't want to be alone during the storm."

The mattress creaked. "Left side of the bed is free."

Myles didn't sound too happy about him intruding, but he couldn't go to his sister's, and he couldn't stomach the idea of sleeping alone. "If you want me to go—"

"No, it's fine, just… I'm just having a pity party."

Casey inched closer to the bed. "Did you want to talk about it?"

"Not much to talk about. Just tired of being dead."

As gently as he could, he sat down on the bed. He didn't know what to say to that. Saying sorry didn't seem appropriate, and saying something like he understood would be a flat-out lie. He sighed and moved to lie down. Jasper had already made himself cozy in the middle of it.

Just as he got settled, thunder rattled the windows and had him sucking in an involuntary breath before letting out a curse.

"You don't like storms?" Myles asked with a little more humor in his tone than Casey would've liked.

"Not particularly, no."

"I love them. They make me giddy and excited, the crashing thunder, the white-hot lightning streaking across the sky. I was tempted to stay out there in it, but when the swell started coming up the beach, I decided to come back in."

"I'm glad you did."

Myles continued after a morose pause, his voice soft and the words hanging between them, baleful and tragic, like the thick clouds outside. "Well, it's not like I can die again."

Casey rolled over onto his side facing him and Jasper. "You're not really dead to me. I mean, I know you are, but you seem real enough. If I close my eyes, it's kind of like you're here with Jaspy and me. And he thinks you're real too."

He heard Myles sigh. "Thanks. A cat and stranger are the only ones who believe I'm real. No offense, but that doesn't exactly cheer me up."

"I thought we were friends."

Casey felt the bed shift slightly, he swore he did, and envisioned Myles rolling over to face him. "We are."

A particularly loud roar of thunder had Casey cursing under his breath. "I can hardly cook without panicking. How am I supposed to handle something that has terrified me since I was a child?" He groaned. "I should have gone to my sister's."

"Have you tried not thinking about it?" Myles offered.

"That's kind of my plan, to keep my mind off it. That, and I just took a pill." He appreciated Myles's concern, but he didn't know what else he could do to distract himself from the extreme weather event taking place above his head. The wind howled outside, and he did calculations about how much damage the nearby trees could do. Maybe shatter the windows or fall on his car.

"What happened, if you don't mind me asking?" Myles asked.

He didn't exactly want to talk about it, but since he'd invaded Myles's room, the least he could do was indulge him. "My grandfather took me sailing a few days after my eleventh birthday, and we got caught in a freak storm. It scarred me for life, in case that wasn't obvious. I thought we were goners. This small boat we were on wasn't really built for riding out a storm in, and I just knew it would break apart under our feet...." The rocking of the boat had him sick the whole time as he clung to the deck for dear life, and he just knew they'd get lost at sea or struck by lightning before the ordeal passed. "That was the longest three hours of my life."

Since then, his anxiety would shoot through the roof when he knew a storm loomed on the horizon.

Another loud crash had Casey squeezing his eyes shut. Hearing Myles laugh next to him didn't comfort him, but something about it made him feel at ease. He didn't want to think about why or the possibility of falling for a spirit. Their relationship only existed as a matter of convenience for Myles. He couldn't leave.

What kind of life would that lead to, anyway? Casey would end up tied to the house too. As far as they knew, Myles couldn't wander out of their little slice of paradise. That meant no dates outside the house, or inside for that matter. Myles couldn't eat, so Casey couldn't truly share his love of food with him. Kids were out. How could he raise children with a ghost? The whole idea sounded so ludicrous that he chided himself for even entertaining it.

"You just need a distraction," Myles singsonged beside him.

Just as he opened his mouth to ask what kind of distraction, a sweet melody filled the small room, drowning out the sound of the rain beating down on the roof. Myles had started to sing. A smile bloomed on Casey's face that he didn't bother trying to stifle. He recognized the song immediately because he loved it as a child, "Kokomo" by The Beach Boys, but he didn't pay attention to the words. He couldn't, not when Myles's baritone timbre penetrated his chest cavity and tugged directly on his heartstrings.

He couldn't help but join in, even though he knew his voice didn't sound anywhere near as good, but he had to admit to its effectiveness in taking his mind off the storm. If he hammed it up a little, no one would ever know but the two of them. When the song ended, the smile stayed cemented on his face, immovable and resolute.

"That's one of my favorites," Casey said, turning his head in an instinctual bid to hide his reddened face even in the near pitch black.

Myles chuckled, and he swore he could feel it. "Mine too. I always loved them growing up. I had all their tapes.

"Oh God, tapes. We're old," he added with a partial groan mixed with his laughter.

"When I was little, one of my life goals was to visit every place in the song."

Casey felt the bed shift beside him again, and Myles sounded closer to him when he spoke again. "How many have you visited?"

"Uh... only Key Largo," Casey admitted. "Kind of pathetic, I know, but the restaurant business is kind of brutal, and I haven't had a proper vacation in, well, ever really."

"All work and no play makes Casey a dull boy," Myles teased.

Casey's fingers twitched, and he shot Myles a mock glare as he reached out to pet Jasper to satisfy the impulse to touch someone who wasn't really there. "Have you been to any of them?"

"I've been to Aruba and Bermuda. Talk about paradise, but I had the others on my list.... Guess that'll never happen now." He sighed, and Casey's heart twisted. "But I have seen some pretty incredible places in my day: Costa Rica, Fiji, Australia, Hawaii. So it's not like I can complain about that."

"Mhm."

"But it would've been nice, though…. You should probably go, while you have the chance."

Several resonant rounds of thunder had the mood threatening to slip back into the dark place they had started in. They spent the next hour bouncing from song to song, but nothing made as much of an impact as "Kokomo." At least they had the same taste in music—eighties retro stuff and alternative rock from the nineties—so they kept up with each other when the songs changed.

He'd ridden out worse storms in his life, but he couldn't remember the last time he'd shared such a terrifying ordeal with someone who spent the entire time trying their best to keep his mind off it. Isabel would cuddle with him, but she'd always make jabs at his inability to get over the past, and he hadn't really dated anyone else long enough to share the experience.

He tried his best not to stick his arm through Myles while he cuddled Jasper. At times he wondered what it would feel like to pass through him. Would they even notice? Could Myles possess him? Myles had touched him a few times, made physical contact, and it had felt real. He even felt every little shift he made rippling through the springs on the mattress.

Maybe it was all in his head, but he swore he sensed the heat coming off Myles. The bed felt less than empty, and he didn't want to give up the illusion of sleeping next to someone again. Not even after the storm passed. He thought about going back to his room once the thunder quieted, but a sleeping Jasper and Myles's presence next to him kept him anchored in place.

In that moment, he realized how strange his life had become. A ghost lay beside him in bed with nothing but a cat in between them. How had he gotten there? At least Myles turned out to be a friendly ghost and Jasper a friendly cat. It felt right, though, so maybe he didn't need dates and kids to have a happy life. But why had it taken a dead man to make him want to live again?

CHAPTER EIGHTEEN
SEE YOU AGAIN

HE KNEW Casey would label him a creep if he caught him staring while he slept, but he couldn't find it in him to care. Myles hadn't been able to tell in the dark of night that he'd shaved, but the sun had come up and the room started to lighten. And now he lay gazing at the face of a different man. He liked the beard, but Casey looked exquisite without it.

He longed to reach out his fingers and stroke the line of his jaw, to glide fingertips over the smooth skin of his cheekbone, drag the pad of his thumb over those bubblegum-pink lips, but he resisted the urge to do so. He didn't want to run the risk of waking him up if Casey somehow felt him, not when he had him so close, not when he looked so at peace.

He studied his face like it held the answers to everything. Who was he to question whether or not it did? He wanted to memorize it, every line, every faint wrinkle forming at the corners of his eyes, the angle in which they slanted just so, and the sweep of his wavy hair over his forehead. It hurt how much he wanted to brush it out of his face. He explained that away as some sort of random pet peeve, but he just wanted to touch. It was as simple as that.

Casey's phone ringing in the other room had his breath catching in his throat. He thought about not waking him, about letting him sleep for as long as possible, but Myles knew the longer Casey stayed in his bed, the more it would hurt when he left it.

"Casey?"

Casey gave a sleepy moan as his reply.

Myles repeated his name a few times, but Casey wouldn't stir. When calling his name didn't work, Myles counted to three and reached out his hand to add a gentle shake. Casey felt warm under his touch, his shoulder solid under his phantasmal fingers—or maybe his mind filled in the blanks with something he longed for. "Wake up, sleepyhead."

Casey rolled over onto his back and stretched as he let out a loud yawn. Myles had to avert his gaze from his lips. Instead his eyes inexplicably followed the line of his neck down to where it disappeared into the white of his T-shirt.

"Your phone rang. I tried to wake you."

"They'll call back," he moaned in a raspy, sleep-riddled voice, bleary eyes blinking a few times before his lids glued themselves back together. He rolled back over onto his side and peeked out through tiny slits, the umber tone of his eyes matching the mocha shade of the coffee he probably needed. "Did it wake you?"

"No, been awake for a few minutes."

"That's good." Casey's eyes slid shut once again, and soft snores soon emanated from his parted lips.

Myles rolled over onto his back, making a point of not watching the man sleep. They had one night of bonding over stupid songs, and now he couldn't tear his eyes away from him. Even if Casey returned the feelings Myles desperately tried to ignore, things could never work out between them. It just didn't seem feasible. Once Casey found happiness and got his life back on track, Myles hoped he'd get to disappear.

AFTER CASEY finally got up for the day, the three of them convened in the kitchen. Casey wore a smile for once while he gathered the ingredients to make breakfast, and he hummed the tune of a song Myles couldn't place under his breath.

"I'm guessing you slept well," Myles teased as he hopped up on the island.

Casey paused and turned to face him. He'd gotten pretty damn good at seeking Myles out, like his eyes were targeted missiles. "I did, and I think your bed might be more comfortable than mine."

Myles didn't believe that for a second. He'd spent the last night of his life in that bed, and if memory served, the damn thing felt like sleeping on a cloud. "It looks like you're feeling more confident today too. That's a good sign."

"It's amazing what a good night's rest can do for a person's mood. For a while there, I thought the storm would keep me up all night." He huffed out a laugh before measuring out some flour in a bowl. "Do you like pancakes?"

"I did," replied Myles, a little more accusatory than he had intended.

"Sorry, I didn't—"

"No, it's fine. It's just frustrating sometimes." He wanted to add how infuriated he felt about life taunting him, moving Casey's life forward while he hung around in another plane of existence. Except it wasn't much of an existence. He couldn't enjoy the fruits of life, only watch as Casey did. The world had moved on without him.

"I forget sometimes that you're… you know, dead. To me, it's like you're—" He spun around and blinked a few times before a smile broke across his face.

Myles had expected him to turn back around, but after Casey stood there staring dumbly, he quirked a brow. "What?"

"It's just… I can see you again."

Myles couldn't help but smirk at that. He didn't know what to say, so instead of saying anything he stuck his tongue out as a test. Casey mirrored him, and they both started laughing, deep belly laughs, the kind that left your stomach burning after they faded away.

"You can see me," Myles said, relieved more than anything. The first time had come as a shock to them both. He didn't know how to respond to it, to being visible after spending so much time in the shadows, but it lifted a burden he hadn't known he carried, some sort of curtain that kept the two of them apart. And by the way Casey's smile lingered, Myles thought he felt the same way.

Casey nodded back. "I can see you… which means I have a tumor that is soon going to kill me or you're—what—becoming stronger somehow?"

"I don't know, but I'll take it."

Casey turned back to his breakfast but tossed a look over his shoulder every so often. Myles didn't know if it was to see if he had gone or to keep proving to himself he hadn't made it up. "Maybe it's because I *want* to see you?"

Myles grinned. "Maybe."

Over breakfast, Casey suggested they take their midmorning stroll on the beach. Myles knew without having to look that the storm most likely littered it with a bunch of seaweed and debris washed ashore by the waves, but their walks had become habit. There was only one problem: his visibility hadn't worn off yet.

"I'm not sure if I'm comfortable with the whole world seeing me," Myles said. He didn't mind Casey and even Mrs. Walton seeing him, but what if he spooked someone and they called a priest or something? It all sounded improbable, but hauntings and weird sightings happened a lot if you believed half the drivel they showed on television these days. He didn't want to take the chance.

He also didn't want to admit it, but he kind of liked the fact that only Casey could see him. Fred must've felt a similar way. Nonetheless, Casey wanted to go down to the beach, and so did he. Being stuck in the house just wouldn't do.

"You don't have to be visible. Can you, I don't know, turn it off or something?" Casey smirked, and Myles didn't want to dwell on how quickly he'd figured out his weak spot for a man with a gorgeous smile.

"Let me try." Myles took a deep breath and tried to think invisible thoughts. He made a terrible ghost.

Casey's smile faltered just a tad. "That did it."

"You can't see me?"

"Nope. Give me a minute to go change, and we'll see if anything interesting washed up."

Myles sat at the table and watched Casey take his dishes to the sink. Jasper jumped up to join him. He and the little fur ball had bonded pretty closely, even Casey had mentioned it, but he knew one day Casey would move on, which was why he gave himself permission to ogle his ass when he walked toward the bedroom. He had to enjoy it while he still could.

THE WALK on the beach always made him happy. A lot of driftwood and trash had washed up like he'd thought, but no lost treasures or secrets to the universe. Unlike the previous walks, Myles stayed a little closer to Casey. The weekday meant the beach sat almost deserted, but he still didn't want people thinking Casey talked to himself or imaginary things.

Casey fell asleep on the couch once they got back to the house. He had kind of a fitful sleep the night before because of the storm, so Myles tried to stay as quiet as he could. He spent most of the afternoon out on the deck and didn't realize how late it had gotten until Casey came out with a sandwich and two beers.

"You out here?"

He tried to make himself visible again, going so far as to close his eyes and concentrate really hard, but he had no success. "Yeah, I'm here," he eventually replied.

Casey picked up on his tone like he figured he would. "What's wrong?"

"Can you see me?"

"No."

"That's what's wrong."

Casey set his plate, the two beers, and the bag of chips he brought out on the table. "You wore yourself out this morning. I bet it's like when you first started talking to me. You couldn't control it, and we didn't know when I could hear you and when I couldn't. It's just like that."

Myles knew he was right, but that didn't mean it didn't frustrate him. "Yeah." Casey bit into his sandwich, and the juice from a tomato squirted out to dribble down his smooth chin. Myles looked away.

"Wanna watch a movie tonight?" Casey asked around a mouthful.

"Which one?"

He wiped the corner of his mouth with the back of his hand and reached for a beer, then twisted the top and sucked down what looked to be a good third of the brew in one go. He followed it up with a very loud and satisfying "Ahh," and Myles had to laugh. "I don't know. Any suggestions?"

"I think I need a few good laughs," Myles said.

"A comedy it is."

After the movie ended, they lounged on the couch for a while. He liked being with Casey. They didn't even have to talk, both content to sit and enjoy the silence, and he wondered if it had anything to do with their inability to communicate in the beginning or if they'd just grown that kind of comfortable with each other. Either way, he didn't care.

Myles hadn't had a crush on anyone in years, not since he'd fallen in love with James, but he knew Casey deserved better than a dead man, a specter caught in between planes of existence. It was unfortunate, but he'd have to find a way to get over the little flurries building up in his stomach before they turned into a full-blown blizzard.

Easier said than done, especially when he could almost smell Casey's scent on his pillow when he went to bed that night. He couldn't smell, not the salt of the sea nor sausage sizzling, but he could imagine them, imagine Casey smelling like the lemon soap he used in the kitchen, a hint of aftershave that lingered on the pillowcase, and possibly a smidgen of musk so uniquely him.

He tossed and turned, not able to get comfortable. Maybe Casey dating would work out for them both, just so long as the person proved worthy of him. It would get Casey out of the house, and distance might help Myles get over his crush. As long as Casey didn't bring his dates back home and didn't talk about them that much, things would probably be okay. But then again, Myles had always had a knack for lying to himself.

CHAPTER NINETEEN
TOUCH ME

THE DOORBELL rang at ten thirty in the morning, and Casey jumped out of bed. He hadn't expected company, but as soon as he looked through the peephole, he smiled to himself. Rachel held baby Will in one arm and had a hold of Tony's hand with the other.

"Hey, Casey, I'm sorry to just drop in like this, but I need a huge favor," Rachel said as soon as he opened the door. She looked frazzled, her raven hair pulled up into a messy ponytail. He steeled himself for bad news. Rachel usually looked more composed, even while wrangling three kids.

Casey pushed the door open farther to let them in. "What's going on?"

Her shoulders looked stiff, and he knew she was trying to hold herself together. "Ethan had an accident at school, and I need to pick him up and take him to the hospital."

"Oh God! Is he okay?"

"I think so. I hope so. He fell on the playground and hurt his arm. The school nurse called and said he should get an X-ray just in case. I was hoping you could watch the little ones for a bit," she said, more like asked, as she bit her lip. He didn't have much experience with children, but he couldn't turn her away.

"Yeah, of course, Rach, anything you need." Her big brown eyes had slipped into full-on puppy dog mode. How could he have said no to that?

She held out the baby, and he effortlessly propped Will on his hip. "Are you sure you're okay with them?" she asked, but she had already started for the door. "They might be hungry in an hour. I really don't know how long I'll be, but I have a bottle in the bag and diapers and…."

"Rach, we'll be fine. I think I can handle it for a few hours." He smiled, attempting to reassure her like she'd always done for him. "Go take care of Ethan."

He ignored the fake smile she returned. She had every right to worry about his babysitting skills, but Ethan needed her. She blew a kiss to the boys and dropped the diaper bag by the door. "Thanks so much, Case. I really appreciate it. I'll be back as soon as I can."

Tony started bawling as soon as she shut the door behind her. He ran over and cried for her to come back as his little fists beat on the wood. At least that's what Casey thought he'd said, but he couldn't make out the words through his whimpering. It broke his heart, but he didn't know how to comfort him. Casey went over to him and dropped to a knee, balancing Will on the other.

"Hey, it's all right, little man. She'll be back. She just needs to go take care of Ethan real quick."

"I w-wan' Mommy," he cried.

Oh God, he was alone with two children and had no idea what to do with them. "You want to watch TV?" he asked, hoping that maybe he could find some cartoons that didn't contain vulgar language. But at that point, he'd take whatever he could get.

In complete contrast, Will seemed as cool as a cucumber on his knee. He gummed his fist and giggled over Casey's shoulder. "What are you laughing at, monkey?" he asked, tickling Will with the hand he held him steady with.

"Me," Myles whispered in Casey's ear. He did a good job of playing off the chill that rocked his body with a gentle bounce of the baby. Rachel had only left two minutes ago, and he was already letting a ghost entertain her children. He wished he could've handed Will over to him so he could figure out what to do with Tony, but that wasn't going to happen.

"T, do you want something to eat? I think I have some cereal."

When that did nothing to stop the whining, Casey sighed and sat down beside him.

After a few minutes, Tony sat down too and stuck his thumb in his mouth. He whined around the digit, cheeks tearstained and eyes bloodred, but the sound no longer pierced Casey's eardrums. He considered it a huge victory. They sat there for a few more minutes, Will giggling away at "thin air" until Tony ran out of steam.

"Why don't we look for some cartoons?" Casey asked in a soft, soothing voice. Tony looked up at him and nodded with a sniffle, snot and tears dribbling down his chin. Casey grabbed a tissue on their way over to the couch. After he wiped noses, he left the TV on the first children's program he came to. He couldn't find anything animated, but he thought puppets would do in a pinch.

"Think the 'monkey' has a present for you," Myles whispered, and that time Casey relished the shiver that trickled down his spine before rebounding up his neck, tiny pinpricks titillating his nerves. He swore he felt Myles's breath against the flesh of his ear, every syllable punched out like the Morse code they'd used in the beginning.

Either Myles had gotten better at interacting with the physical world, or the weird stirring in Casey's stomach had bloomed into a ridiculous and unequivocally inappropriate crush. Third option, he needed to drive himself to the closest asylum and have himself committed, because it felt too real for something his mind made up. He knew that if he turned around, his eyes would land on pale blue paint and a few pictures of starfish hanging on the wall, and he didn't think he needed that kind of disappointment at the moment.

He scrunched up his nose as he gave a hesitant sniff in Will's direction. The tyke seemed entranced by the green puppet on television and content to sit on his thigh as he marinated in his own waste. "Eww… I thought we were friends," he moaned, picking up Will and scurrying over to the diaper bag.

They went into the guest room, and he laid the baby on the bed. "Sorry, Myles. I'm using your room because you can't smell. Lucky bastard."

"I heard that."

Myles's voice came from over by the doorway, and Casey turned his head to look in his general direction. "I know. Now be useful and keep an eye on Tony. Rachel said he liked to wander."

"He's fine," Myles replied after a moment. "Do you want kids?"

"At this exact moment?" Casey asked, peeling apart one of the sticky plastic fasteners of the diaper. "Definitely not."

"I do… did."

"Uncle Casey, what are you doing?" asked Tony as he ambled into the room.

"Changing Will's diaper… I hope."

"He likes the powder."

"Oh, okay," Casey replied, turning his attention back to the stinky diaper. At least he thought to reach in and grab a new one before he took it off completely. Will rolled over a few times and tried to worm his way out of Casey's grip, but he eventually got everything ready to complete the change.

He undid the second plastic tab and peeked inside. Thank God he had his mouth shut because the little shit started giving him a golden shower. "Sonuvabitch," he hollered, folding the diaper back over. "Oh God, oh God!"

Tony started in on a lecture about using swears, and he heard Myles cackling in the corner as he reached for the wipes. He popped open the package and yanked, pulling all of them out as he did his best to clean the pee off his face. "It almost went in my mouth!"

"Don't fo-get the powder, Uncle Casey," Tony reminded him.

"Can I change my answer to hell no?" he asked, turning his head in Myles's direction.

"You said a swear!"

It took a few tries and the whole bag of wipes, but he eventually got Will squared away. Tony had insisted on pouring on the baby powder, which ended up going all over the place—the guest room looked like it had snowed—and Myles had whispered in his ear the whole time, instructing him on the proper way to hold Will down while adjusting the plastic sticky tabs. He wanted a shower, but he settled for scrubbing his face while the kids ate cereal.

He made them peanut butter sandwiches for lunch and had just gotten situated on the couch when Rachel texted.

Broken. :(Needs a cast so maybe an hour or two. How's my babies?

Casey assured her the house hadn't burned down just yet and told her to take her time. He regretted that as soon as Will started fussing ten minutes later. Rachel had mentioned naptime, but he had no idea how to do that. His brilliant idea was for all of them to sleep on his bed, because he needed a nap too after their morning, but Tony pitched a fit.

"Kid, in ten years you're gonna wish you could nap." Casey sighed, unsurprised that reasoning didn't work. But it did send Will into a crying fit. Casey picked him up and started bouncing and shushing him as Tony threw a tantrum on the floor, complete with leg kicking and fist pounding.

"Want me to try?" Myles offered, but Casey had no idea what he could possibly do.

He shrugged, mostly in defeat. What did they have to lose?

Myles flashed transparent as he walked over to Tony, but something seemed off about him. He crouched down beside the screaming toddler and squinted when Tony let out a particularly high-pitched wail.

"Hey, kiddo," Myles said, startling Tony. Or maybe he just scared the crap out of him because he immediately froze, his eyes going wide as he sucked in his sniffles. Tony sat up and scooted away a few feet.

"It's okay. He's a friend," Casey said as he moved over to them. Just then he realized Will had also stopped crying too. "I think they can both see you."

Myles smirked up at him before turning his attention back to Tony. "Your uncle Casey is very tired today. So why don't we lie in bed and I'll tell you a story while he and Will take a nap? Can we do that?"

Tony stared at him for a moment then looked to Casey, who gave him an encouraging nod.

"Okay... but I'm not gonna go to sweep."

Myles smiled up at him, and Casey melted. If he'd had ovaries, they might've exploded.

"Of course not. My name's Myles. What's yours?"

"T-Tony," he replied, his little shoulders relaxing just a tad. When he went to stand up, he wobbled and fell forward.

Casey held his breath, fully expecting him to fly right through Myles and land on the floor, but his hands found purchase in the polyester of Myles's board shorts. He looked up and saw Myles staring back at him in shock, but he didn't have time to think about what it all meant before Tony started pulling Myles over to the bed by the hand.

Will grunted around his fist, which broke the confused state Casey had fallen into. "Oh, now you want to go to bed?" He scoffed out a laugh and took Will over to the bed to plop him down beside Tony. Myles had already perched himself on the far edge, so he followed suit on his side, their bodies caging in the kids.

He couldn't help but stare a little in awe as Myles recited the story of Peter and the Wolf. The story captivated Tony from the beginning—the silly voices Myles used helped—but after a while, Will began to yawn and babble until he talked himself to sleep halfway through. Tony joined him as soon as Myles said, "The end."

How had he gotten both children to not only stop crying but to fall asleep so fast? Apparently his ghost was a child whisperer. And a lot less ghostlike than usual.

"Thanks," Casey whispered, rolling over on his side to face Myles and the kids. He kind of wished they had the bed to themselves, since he itched to see what Myles felt like. But no such luck.

"The crying hurt my ears," Myles whispered back. "They're still ringing."

Casey held in a snicker as he nodded. "You could've just left, you know."

"I like kids."

"You're really good with them."

Myles huffed out a quiet laugh. "I just told them a story. You changed diapers."

"Ugh, don't remind me."

A comfortable silence settled in as they gazed at each other. Myles looked different—real, solid—and Casey wanted to touch him like Tony had, but he didn't want to weird him out. Myles had gotten stronger and stronger since they'd met, but this took things to a whole other level.

"You look… different," Casey said, hoping for a distraction from the X-rated thoughts trickling in from his subconscious. He chided his brain for being inappropriate with two kids between them. Not to mention the whole ghost thing. But to be fair, sometimes Myles seemed so real Casey forgot about that.

"I could feel it when Tony touched me. His hands are sticky."

Casey buried his face in a pillow to smother his laughter. He looked back over to Myles in time to watch his fake glare turn into a grin.

"Kids are always sticky."

Myles hummed an affirmative as his grin slipped away. "Did you wanna… touch me?"

He did, but only if Myles gave his okay. "Are you sure?"

"Of course," he said a little too loudly.

Casey felt Will wiggle next to him and held his breath in hopes he wouldn't wake up. Thankfully he rolled over, coughed, and started letting out little baby snores. Casey sighed in relief. They all really needed a nap.

"Sorry," Myles whispered.

"It's fine. He went back to sleep."

"So…."

"So?"

Casey watched Myles stretch out his arm above the boys' heads, palm up in invitation. He only hesitated for a moment before he reached toward him, the tips of his middle and index fingers giving a few experimental touches of Myles's hand. He shot Myles a skeptical look.

How did he feel so real? Yesterday Casey watched him disappear through a door, and now he felt warm to the touch.

He looked back over to Myles's hand and traced the lines on his palm with the pad of his thumb. "How?" was all he could think to say.

"Hell if I know."

Casey drew his fingers down each one of Myles's digits before skimming them back over his palm.

"That kind of tickles."

"You can feel me too?" Casey asked.

"Yep," he replied, closing his hand and squeezing Casey's fingers.

Myles's hand felt real, which left Casey wondering how the rest of him felt. He wanted to run his hands all over him, wanted to see if his lips felt softer than the line of his jaw or if his earlobe felt different between his teeth than his collarbone. So much for a distraction from his inappropriate thoughts.

He watched Myles thread their fingers together and couldn't help but smile. If he really had descended into madness—and holding hands with a ghost sure fit the bill—he never wanted to come back up.

CHAPTER TWENTY
PAST THE BREAKERS

MYLES WATCHED Casey while he slept: his lips puckering when he breathed out, the fluttering of eyelashes when he went into REM sleep, the twitch of fingers sandwiched between his own. The first two he was reluctant to admit he'd studied before, but now he could *feel* the digits dancing on his skin. And not only that, but he could feel the bed underneath him and the elbow to the ribs Tony gave him when the slumbering toddler rolled over.

When Tony had slipped, Myles braced himself for more tears and the inevitable fall, but the tiny palms hit his thighs instead and sent him into shock. He knew he'd grown stronger by the day, but he never expected to interact with the living world again on a physical level. As soon as he knew he could, thoughts of touching Casey consumed him like a ravenous hunger. He'd forgotten what that felt like.

He had hesitated to ask if Casey wanted to touch him. They'd become friends—as much as the living and the dead could be—and he didn't want to risk things getting weird between them. But he asked Casey anyway, because in the end, they *were* friends. Just friends. The decision had nothing to do with his craving for human contact.

Casey looked in awe of him when he stretched out his fingers and grazed over the flesh of his palm. He hadn't expected such delicate attention, but he knew neither of them had experienced anything like it before. He understood Casey's need for exploration, if only to prove it really happened, but the longer they touched, the more he dreaded the empty ache that would set in when Casey pulled away.

But Casey didn't pull away. He fell asleep, their fingers vined together as if they'd always belonged. He knew he shouldn't get attached or let his feelings grow out of control. Casey had a life to look forward to, while he had no idea what his future held. He might disappear tomorrow into the Beyond without having a chance to say good-bye.

Every time he ran the metaphorical numbers in his head, a relationship between them didn't add up. Casey would have to stay in the house forever, and although he liked the thought, Casey might not feel the same. But even if Casey wanted to stay, other impracticalities remained. They couldn't go out on dates, Casey couldn't introduce him to friends and family, and they probably couldn't start a family—not that Casey wanted one after their day.

Casey deserved so much more than he thought he did, and he certainly deserved better than an apparition he couldn't touch.

Then again…. He held Casey's hand in his own, Casey could see him and hear him, and he'd already won over the nephews and a very fickle cat, so maybe it wouldn't be as impossible as he originally thought. After all, the Waltons made it work. They had a long-established relationship beforehand, but they seemed happy now. As happy as Mrs. Walton could look. But then he'd have to watch Casey grow old. He could do that, perhaps.

Just as his optimism solidified, he felt his body start to weaken. It ached down to his core when the last trickle of feeling leached away, Casey's body heat no longer registering to his senses. He'd never felt colder than he did in that moment. He forced himself out of bed, unable to push down the sadness welling up inside him.

Just a crush, nothing more. It would fade eventually like he always seemed to, like the light after sunset, and he'd help Casey get better, help him start to cook again so he could get back on his feet. He considered himself Casey's guardian spirit, and he had a job to do. He'd just have to do a better job of keeping his silly emotions under control. If not for him, then for Casey's sake.

MYLES SPENT the rest of the afternoon out on the deck. He heard the doorbell ring at one point and knew Rachel had arrived to pick up the kids. For a moment, he thought about sneaking inside to see what the kids had to say about him, but he thought he'd let Casey handle it.

A little while after that, he heard the door slide open and Casey stumble out with dinner: a sandwich, chips, and beer. "Myles, you out here?"

"Yeah, I'm over here," he replied, doing his best to pop into sight.

Casey took the seat beside him and arranged his dinner on his lap as he twisted off the cap to his beer. "Man, what a day. Jasper looks exhausted. I didn't know he liked kids."

He chuckled as Casey bit into his sandwich. "Yeah, you look a little worn-out too."

"Mhm!"

Myles waited for Casey to swallow his bite. "So what'd you tell Rachel?"

"Told her a neighbor came over and saved me." Casey chuckled before taking a swig. "She kind of looked at me funny when I told her your name. Couldn't tell if she put it together or not."

Myles hummed in acknowledgment and let Casey finish his meal in peace. The sound of chips crunching next to him soon drowned out the ever-present roar of waves in the distance, but he didn't take his eyes off the horizon. God, he wished he could just run out there and catch a set, but an unmanned surfboard shredding waves might attract too much attention.

He hadn't realized he'd sighed until Casey asked him what was wrong.

"I miss it, you know, surfing. It literally used to be my whole life, and now it's like the ocean is taunting me." He looked over to find Casey frowning at him. "What?"

"Nothing… it's just that I… I had wanted to ask if you'd teach me, but I can understand if you aren't up for it. It actually makes me kind of feel like a jackass for asking."

"Well…," Myles teased, and Casey shot him a disgruntled look. "No, yeah, I mean, what better way to learn than right from a pro, and you should learn. Surfing is amazing. I think you'd really enjoy it."

Myles smiled so Casey would know he'd meant it. He had a vested interest in Casey's happiness, and surfing always seemed to raise his own spirits. It might sting a little at times, watching Casey enjoy something he couldn't, but he'd do it.

"How about tomorrow? After wrestling the kids, I just want a nice quiet night in tonight," Casey said.

"You're on."

They talked about the kids and Myles's ability to feel things while Casey finished eating. Afterward, they went back inside to watch a movie. If Casey noticed he'd sat beside him on the couch instead of in his usual chair, he didn't comment on it.

MYLES BEAT Casey into the kitchen the next morning and perched on the island to watch him cook. He noted how Casey's confidence had grown by leaps and bounds since he first arrived, especially over the last few weeks, and he found himself looking forward to the way he buzzed around the kitchen with controlled chaos.

He wondered if he'd ever get his sense of taste back, because everything Casey cooked looked delicious, and after the whole feeling thing, he had a little more hope about things like that.

"You're staring again," Casey said without turning around to look at him.

Myles's eyes jerked up from Casey's ass, and he could almost feel the tips of his ears growing warm, but he knew Casey had meant it about the food.

"How else am I going to learn how to make crepes?"

"The Internet?"

"But yours always look so good. You should put your recipes on there," Myles said as he hopped down from the counter. He moved over to Casey and leaned his hip against the dishwasher as Casey poured some more batter into the hot pan.

"I doubt anyone would be interested."

Myles looked up from the pan just enough to see Casey's profile, and a thoughtful expression had replaced the frown that usually resulted from very similar conversations. Casey met his eyes, and his heart would've fluttered if he'd still had one.

"Would they?"

He nodded and gave an encouraging smile. "Of course... but I might be biased because you're my best friend right now."

"Your only friend," Casey corrected.

"You wound me," Myles said, feigning hurt as he clutched his chest. "And I'll have you know Fred next door and I have become pretty good friends, and also me and Jasper."

Casey followed his eyes down to the tabby rubbing up against his calf. "*Et tu*, Jasper?" The cat meowed, and they both laughed. "Guess I can't argue with that."

After he finished cooking, they sat down at the kitchen table while Casey ate. Myles tried to give him a few surfing tips, but Casey hadn't surfed before and didn't really understand him. Hopefully things would go better once he had a board underneath him.

"SHOULDN'T I wait thirty minutes first?" Casey asked, an apprehensive frown on his face, once they made it down to the beach.

"We won't be going in the water for a while. First you need to learn how to stand up before we take it out there," Myles replied.

Casey had grabbed a long board from the storage area downstairs and ended up dragging it halfway down the beach. He looked somewhat winded already, but Myles had confidence he could whip him into surfing shape in no time. Maybe he would get some sort of secondhand excitement watching Casey do something he had loved so much.

He looked to make sure no one was around before he came into view. "Okay, just lay the board down right there," he instructed, pointing to a relatively flat spot in the sand. "Watch me do it a few times, and then I'll walk you through it."

Casey nodded, and then Myles lay down on the board. "So… say you see a killer wave coming in. First thing you do is start to paddle toward the shore. When you feel the wave start to lift up the back of your board, you put your hands on the deck, right about here under your chest, push up and arch your back, then… pop up."

He looked at Casey once he'd gotten to his feet, only to find him shaking his head.

"It's really not that hard. It'll just take some practice. Let me do it again." Myles lay back down on the board before walking him through everything once more. He tried to go a bit slower, but he could tell most of what he said went in one ear and out the other. "Okay, one more time, and then you can try."

After the third demonstration, Myles made himself disappear. The beach looked deserted, but he didn't want anyone to recognize him if they happened to walk by. He knew everyone in the small town had seen his dead face in the local paper.

"Let's just go through it slowly so you can get the hang of it," Myles said.

"I'm not sure I can do this, but I guess I can try."

"You'll do fine. I'll walk you through it, okay?"

"Okay."

"Let's imagine you're out on the water and a nice set of waves comes rolling in. You start to paddle toward the shore, wait until the tail of your board starts to move upward with the wave, give a few lasts strokes, then hands under your chest… move them under you a little more."

"Like this?"

"Yeah, that's good. You don't want to grab onto the rail. Now when you jump up, make sure your left foot lands under your chin, or right between where your hands are now."

"Got it."

"Ready?"

Casey gave a nod.

"Now, pop up."

Casey stumbled and almost fell over before getting to his feet. "That was terrible."

"You think I became a pro after one day? No, so lay back down and try again."

His second attempt looked just as bad, and he let out a frustrated growl. "This was a bad idea. My stomach's too big." He wrapped his arms around his waist and stepped off the board.

Myles didn't think he had anything to worry about. Casey looked cute and very handsome regardless of the extra baggage he carried around, but he understood the concept of feeling inadequate. James made him feel that way a lot, only he never realized it because he hid it behind backhanded compliments and the illusion of love.

"Casey, I've seen guys twice your size out there ripping killer waves, so that doesn't matter. You can totally do this."

Casey shrugged and looked away.

"You know, you really don't give yourself enough credit. You've been through a lot lately: a breakup, your restaurant burning down, a move you didn't want to make. But look how far you've come. Do you remember the first time you tried to cook here? You had a panic attack, but this morning you cooked yourself a gourmet meal. That's progress.

"I believe in you. And maybe I don't count because I'm not really a person anymore, but if you want to cook again, I know you can do it. If you want to learn to surf, I know you'll be good at it, and if you want to share your cooking with the world, I know people will love it. So just give yourself a break, okay?"

Casey turned back to him and gave a shallow nod. "You do count."

Myles smirked. "Good, now get back down there and do some more pop-ups before I drag your ass out past the breakers."

"All right, all right. You don't have to be so pushy," Casey teased.

Several more tries later and they discovered Casey preferred a goofy stance with his right foot forward, and it made a huge difference. Once he got the hang of standing up on the board on land, Myles convinced him to head out into the water. It took hours before he could stand up without toppling off, but Myles was just as excited as Casey when he rode his first wave.

CHAPTER TWENTY-ONE
TIE YOU BACK

CASEY HAD surfed almost every day since Myles taught him two weeks ago. He'd get up, make some breakfast, then catch a few waves before he tired himself out. It was good exercise, and he thought it had already started to show. His shirts felt a little looser, anyway. He put off starting the food blog Myles bugged him about incessantly, but his confidence as of late had increased to the point where he felt ready to give it a try.

He had already set up his website, *Cooking with Casey*, and posted a few cooking tips, but today he decided to take pictures as he made chicken cacciatore—one of his most popular dishes at his restaurant. He also liked the idea of sticking with the *C* theme. Plus he knew the recipe inside and out. He kept telling himself it didn't matter if he messed up because no one but him would have to taste it, but it felt like such a big deal, his make-or-break moment, and he wanted things to go well.

Myles claimed his spot on the counter as Casey prepped his ingredients, and Jasper jumped up beside him. Usually he didn't like Jasper on the counters, but today he needed all the moral support he could get.

"I told you it's not that big of a deal. Just pretend you're teaching me," Myles offered when he'd dropped a bowl for the second time.

"I'm not usually so clumsy."

Myles slipped off the counter and approached him, then placed a hand on his shoulder. He'd gotten stronger every day, and Casey's tension dissolved as soon as he made contact. "You're doing fine."

"Were you always this patient?" Casey asked, turning back to the island.

"No, not really, but it helps when the person you're with actually listens to you. Also, death tends to change your perspective on things."

Casey huffed out a laugh as he poured some flour into the bowl he'd finally managed to set on the island. Then he got busy dredging chicken. He fried it up, talking Myles through every step, which really helped settle his nerves. When the chicken had browned, he started in on the vegetables and sauce before placing the chicken back in the pan to simmer.

Along the way, he took pictures, and while the chicken cooked, he started working on the blog post, uploading the pictures and adding captions. It didn't look very sophisticated, rather plain and simple, but he never claimed to be a whiz with computers. He preferred his kitchen gadgets, anyway.

When the kitchen timer went off, he removed the pot from the heat and started to plate the meal. It smelled delicious, and he couldn't wait to have a bite, but he needed to photograph it first.

He placed one last torn basil leaf on the top of each piece of chicken and stood back. "How does it look?" he asked.

Myles leaned over the plate. "Like I'd come back to life just to eat it." He snickered when Casey shot him a concerned look. "It looks amazing."

"Thanks."

Casey took several pictures from different angles before deciding he'd had enough. He set down his phone and picked up a knife and fork to cut off a piece. He felt Myles watching him from off to the side as he opened his mouth and took the first bite. The flavors popped in his mouth, and he hummed his pleasure as he pulled out the fork. Just as delightful as it smelled.

"How is it?" Myles asked, his voice a little strained. Casey thought he might soon run out of steam—not uncommon during the evenings— but when he made eye contact, Myles looked as real as ever.

"Think I went too easy on the garlic."

Myles cleared his throat. "You have sauce on your face."

Casey stuck his tongue out and licked the corner of his mouth. "Did I get it?"

"Uh no, it's right…."

Myles's finger hovered over his skin, like he was asking for permission. Casey smiled and gave a jerky nod, a silent answer to a silent question. He felt Myles's thumb glide across his skin right under his lip, the touch light, almost hesitant, and it drove a tingling sensation all the way down to his toes.

"There," Myles said as he pulled his hand away, but Casey reached for it, wrapping his thumb around Myles's.

He stared at the red streak and wondered briefly about what would happen to it if Myles disappeared right then. Because he felt so real, looked it too. Maybe Casey should rethink committing himself. He definitely had something wrong with him if he had trouble keeping himself from plunging a dead guy's thumb into his mouth. He wanted to suck off the sauce, but he wiped it away instead, the pads of their thumbs brushing in the process.

This felt like a date, his brain supplied. Cooking dinner, idle chitchat, the way Myles's eyes focused so intently on him. He didn't want to remember the last date he had, but despite Myles's current condition, he couldn't help but compare the two. He much preferred this one, which led him to question whether they should make out. Or perhaps end the evening with a good-night kiss?

Casey chided himself at the utter ridiculousness of that idea. Was he so repulsive to the living that no one on earth would want him? Out of all the billions of people on the planet, he couldn't find anyone willing to give him a chance other than a ghost... a sweet, gorgeous, and strangely physical ghost? A ghost who he swore flushed pink before turning away.

Not a date. Like usual, he'd made a mountain out of a molehill. The ghost in his kitchen kind of proved he had a habit of seeing things.

To keep his mind busy—and off things like how close Myles liked to stand next to him—he got back to work on his blog post. It needed more polishing, so he decided he should sleep on it before he published it. He closed his laptop and went back to the kitchen to eat his chicken as he cleaned. Myles and Jasper had already claimed their spots on the couch by the time he finished, and he sat down with them to watch a ballgame. He didn't care much for baseball, but Myles liked it.

He didn't mind suffering through a boring game after Myles gave him so much support in the kitchen. His last freak-out happened weeks ago, and he felt better than he had in months. Time helped, so had the move back to Land's End, but the ethereal presence pressed against his side had a lot more to do with it than he wanted to acknowledge.

CASEY WOKE up on the couch the next morning, not really remembering when he fell asleep. When he opened his eyes, he came face-to-face with Myles and the realization he hadn't slept there alone. He felt Myles's legs twisted together with his own, the light pressure of an arm thrown over his side as it draped down his back. Myles didn't put off much heat, but Casey's skin buzzed everywhere they touched. The odd but pleasant sensation had him once again wondering what a kiss would feel like.

He hadn't noticed when Myles's eyes opened because his own had locked onto his lips, plump and pink and devilishly inviting. But he startled from his musing when Myles spoke.

"Morning," he said, bleary eyes twinkling with amusement.

"Morning."

A brief silence hung in the air before Myles continued. "I had a great time last night."

Casey laughed and shook his head. "No, don't say it like that."

Myles looked confused, his brow pinching. "Like what?"

"Like it was a date. I'm still not, I mean I can't, and you're a ghost."

"That certainly clears things up," Myles huffed as he pulled back, his form fading away in the morning light until Casey could no longer feel him.

"Don't be mad, Myles. I-I didn't mean it in a bad way. It's just...." Casey sighed as he sat up, his back popping after sleeping on the couch all night. "Maybe I've just been thinking about things lately."

"What kind of things?" a disgruntled voice said from across the room.

"I don't know... things. Maybe... what it would feel like to kiss a ghost," he blurted out. He honestly had no idea where his newfound bravery had come from, but he had a few suspicions.

"You want to kiss me?" Myles asked with surprise.

Casey could tell he'd moved closer, relief flooding through him that he hadn't stormed out already. "I'm curious is all... but from a practical standpoint—"

"It doesn't make sense."

"No... I still struggle with whether or not you're real, so how exactly would that go?"

Myles popped back into view, elbows coming to rest on his knees and fingers interlocked as he sat on the coffee table. He sighed, sad eyes meeting Casey's. "Wish I'd met you before."

Casey nodded. "Me too."

"But I'm dead now, and even though you can feel me, nothing could ever come of this. You have a chance to live, to go out and do things, and I'd just hold you back. I can't leave, I can't really talk to anyone or make my presence known, hell, I don't even know if I'll age, but you will. It won't be fair to either of us."

"You've thought about it, then? About us?"

Myles looked down at his hands. "You're kind of all I have."

"That's not true. You have Joe and the Waltons next door, and I'm sure Bobbie could round up a few friends for you, if you want." He smiled when Myles glared at him. "Just a suggestion."

"Yeah, but—"

"You're dead, I know, but you're still here, with me."

"For how long? And besides, don't you want to move back to LA?"

It should've shocked him that he didn't. Even that near-incessant pull to New York had started to wane. Casey shrugged and turned his head toward the window. The ocean outside looked as blue as he'd ever seen it, and his body itched to get out there and enjoy it. He tore his eyes away and turned back to Myles. "I may regret saying it, but this place is growing on me."

"You spent the first seventeen years of your life trying to get away, Casey. I can't be the thing to tie you back to it."

"That was a long time ago. It's not the same place. I'm not the same person. But it doesn't matter. I'm sure I have some kind of brain tumor, since I see dead people, so I figured I'd be joining you soon anyway."

Myles rolled his eyes. "For the hundredth time, you don't have a brain tumor."

"Then how can I see you? How can I touch you?"

"I don't know."

"If it's not a brain tumor, then that means you're real, okay? Real to me, real to Jasper and to Mrs. Walton. You've helped me through the darkest time in my life, and I'm finally to a point where I can breathe again. I can see the light again. And do you know what else I see?" Casey paused until Myles looked at him. "I see you, sitting right in front of me."

"I could disappear tomorrow."

"Then why are you fighting me today?"

"Because I know what it's like to have to say good-bye to someone you care about."

"But if you do disappear, I'd like to have the memories at least. You taught me how to surf, you helped me get back into the kitchen, you chased off an asshole, and God, you helped me babysit two toddlers. How could I not fall for a guy like you?"

"A *ghost* like me," Myles corrected.

"Do you think that matters to me? I'm pansexual, remember? I'll fuck just about anything," he joked, hoping to lighten the mood, but Myles didn't laugh.

"It should matter to you. It should matter that any kind of relationship we have won't be good enough for you."

Myles obviously didn't want him getting hurt. That made his heart ache.

"Yeah, but it doesn't… and I want to kiss you even more now."

He could tell he'd made a dent in Myles's defenses, and he could also see the glimmer of want hiding just under the surface. He wanted too, wanted Myles, and he didn't know when exactly he'd had the revelation—two minutes ago, maybe two weeks ago—but his stubborn ass wasn't about to let it go.

Casey slipped off the couch and onto his knees.

"You know this won't end well," Myles said, his eyebrows furrowing as Casey inched closer. "It can't work because I'm fucking dead, Casey."

His voice sounded angry, but he hadn't popped out of view, so Casey took that as a good sign. He covered Myles's hands with his own and nodded his understanding. It took him a moment to gather his thoughts, but he wanted to try one more time to explain to Myles how he felt.

"I've spent months convinced I'd lost the only thing that ever really mattered to me, and I know without a doubt I wouldn't have pulled myself out of that dark place if it hadn't been for you. And I know you know how weird this whole ghost thing has been on my fragile little brain, but I can *feel* you and see you, and yeah I know this is a really fucked-up kind of situation, you being dead and all, but can you please just humor me?

"I don't fall in love easily, never have, and I'm not going to say I'm in love with you now, but I could see myself getting there. And it fucking sucks that you don't have a body and that things would be far from normal going forward, but I've gotten to know you since moving in, and I like it. I like you. I like how you make me feel and how you calm me when nothing else can.

"And I can tell you're just as scared of this as I am because it's not conventional, but I've had conventional relationships, and to be honest, they weren't that great.… I don't know, maybe it's selfish of me to even ask, but I'd really like to kiss you now, and not just because I'm curious, but because I know that if you were alive, that's what I'd want too."

Nothing he'd said sounded like he wanted it to, but Myles had relaxed a little and took his hands, so maybe the message got through despite his lack of finesse. The message of course being that he wanted to date a dead man. Geez, he couldn't believe how optimistic Myles made him, but at the same time, he understood Myles's apprehension. He did kind of spring everything on him.

Myles slipped off the coffee table to kneel in front of him. "It might not be very good. I've never kissed anyone in this... *state* before."

"If it feels anything like the way it does when you touch me, I don't think it'll be a problem," Casey replied, biting his lip when Myles gave him a shy smile.

Casey licked his lips as Myles moved closer, their bodies almost touching as they leaned in. His eyes fluttered shut right before they made contact, the spark of electricity not surprising him as their lips met for the briefest of moments. It was probably the shortest first kiss Casey had ever had, a sweet little peck, but it would be one he remembered till the day he died.

"Yeah, definitely nothing to worry about," Casey rasped, a smile breaking across his face that Myles returned. "But I'll understand if you don't want to kiss me a—"

He didn't get to finish before Myles surged forward like the tide and kissed him again, his whole body pressing against Casey as his fingers threaded through his hair. And with his eyes shut so tight, he couldn't tell the difference between Myles and everyone else he'd ever kissed, except for the fact that Myles blew them all out of the water.

CHAPTER TWENTY-TWO
A GODDAMN SUCCUBUS

MYLES COULDN'T believe Casey kissed him, or had even wanted to kiss him. He might've hoped he did, but he never thought it would happen, not to mention that Casey would actually enjoy it. And he did, judging by the little moans he let out when Myles ran his tongue along his upper lip. The sound had his whole being going up like tinder.

He never imagined a kiss could feel so real since he didn't have his body anymore. Regardless, he felt something between them—like an invisible force field or a whole dimension perhaps—and it managed to amaze him nonetheless. Casey had a way of making him feel alive to the point he'd forget otherwise. Kissing him only intensified the feeling.

Casey pulled back, a little breathless, lips plump and shiny, and looked at him with pupils blown wide. His heart burst with a bittersweet feeling at the thought that things wouldn't work out between them, despite how much he wanted them to. His untimely death sucked so much ass, and he thought he deserved more than the realization his boyfriend had cheated on him and a seemingly permanent connection to a beach house he'd only spent one night in.

The afterlife was supposed to come with perks. He'd lived a pretty decent life. What happened to the streets of gold and the endless happiness he'd heard so much about? Or had they sent him to the nonbeliever section? To a place he kind of liked only to get stuck with someone he couldn't have? But he could have Casey, for a moment at least. They'd kissed, Casey wanted him, and maybe he could find contentment with him, even from the Between.

Fuck!

Why'd he have to fucking die before he found some semblance of true happiness? It just didn't seem fair.

THEY SPENT the morning in the water as Myles watched Casey surf, shouting out pointers every now and then. Casey had improved some since the first day, but more importantly, he looked like he'd started to enjoy it. Myles had noticed the change in him over the past few weeks. His confidence had grown, and it made him happy to see, but it had been one of the reasons he'd hesitated when Casey asked to kiss him.

Casey deserved so much that he knew he couldn't give him, but he decided he should embrace Casey's attention and affection while he had it because he had no idea if the next renters would accommodate him in the same way Casey had. No doubt Casey would find someone worthy of him eventually, and he knew it would sting when he did. So he had to make sure he didn't fall too hard in the meantime.

After Casey wore himself out, they climbed the stairs to the house. Myles anticipated their typical lazy afternoon, but Casey decided to work on his blog post some more. He watched him tinker with it for a while before he went on his usual round with the mailman.

He waved to Mrs. Walton, who had taken Mini out to do her business on the front lawn. She didn't glare as hard at him anymore, but he figured he wouldn't get anything even closely resembling a smile, so he didn't bother. He thought about asking for advice from her and her husband about what to do about Casey, but he knew they had a completely different relationship. They'd married years before Fred died, and he expressed his contentment many times to wait for his wife to join him on the other side.

Casey, on the other hand, had his whole life ahead of him. And as much as he liked the idea of spending eternity with him in the Beyond, Myles didn't want him to suffer an early death.

"It's unlike you to slouch, kiddo," Joe said as he leaned against a random car parked on the street. He'd stopped popping in and out of nowhere when the novelty wore off. "What happened?"

Myles shrugged back. "Nothing."

"So you're just gonna lie to me? I'm hurt," he teased. When Myles didn't react, he sighed. "I'll be around when you're ready, then."

The loud groan Myles let out had Joe frowning at him.

"That bad?"

"It's Casey."

"Your living friend."

"We kissed. He wanted me to kiss him and I wanted to kiss him, so… we kissed."

"I see…. Hmm, maybe I don't see."

"I'm dead, Joe. In case you've forgotten!" Myles yelled before shrinking in on himself when he realized he had. "Sorry, I just… what kind of life would that be for him, loving a ghost? I'm a goddamn succubus!"

"I think males are referred to as incubi."

"Didn't stop me from getting the sucking part down," he huffed under his breath.

He went on and on, baring his soul and all his fears as Joe listened to every word. It felt good to get everything off his chest, everything he should've said to Casey but didn't have the heart to. When he had finished, he folded his arms as he leaned against the car next to Joe.

"That's quite a mess you've gotten yourself into, kiddo."

"I know, but it's just not fucking fair," he whined.

Myles sank into his embrace when Joe draped his arm over his shoulder. "Do you make him happy?"

He thought about it for a moment, because he didn't know. It could've been the move that had Casey feeling more confident and happy the past few weeks. The salty air and the sea always did wonders for him. But he remembered the first time Casey had a panic attack in the kitchen, how scared he'd looked. Then he remembered the last time he'd had one and how he looked to Myles for help to get him through it, like he'd die without him.

"I think so. He said I helped him through a lot, but what if it's just this place? What if he healed on his own without me?"

"So you don't believe him?"

He really hated when Joe answered his questions with a question of his own, but he had to admit, it proved effective. "No, I do. He's the one who initiated everything, but I'm just worried I won't be able to give him what he needs."

"Maybe what he really needs right now is you. Myles, you know how fragile life can be, how short and fleeting it really is. If you can make him happy, even for a short time, don't you think he deserves that?"

Myles sighed as he nodded. "He does." Casey deserved the world, and he'd give him as much of it as he possibly could. "Thanks."

Joe squeezed his shoulder and gave him a gentle head butt. "Always happy to knock a little sense into that thick skull of yours," he said, chuckling when Myles glared at him. "Now go on. Maybe you've finally found your purpose."

"Yeah… yeah, maybe I have."

As soon as Myles walked through the door, Casey insisted he take a look at his blog post. He'd already gotten a few likes and a comment from someone wanting to try it out, which had him beaming like the sun.

"It looks really awesome! I'm so proud of you," Myles said, peering down at the computer over Casey's shoulder.

"Couldn't have done it without you."

Myles smiled and turned to look at him. "Happy I could help."

"Okay," Casey said, pushing himself away from the desk. "I'm going to run to the store. I was browsing recipes and found a chicken parmesan ravioli I want to try out tonight."

"Sounds wonderful."

Casey leaned in and pecked him on the lips before Myles had a chance to react. "I'll be home soon."

"Good, because I was hoping we could practice some more of that kissing stuff after dinner."

That had Casey spinning around and strutting back to him, the movement of his hips filling Myles's head with delightfully dirty thoughts. He met Casey halfway, and they shared a heated kiss that would've left him breathless if he had still needed air.

"Dinner is never complete without dessert," Casey said, winking before he started for the door.

Myles just hoped he'd have some strength left.

THEY SLEPT in Casey's bed that night, but that had happened more and more as time went on. Casey said he slept better having him close by. Myles didn't mind watching over him since he didn't sleep, even though it meant balancing Jasper on his chest all night. But unlike previous nights, they curled up together, limbs tangled until Myles's body faded away.

Casey slept like a log, and before Myles knew it, the sun had started to rise. He'd gained his strength back by the time Casey woke up, their bodies fitted together as if they'd stayed that way all night.

"Good morning," Myles muttered right before he pressed a kiss to the tip of Casey's nose.

"Very good morning. How's the swell look?"

Myles laughed at him. "Pretty flat, I'm afraid."

"Do I sound like a real surfer now?" Casey teased.

"You're getting there."

"Maybe tomorrow."

They shared a few languid kisses, and Myles couldn't remember a time he'd smiled so much before breakfast. With James, he'd thought they'd simply passed the honeymoon phase, but he realized the last few years of their relationship hadn't meant as much to James as they had to him. The signs were there, but he'd ignored them.

"So I'm thinking I need a shower and was wondering… if you'd maybe like to join me?" Casey asked. Myles's eyes opened wider at the request, and he zeroed right in on the lip caught between Casey's teeth, now red from worry.

Myles smiled, and his face probably would've hurt by then if he'd had muscles to pull. "I would love to. Not sure if I'll be good company, but we can give it a try."

Casey's cheeks pinked up as he threw off the sheets, and Myles felt things he hadn't since he died. He swore he had a physical reaction to the prospect of seeing Casey naked. He remembered what it felt like to have his pulse skyrocket when he became aroused and the way his cock started to fill with anticipation.

They made their way into the bathroom, Casey pulling him along by the hand. Casey turned on the shower and leaned in to adjust the temperature. Myles didn't feel as guilty for checking out his ass as he usually did, but Casey flushed when he caught him staring.

"I know I'm probably not what you're used to," Casey said, shoulders pulling in.

"What do you mean?"

"You're an athlete, and I'm a fat chef with a potbelly. I just didn't want you getting your hopes up."

Myles chuckled and ran his hands down Casey's arms. "I think you're pretty hot the way you are, but that's really not why I like you."

Casey pressed a kiss to his lips before discarding his shirt. He took a deep breath and pushed his boxers down past his thighs so they could fall to the tiled floor. "You can… look, if you want."

Myles smiled and let his eyes drift down Casey's body. He'd gained a little color since his arrival, his skin now a golden olive, and despite his insecurities, he looked healthy. And his cock, half-hard with a slight curve, had Myles even angrier than usual that he'd died before they met.

"Kind of wish I could see you naked. It's a little unfair, don't you think?"

Myles had learned he couldn't take his clothes off the first day. Just like when he tried to escape the radius of the house, as soon as he'd strip, his clothes would appear right back where they started. "Kind of wish I wasn't dead right now."

"Okay, you win, but you can't use that line every time," Casey said, smirking before turning around, stepping into the shower, and leaving Myles to unabashedly ogle his ass. "Are you coming?"

Myles didn't think he still had *that* capability, but the smoldering look on Casey's face had him willing to try. "God, I hope so."

He could feel the pressure from the water drops as they pelted them from above when he moved into the shower. Casey reached around him to close the door, pressing his chest against him in the process. Then they shared a kiss under the water, and while he couldn't feel the water cascading down his skin, he swore he felt every inch of Casey's naked body where they touched.

Casey's fingers burrowed under his shirt to slither up his spine. "I'm so glad I can touch you."

Myles brushed back a strand of hair that had fallen on his forehead. "Me too."

A few more experimental touches and several kisses later and Casey grabbed the shampoo from the caddy to wash his hair. Myles helped him rinse it. Then he went for the body wash. He squirted some on a washcloth and lathered it up to clean his body. And that's when the real show began.

Myles leaned against the wall and watched him draw the washcloth up one arm and across his chest. He moved down the other, looking at Myles as he bit his lip. Myles wouldn't have pegged him as such a tease, but he liked this Casey. The playful flirting, the way his eyes crinkled when he smiled. He almost seemed like a different man, and it warmed Myles's spirit to know he'd helped to bring it out of him.

Casey moved on to his chest before spinning around and washing his sides, but Myles didn't think he could reach all of his back. Instead he squeezed some soap over his shoulder, and Myles took the opportunity to rub him down. He didn't know how much washing he actually did, but he loved the contact nonetheless.

"Is this okay?" Myles asked.

"Mhm, feels good."

Myles pressed a kiss to the skin behind his ear and felt a tremble course through Casey as he sucked in a stuttered breath. He slid his hands from Casey's hips around to his stomach and kissed a trail down the tanned expanse of his neck, dragging his teeth over the corded muscle of his shoulder.

He felt something akin to arousal when Casey rocked his ass back into him, but he figured the muted sensation would be enough.

Casey leaned a forearm against the wall and interlocked their fingers with his other hand. "Will you touch me?" he asked, voice throaty and hoarse.

Myles didn't answer with words, choosing to move their hands downward and curl them around the base of Casey's cock in response. He thought he could feel the heat of it, the weight of Casey in his palm, and he didn't want to debate whether or not he could. So he did his best to shut off his analytical brain and concentrate on the increasingly desperate moans that poured out of Casey as he ran their joined hands up to the head.

He didn't know how Casey liked things, and it had been far too long since he'd jacked himself off, so he let Casey set the rhythm, slow and easy to start. The familiar movement came back to him quickly, and even though the pleasure seemed duller than he remembered, he enjoyed every gentle stroke.

Casey let go to rest both arms on the wall and began to work his hips a little more, rocking them back into Myles before thrusting into his fist, his moans mingling with grunts when Myles squeezed a bit harder.

After turning to face him, Casey lunged forward to hook both arms around Myles's neck. "Just wanted to see you," he panted out.

Myles smiled and took him back in hand, Casey hissing as he picked up where they'd left off. He let himself relish every fluttering kiss, the seamless way their bodies fit together, the tightening grip around his neck. This could be enough for him: watching Casey's face contort with pleasure, feeling him edging closer to his breaking point. It didn't matter that he had to do most of the work. He considered himself a giving lover, and if anyone deserved to be pampered, it was Casey.

"I'm about to come," Casey warned, hands slipping from Myles's shoulders to fist in the wet fabric at his back. Then Casey muttered his name a few times, giving him the go-ahead to speed up his strokes. He wanted to see what Casey looked like blissed out of his mind, to see if it matched his fantasies. But he should've known they wouldn't compare to the real thing.

Nope, not even close.

He watched in awe as Casey let out a strained whimper, cheeks hollowing out when his lips formed a perfect *O*. Casey's cock twitched in his hand, and he knew he'd finished all over his board shorts. His clothes never soiled, but the water would've taken care of most of the mess anyway.

They stood under the spray for a while, Myles holding him up until Casey could stand on his own again. Then Casey started laughing out of the blue, and Myles shot him a curious look. "What?"

"It-it's just...." Casey had to pause while he composed himself. "I think I just had the best sex of my life, and it happened to be with a dead guy."

"Best sex of your life?"

"Don't get me wrong, I've had some great orgasms in my day, but that—" He pressed a kiss to the corner of Myles's mouth. "—that was something else entirely."

Casey turned off the water and pushed open the shower door. Myles moved to the side to let him out before following his lead. He didn't think the towel was necessary—he'd grown quite fond of the salacious view—and it must've shown on his face when Casey wrapped one around his waist.

"Shit, was it okay for you?" Casey asked, obviously having misinterpreted his frown.

"Yeah, of course. I guess dead people don't orgasm, which sucks, but I thoroughly enjoyed watching you." He smiled as he ran a hand through his already dry hair.

Casey ducked his head. "I just hope I can be enough for you... without *that*."

"Casey, I didn't get a happy ending, in fact my life kind of ended on a pretty big downer, so this," he said, moving into Casey's personal space and tilting Casey's chin up with the tips of his fingers, "*this* is so much better than anything I had when I was alive... and maybe dying wasn't so bad since it brought me to you."

He could feel himself starting to weaken as they fell into another round of passionate kisses, each one leaving him more numb than the last, but the way Casey's eyes continued to track him long after he'd faded back into the Between gave him hope that they could make this work.

CHAPTER TWENTY-THREE
A WORK IN PROGRESS

CASEY MADE sure to invite Myles into the shower every morning after their first time. He'd wake up with Myles beside him and watch as the morning light glittered against his bronzed skin. Jasper liked to sleep on him, which they both found odd since he didn't put off any body heat, but Casey knew they shared a strong bond.

He'd pet Jasper first thing before letting his hand trail down to Myles's chest. Myles didn't exactly sleep, but sometimes he could rouse him from hibernation. Then they went into the bathroom, Casey stripping off his clothes. He no longer had the compulsory need to suck in his gut, partly because he'd grown more comfortable in Myles's presence, but also because he didn't have much to suck in anymore.

With Myles's encouragement, he started going for runs before sunset. Myles tagged along, so he made sure to turn around before they made it outside his radius. Running, combined with his newfound love of surfing and healthier meals, had him dropping weight like crazy. Myles told him several times that he didn't care what he looked like, but his new routine had him feeling better about himself. They both agreed that mattered most.

So went most days. Though sometimes Casey would go down to the farmers' market and get fresh seafood. He started posting recipes for "Seafood Saturday," as he called it on his blog. Rachel invited him over for dinner every once in a while. He liked visiting with the kids, but Tony always asked him about Myles. Tony's curiosity tickled him, but he never knew how to respond to him.

Sundays went a little differently. He considered it his day off and had started meeting Rachel for brunch at a small cafe. The first time he called to set it up, she asked if he was feeling okay. Honestly, he hadn't felt this good in years, and she encouraged him to keep up whatever he'd done that had him smiling again.

"How are the kids?" he asked as usual when they met outside the cafe. He gave her his customary kiss on the cheek and held the door as she went inside.

"A handful," she said, sighing. In spite of the circles under her eyes, he knew she meant it in a good way. "But I'm really starting to enjoy this time we have together. At first I felt guilty for leaving them, but Gary's perfectly capable of parenting his own children for a few hours a week."

Casey laughed as they settled around their table by the window. He ordered waffles with Nutella and banana slices and a mimosa, scoffing good-naturedly when Rachel decided on the same.

"You're the chef of the family. I trust your judgment," she conceded when he gave her a knowing look.

"How's your week been?" he asked.

"Ethan's ready to get that cast off. Just two more weeks, but he complains it itches too much. And the little ones are starting a music class next week, so we had practice in the living room a few mornings so they know what to expect. And Gary had to work late again one night, but he made it up to me with breakfast in bed yesterday."

It only stung a little when he thought about not being able to do that for Myles.

"Well, it sounds like you're going to be even more busy." Casey smiled as Patrice, the waitress, brought over their drinks. "Thanks."

"Anything else I can get you while you wait?" Patrice asked, a syrupy sweet grin aimed right at him.

"No, we're fine, thanks."

"Your order will be right out."

"I think she likes you," Rachel whispered after she'd walked away.

"She's cute," he admitted, "but I'm not sure I'm ready for that." He hated to lie about it, but he didn't feel ready to go around telling people about his ghost boyfriend.

"Are you sure it has nothing to do with this Niles guy my kids keep talking about?"

"Myles," Casey corrected before blushing at his blunder. "And no, it doesn't."

Her smirk told him she didn't buy it, but she didn't press. "Well, when you *are* ready, I have a lot of friends who would love to get to know you better."

"I'll keep that in mind."

Luckily, a few people he'd gone to high school with came up to make conversation, saving him from any more embarrassment. He'd gotten used to running into people from his past, which seemed to happen almost every time he left the house. The awkward reunions had been one of the reasons he preferred to stay home with Myles, but his arrival soon became old news, and they'd become more bearable.

Their brunch arrived shortly after, and they talked about Casey's next blog post as they ate. He wanted to try the clam chowder their mother used to make them and wanted to run it by her. He only remembered half the recipe, but between the two of them, they managed to recall enough of it for him to experiment with.

They settled the tab, and Casey walked her to her car and kissed her cheek. The kids had to go to a birthday party next Sunday, but they made plans for the week after that. He waved good-bye before making his way to his car and taking the scenic route along the coastal highway back home.

When he arrived, he found Myles lounging on a deck chair looking out at the ocean. Casey greeted him, and he turned his head and smiled like Casey was the only thing in existence, which sent his heart into spasms. Casey forwent his own chair to curl up with him, and they snuggled in for an afternoon nap. Sundays were without a doubt his favorite day.

THE NEXT morning, Casey had an appointment with his psychiatrist. Dr. Roberts insisted he come in once a week, but Casey had canceled the last two times. He didn't see the point with his improved mood. Unfortunately, she called his doctor in LA and tattled on him. So to appease both doctors, he had to go show his face.

"You'll be fine," Myles said as he sat across from him at the breakfast table.

"I just don't know why I need to go talk to her. Everything is great right now."

"She probably just wants to check on your progress. You've made a lot lately, and maybe she wants to see it for herself."

Casey absentmindedly stirred brown sugar into his oatmeal. "She's gonna ask how I'm doing and what I'm doing, but I already told her over the phone."

"Hmm… maybe she wants to see how hot you look in your jeans now," Myles teased.

He scoffed and tried not to blush. "I still need to lose twenty pounds."

"Everyone's a work in progress. Just tell her you started eating better and working out. And having sex with your ghost boyfriend."

"Wonder how that would go over?"

"Maybe just stick with the first two. If they put you in the psych ward, I won't be able to visit."

"That's a pretty big incentive to keep my mouth shut," Casey said with a smirk. He blew on a spoonful of oatmeal and took a bite. "Speaking of my hot ghost boyfriend… I was thinking about maybe inviting my sister over one morning, maybe Saturday. I'm sure the kids would love to see you again. Rachel said Tony asks about you all the time."

"Really?"

"Yep. And I know you're at your strongest in the mornings. You could totally pass as alive for a few hours. But only if you want. No pressure. Heh, I think I just asked you to meet the family."

"You've met Joe… sort of. He approves."

Casey smiled as he glanced at the clock on the stove. "Shit, I better hurry or I'll be late. Dr. Roberts is already pissed at me. No need to make it worse."

CASEY ENDED up arriving a few minutes late, but he blamed that on Myles. He went to kiss him good-bye and things got a little out of hand. One kiss had stretched into several when Casey pushed him up against the wall. Thank God he didn't fall through it. Regardless, he'd gladly take the disappointed look he got from Dr. Roberts in exchange for Myles's kisses.

"Sorry I'm late. Monday morning traffic," he said, slipping past her into her office.

"I'm just glad you made it." She motioned for him to have a seat on the sofa before picking up a pad and pen from her desk and taking a seat in a comfortable-looking chair. "It's been a few weeks, so let's dive right in. Tell me what's been going on with you."

He hummed and thought about where to start. "Well, I started running again. Haven't done that in a while, since I lived in New York years ago, through Central Park, so what does that tell you? I didn't go very far last week, but I think I've improved some this week."

"Wow, I'm impressed, Casey. Exercise is a natural mood booster, and I'll encourage you to keep it up. Is this something you've been wanting to do?"

"Yeah, but my previous work hours didn't really allow for runs on the beach. I guess I figured I might as well use the time I had to pick it back up."

"That sounds pretty reasonable to me," she said, writing down something on the pad. "And how are things in the kitchen? You mentioned your blog the last time we met. Any new posts?"

Casey nodded. "Yes, a few. I kind of feel my confidence coming back with each one. I don't think I'm anywhere near ready to go back to work, but I finally feel like I'll get there, you know."

Dr. Roberts smiled. "I'm really liking this optimism, Casey. Since we're on the topic of work, have you started thinking about what you want to do about that? Do you see yourself going back to work in a restaurant?"

"Well...." He paused to think about it for a moment. He did like the idea of opening another restaurant someday, but the thought of going through something like he did with Cinder turned his stomach. Myles could help him through it, but the fact that he couldn't leave the house kind of put a damper on that.

"I guess I would like to open up another restaurant eventually, but I think the blog is enough for now."

"Small steps add up, and I think that's a good plan. You've come a long way since you arrived, and I think the best thing you can do is try to continue moving forward." She wrote something else down on her pad. "What about your plans to move back to LA? Is that something you're still struggling with? Over the phone, you mentioned the possibility of staying here for a while."

"I'm definitely leaning toward staying. Things with my sister are going really well. We've kind of had to get to know each other again. And my nephews are pretty awesome little dudes, so...."

"Family is important, as we've talked about before, and it's not uncommon for estranged siblings to have that period of adjustment, especially when they have to get to know each other as adults."

"We've set up brunch every week, and I really look forward to it."

"I'm sure she does too. A break from the kids is always nice."

Casey had to agree.

"And how are you doing with your meds? Are they still working? Any side effects?"

"I haven't needed the anxiety medicine as much. I told you I started surfing, and that's really helped. It's kind of like meditation, I think." That's what Myles always said. "And I have been working on eating healthier."

"Those are all excellent things we've talked about that can help combat your anxiety and depression. It's good to hear you're taking a more active role in your recovery. For a while there I know you struggled with getting out of bed some mornings."

That was still the case some days when he woke up to fluttering kisses on his neck. But he didn't think that's what she meant. "I have more good days than bad, so I'm getting there."

"It sounds like it. And it's great you're feeling good again. That's been our number-one goal, to get you back to feeling like yourself. I think we should keep you on the medicine a little while longer. It seems to be working, and taking you off too soon could send you into relapse. We want to avoid that."

"Yes, I don't want to go backwards."

"No, you don't." She flipped through a few pages in her notes as he looked around at the photos on her desk. He'd seen them several times now, but the silences always made him feel awkward. "And how about the hallucinations?" she asked. "Have those stopped?"

He wanted to protest the insinuation that Myles was a hallucination, but he bit his tongue and smiled as he nodded.

"Wonderful news," she said as she jotted down another note. "Are you having any suicidal thoughts or thoughts about harming yourself or others?"

"No, can't say that I have."

"Very good. Is there anything else you'd like to talk about? Any concerns you've had since we last met?"

"I don't think so. I'm doing pretty good right now."

"I'm so happy to hear it, Casey. And I'm glad you came in. I know people tend to stop taking their medication and visiting their doctors when they start to feel better, but sometimes that can derail you more than anything."

"I think I'm on the right track, though."

"I do too. You sounded good on the phone, but I needed to see it for myself," she said, clicking the end of her pen. "This kind of feels like a short session, but I think we can wrap it up, unless there's anything else?"

"No, I think I'm just going to keep doing what I'm doing."

"I think that's an excellent idea. And if you like, I think we can bump down our sessions to every other week unless you feel the need. How's that sound?"

"Sounds good," Casey replied.

They both stood and shook hands before she led Casey back into the waiting room. He paid his copay and started for his car, chiding himself for putting off the painless visit. Dr. Roberts hadn't said anything revolutionary, but it felt nice to check in and get some positive feedback for all his hard work.

On his way home, he stopped by the store and picked up the ingredients for his mother's clam chowder and some fresh fruit to make breakfast smoothies. The warmer weather had him detesting oatmeal.

He wanted to hurry back, though, because mornings gave him and Myles the best time to pretend they had something akin to a normal relationship. They had to improvise on certain things, in and out of the bedroom, but they were making it work, and despite the odds, he felt happy. Then when the cucumber fell out of his bag as he loaded up his groceries, an idea struck him.

Myles had no use for worldly possessions, but Casey had finally thought of something he could buy that they both might enjoy.

CHAPTER TWENTY-FOUR
WHO'S HUNGRY

MYLES HADN'T known what to say when Casey suggested they invite his family over on Saturday. Casey said he didn't want to pressure him, but it felt like a big deal. He wanted to make Casey happy, and he figured doing normal couple things might make him more comfortable with their relationship. So despite his fears of screwing everything up, he agreed to brunch at the house.

"She's going to love you, you know," Casey said as he whipped some eggs together for a quiche. "And I know you're worried about fading in and out, but we made sure to time you this week and know about what time you get fatigued. As long as they leave by one, we should be fine."

"Yeah, I know," Myles said, sighing as he let his head smack against the cupboard. His dangling feet made a thud against the ones below.

Casey looked over at him and rolled his eyes. "I'm never going to break you of that habit, am I?"

"I was here first," he replied with a smug grin.

"I can't argue with that."

Myles jumped down and watched over his shoulder as Casey poured the egg mixture on top of the sausage, cheese, and peppers he'd already placed in the pan. He'd made a few quiches in his day, but he knew Casey's probably had his beat. "You should put this in the blog."

"I think I have enough to worry about today. Maybe next time."

Casey carefully moved the pan into the oven before pecking Myles on the lips and heading into the bedroom to get ready. They'd forgone their regularly scheduled shower activities that morning in the hopes it would give him more strength, but he still couldn't manipulate objects very well, which meant he had to go through the door to get out onto the deck. He'd have to remember not to do such things when company arrived.

When he went back inside, his nose scrunched up when he caught a whiff of something for the first time since he died. It smelled like bleach or some other kind of cleaning solution, and he assumed Casey had tried to clean up the kitchen a little. While he would've preferred the musk of a thoroughly fucked Casey to harsh chemicals, the fact that his nose had started to work gave him hope that his other senses would continue to heighten.

Before he could mention it to Casey, the doorbell rang. If he had a heartbeat, it would've quadrupled, though he could almost feel his palms getting sweaty.

"They're gonna love you, because you've already won over the kids. Tony, anyway," Casey said, giving him a quick kiss before scrambling for the door. "Hey, guys!"

"Uncle Casey!" Tony and Ethan screeched, throwing their arms around his legs as soon as he'd opened the door.

Myles hung back while Casey greeted everyone and ushered them inside.

"You must be Myles," Gary said, positioning Will a little higher on his hip.

"Yes, this is my friend Myles," Casey said, introducing him to the rest of the family. "He's, uh, visiting from LA. He used to work in my restaurant."

It took Rachel a moment to greet him as she fumbled with the diaper bag, but when she finally had the chance to study him properly, the face she made, like she was trying to place him, had Myles worried.

"It's nice to be able to put a face to the name," she said, flashing him a curious smile. "I'm sorry, have we met before? You look familiar."

"Uh, no, I don't think we have, but I get that a lot," Myles replied.

"He has one of those faces," Casey added when Myles looked at him for help.

"Maybe it's because the kids gushed about you. Well, Tony, anyway. He insisted on hearing the story of Peter and the Wolf every night for weeks after you two babysat."

"It's a good story, Rach. So who's hungry? I made quiche," Casey announced. Myles appreciated his attempt to steer the conversation elsewhere.

AFTER BREAKFAST out on the deck—complete with a side of awkward conversation—they took the kids down to play in the surf. It was the first time Myles made himself visible on the beach, and he felt a little self-conscious. He made sure to stay out of the water because he didn't want to explain why his clothes never got wet, but he had fun helping Tony build a sand castle.

He thought playing with the kids would offer him a safer haven than interacting with Rachel. She kept watching him and asking questions. Casey dismissed it and insisted she stop interrogating him, but Myles knew it must've killed her that she couldn't place him. Though he didn't know what would happen if she succeeded. In all honesty, he had no idea how he would've reacted if the roles were reversed. He hadn't believed in ghosts until he'd woken up as one.

Luckily the kids started to get cranky around noon, and Rachel decided they needed to head home for naptime. They exchanged pleasant good-byes, made open-ended plans for the future, and then Casey helped them put the kids in the car. Myles waved from the door.

Overall, the morning had flowed smoothly. Myles's paranoia got the better of him a few times, but Casey talked him down and assured him things were going well. He enjoyed seeing the kids again too, and he had a nice chat with Gary about baseball at one point. But the morning left him exhausted.

Casey looked it too when he made it back inside, flashing a frazzled smile. "That wasn't so bad. I think they bought the whole 'juice cleanse' thing."

"Yeah, how'd we forget I can't eat?"

Casey shrugged and shook his head.

"How do you think she would've reacted if she'd figured out I'm dead?"

"I'm not sure, but I think she'll find out eventually. I'm surprised she and Gary didn't put it together. I'm so used to the big city that I forget how small Land's End is. A celebrity death in town isn't something that's easily forgotten."

"I'm not a celebrity," Myles said, leaning over to kiss Casey once they'd settled on the couch.

"You had fans, though, right? I saw a picture of you online signing autographs."

"Yeah, but—"

"And the cover you did on *SURFER* magazine."

"Okay, you win. I might've been a Z-list celebrity."

They shared a laugh, soon interrupted by the doorbell.

"Shit, did they come back?" Myles asked. He didn't think he had any more strength for socializing after the busy morning they had.

"Relax! I think it's the delivery service. I'm expecting a package," Casey said as he stood. Myles faded as Casey walked to the door. He peeked out the peephole and nodded, smirking back at him before answering the door. "Yep, just your present."

"My what?"

"Shh!"

Myles's curiosity got the better of him, and he joined Casey at the door to watch the swap of his signature for a nice-sized box.

"Thanks. Have a good day," Casey said with a small wave to the deliveryman.

"What is it?" Myles asked once Casey shut the door.

He got a wicked grin in reply as Casey strutted toward the bedroom. And his nonexistent heart beat a little faster at the seductive wink Casey gave him just before disappearing over the threshold. He knew because it matched the beeps he heard in the distance right before the delivery truck rumbled down the street.

But he didn't pay it much attention, as he'd already started for the bedroom. Casey lay sprawled across the bed when he walked in, the package in front of him as he propped himself up on his elbow. Myles had a feeling he knew what lay hidden inside, but he asked anyway. "So... what is it?"

"It's uh... well, I think it would be better if I showed you," Casey replied. He wore a nervous smile, and Myles didn't know what to think.

Casey patted the bed beside him, and Myles took the cue to sit down. Once they'd gotten situated, Casey opened the box with a blush on his cheeks, tossing the ripped tape on the floor as well as the pillow-like packing material from inside.

"Ohhh," Myles said when his eyes landed on a nice-sized glass dildo complete with a blue spiral ridge running up the shaft. The whole thing reminded him of a wave, and it kind of ached, how much he wanted it in him, although he knew that would never happen.

"I was wondering if you'd like to help me test it out," Casey mumbled, his head hung low and his cheeks an adorable pink.

That put an end to his pity party, because how the hell could he turn down an invitation like that? "I'd love to."

He liked watching Casey touch himself despite the fact he didn't get aroused exactly. Casey enjoyed his presence when he got off, and that gave him a sense of satisfaction about their love life he could live with. And as long as Casey felt satisfied too, they would be okay.

"Are you sure? Because I thought it might be a fun surprise, and I guess I was hoping it would help you feel a little more included in *things*."

Myles bent down to kiss him gently on the lips. "We're good, but I'm totally into trying new things."

"Good to know," Casey said. "I'm just going to rinse this off in the bathroom."

Myles nodded and lay down on the bed. He did his best not to fade away as he listened to the sound of water splashing in the sink. They were pushing it in terms of timing. He knew his limit on visibility and physicality diminished come noon, and the clock read half past.

Casey came out of the bathroom naked, and Myles took a moment to drink him in. He looked sexy as hell even if he didn't think so, but if he kept up his exercise routine, Myles knew he'd agree before long. Paddling on his surfboard had already started to tone his arms, and running combined with the absence of junk food had shrunk his beer belly tremendously.

Myles could sense his lingering self-consciousness, though.

He quickly joined Myles on the bed and lay down facing him, letting out a deep breath. His nervousness was obvious. Even though he couldn't quite participate physically, the emotional aspect felt very much like their first time.

"Are you sure you want me here?" Myles asked.

"Yes, I really do," Casey assured him. He rolled over and plucked a bottle out of the box he'd placed on the floor earlier. "Bought lube too. It's been a while since I've done this, or even been with a man, but I think I remember the process."

They both let out a nervous laugh. Then Casey twisted the cap off the lube and coated his fingers. Myles watched as his mouth fell open into a little *O* when he moved his hand around to his ass. That left him slightly disappointed, because he'd kind of hoped to watch.

As if he read Myles's mind, Casey asked, "Did you want to see?"

"If you're okay with it, then yes."

"Y-yeah, I'm okay with it."

Myles smirked. "Good, then roll over."

Casey obliged, and Myles watched as he swiped his index finger over his hole, drawing a few tiny circles before he started pushing into himself. His breath hitched when he reached the first knuckle, and Myles felt a sense of warmth wash over him. Casey looked over his shoulder at him when he let out an unstoppable moan, because wasn't that a fucking sight?

He didn't get any closer to arousal than that these days, and he kind of hated it. But they'd make it work.

"This is so much better than porn," Myles said. "How is it?"

"Feels good," Casey replied, his voice low and sultry.

Casey shuddered when Myles placed a hand on his hip and gently moved it up and down Casey's side. He inched a little closer until their bodies molded into one, making sure not to disrupt Casey's rhythm.

Casey slipped another finger in and continued to work himself open. Myles enjoyed watching, but he really wished he could've stuck his fingers inside that tight heat instead. God, he missed what that felt like, to take someone, to be taken by someone, the foreplay, the smell of it—of sweat and lust—the high afterward... but he could live with just the view. What other choice did he have?

A few moments later, Casey grabbed the dildo. He lubed it up and moved it into position, Myles scooting back some so he had room to work. He let out a hiss as he pushed the tip inside. Myles bit his lip and watched it sink farther and farther into him. Casey's body arched, and he moaned when he'd slid it all the way home.

"You're so fucking hot," Myles whispered into his ear. He smiled when he felt a shiver move through Casey's body.

"Just need a minute."

Myles pressed kisses to his neck as they gave him time to adjust, his fingers thrumming over Casey's hipbone. "Take your time. Just pretend it's me inside you."

Casey huffed out a little laugh. "Already am."

When he felt ready, Casey began to work the toy in and out of himself, quiet moans increasing in volume the faster he went. Myles wanted to help, but his strength had started to wane. He didn't know how much Casey still felt of him when he reached in front to take him in hand, but Myles liked to think he contributed greatly to the pleasure coursing through him and the moans pouring from his lips.

Casey cursed, and Myles assumed he'd hit a good spot. A hand covered his on Casey's cock, fingers twisting together as they stroked him. Casey's hips rocked back against him, and there must've been enough resistance against the dildo because he rasped out Myles's name before repeating the motion over and over.

Myles helped, driving his hips forward to meet Casey's. It surprised him how much he could feel, how close the pressure bubbling up inside him was to the way his living body responded before. Maybe the visual Casey had just given him had him especially excited—his hole stretched around the dildo—or maybe it had to do with some kind of psychological response.

Either way, it kept building within him until his own blissed-out moans mingled with Casey's. Then it broke like the perfect wave, his body convulsing right along with Casey, who had spilled out in his hand, and he knew that because he could *feel* it, warm and wet and so fucking perfect. His whole body had lit up, and for a brief moment he felt truly alive again.

"God, Casey," he whimpered into the crease of Casey's neck, both arms pulling Casey against his chest. He could almost fucking smell him too, the bacon leftover from brunch mixed with the salt of the sea, but as his postorgasmic haze lifted, his senses started to dull.

"Was that okay?" Myles asked, holding on as best he could, not wanting to let any of it go.

"Perfect," answered Casey. "You're about to disappear, aren't you?"

"Yeah, think so."

Casey reached back to pull out the dildo, carefully placing it on the nightstand before rolling over. "Just as long as you come back, because we definitely have to do that again," he said with a sleepy smile. They shared a sweet kiss before Casey sighed in contentment and nuzzled against him.

Myles kissed his forehead. "I wouldn't leave you even if I could."

"Good," Casey said on the tail end of a yawn, "because I love you."

CHAPTER TWENTY-FIVE
A RIGHT TO MOURN

CASEY WOKE with a start when his phone rang. He scrubbed a hand down his face and glared across the room at the offending device on his dresser. When it stopped its high-pitched wail, he groaned and rolled over, his eyes catching on the twisted blue glass of the dildo he'd had inside him a few hours earlier. He smiled at the memory and called for Myles but received no answer.

Just as he had resigned himself to getting out of bed, his phone went off again. He threw off the sheet and padded over to the dresser to pick it up. He didn't recognize the number, but since they'd already called twice, he decided to answer it.

"Hello?"

"Is this Casey North?" a man asked.

"Yeah, who wants to know?"

"Uh, yeah, this is James. I don't know if you remember me, but you called a few months ago and said that you could talk to my deceased boyfriend, Myles Taylor."

He could do a whole lot more than talk, the ache in his ass reminded him.

"Yeah, I remember you, the cheating bastard," Casey couldn't help but snap.

"Excuse me?"

"Myles told me you were cheating on him. He was going to propose to you the day he died, but you were probably too busy fucking your agent."

He heard a scoff from the other end before James continued. "I don't see how any of that is your business."

"Myles is my business."

A long silence stretched out between them, and Casey gave serious thought to hanging up, but his curiosity got the better of him. What on earth did James want? Myles had moved on, and from the sound of the whispering in the background, James had too.

"Look, I'll be in Land's End next weekend, and I was wondering if…. God, this is stupid…. If you can really talk to him, then I would like to come by and apologize to him, maybe get some closure."

"You changed your mind?" Casey asked, skepticism evident in his voice.

"My boyfriend of four years died. I think I had a right to mourn him however I liked. But now that I've come to terms with his death and the possibility that you might be telling the truth, I'd like to talk to him. So… I would like to come by. If the offer still stands, that is."

James's sudden change of heart had Casey wary of his sincerity. But on the other hand, if someone had called him telling him his dead lover had decided to haunt their house, he might take a while to warm up to the idea too.

"I'll have to get back to you."

James snorted in derision. "What? Do you have to ask the spirits for permission?"

"Yes," he deadpanned. "Otherwise we might summon a demon from hell that'll attach itself to your dick." Casey hung up on him before he could reply. "What a douche."

He set the phone back down on the dresser and opened the drawers to grab some clean clothes. Once he got dressed, he gave Jasper a good rubdown and went to look for Myles. He wouldn't invite James over unless Myles gave him the go-ahead.

"Are you around?" he asked when he walked into the living room. He sighed when he got no answer. He'd check the deck, but if Myles wasn't there he'd have to trek all the way down to the beach. Or he could sit his ass down and wait for him to come back, but he kind of wanted to tell him about the phone call.

He slid open the door and stepped out onto the deck. "Hey, babe, you out here?"

No answer.

"Oh, come on!"

With a grunt, he started down the steps to the beach. The warmer weather had started to lure the crowds out on the weekends, so he knew he wouldn't be able to see Myles. He didn't want to call attention to them either, so he refrained from shouting his name. Instead he walked the beach for a while in hopes that Myles would find him.

They'd gone through this many times before, including once when Myles got upset after Casey called him Casper during a fight. Myles followed him around in silence for a while before Casey gave up, sat down, and yelled "I'm sorry" into the sea. But at that point, Myles couldn't contain his laughter and gave himself away.

Casey still had an hour before he planned to start dinner, so he didn't mind combing the beach while he waited for Myles to approach him. He picked up an unbroken sand dollar to add to his growing collection and almost got knocked over by a dog chasing a Frisbee, but at least the weather cooperated. He'd heard they'd get some storms later in the week, but he didn't want to think about that yet. As long as he had Myles, he could handle it.

His stomach rumbling had him heading back to the house earlier than expected with no sign of Myles. He figured they'd just missed each other somewhere along the way. That or Myles had gone over to the Waltons' for a visit. He knew Myles enjoyed listening to Fred's stories and could easily spend hours over there unless Mrs. Walton ran him off. Casey would've liked to join him a time or two, but Mrs. Walton kind of scared him.

Jasper greeted him with a meow when he got inside. He looked around, hoping to spot the slightest shimmer to indicate Myles had returned, but he came up empty. Casey shrugged off the nagging feeling in his gut that something was wrong and started the prep work for dinner. It wouldn't take long, grilled tilapia and vegetables.

But the later it got with no word from Myles, the more concerned he became. His appetite left him halfway through his meal, and he abandoned it to pace in the kitchen.

"Myles?"

Nothing.

"Okay, I know this morning took a lot out of you, so I'm not going to freak out until tomorrow morning, but if you can just give me a sign that you're still here, I'd appreciate it... maybe kick the cabinets for ol' time's sake... pull Jasper's tail?"

He told himself to stop overreacting. Myles had spent the longest amount of time visible that morning that he ever had before, which Casey knew had exhausted him. Casey just needed to be patient until he regained his strength.

Only that seemed hard to do when the place sounded so quiet without him.

Casey tried to keep himself busy by cleaning. The seagulls had finished off his dinner on the deck, but he had to scrub down the grill. Then he piddled around in the kitchen, wiping down the counters and emptying the dishwasher. He even got his old toothbrush out to clean the grout, anything to keep his mind off the deafening silence of the house. The counters shone by the time he finished.

He thought about moving on to the bathroom, but he knew the shower would remind him of Myles. Instead he sat down on the couch and turned on the television, but the only thing worth watching was baseball. He decided to leave it for when Myles returned, though his optimism had faded hours ago.

By the time ten o'clock rolled around, he decided to call it a night. "I'm going to turn off the TV, if no one objects." He waited a moment for a thud or something, but it didn't come. With a sigh, he pushed the Power button on the remote and hefted himself off the couch.

After several weeks of sleeping with Myles, he'd gotten used to having him close. Tonight the bed felt empty. How had a ghost woven its way so completely into his life without him realizing it? He knew he'd fallen for Myles, he'd admitted it several hours prior, but how had half a day without his presence gotten Casey so worked up?

He'd never stayed in the house without Myles, and while the possibility existed that Myles just didn't have enough strength to communicate with him, Casey knew deep down he wasn't there. But he hated not knowing why. Had he scared him off with the whole "love" confession? And what could he do if Myles didn't come back? He couldn't exactly file a missing ghost report or stick Myles's face on a milk carton. Did the Beyond have a hotline you could call when you lost your ghost boyfriend?

If Myles didn't show up in the morning, Casey could go down to Bobbie's and see if she knew anything. He thought he could even persuade her to hold a séance if she felt it might help. Another option included asking Mrs. Walton if she'd seen him, but he didn't have high hopes she'd help. Maybe Fred would.

He sighed and started to get ready for bed. His brain had taken off like a runaway train, and he needed to reel himself in before he drove off a cliff. It had only been half a day, and he knew Myles would have a perfectly good reason for scaring him half to death when he showed back up.

Despite his best efforts to dismiss the intrusive thoughts, it took hours of sifting through what-if's before his mind shut off enough that he could sleep, but one thought persisted to the point of penetrating his dreams. What if Myles had finally moved into the Beyond?

"MYLES?" CASEY called out upon waking, but Jasper camping out on his chest made it painfully obvious Myles hadn't shown up. "If you think you're sparing my feelings, you're wrong. I don't care that you're a ghost."

He only got Jasper's meow in response.

The sun had just risen, judging by the pink-orange of the sky out the french doors, and he thought about getting up and going for a run, but after listening to the eerily quiet house, he pulled the covers tighter around himself.

"Myles, please! I just need to know you're still here." He groaned into the silence when he received no reply. "Did I do something wrong? Are you mad at me? Do you need a break from me? You know I'd understand that."

He glanced at the clock on the side table before convincing himself to climb out of bed. He knew he wouldn't have any luck falling back asleep, which meant he'd lie there agonizing over Myles until he had to get up and meet Rachel for brunch at the cafe. He wondered how upset she would get if he canceled on her at the last minute. They'd finally settled into a nice routine, and he'd hate himself if he blew her off, but he'd already slipped into crisis mode.

Myles had become his rock since he'd moved back home, and he didn't know what he'd do without him. He loved him, after all. But what if his declaration had scared him off? The more he thought about it, the more he convinced himself Myles just needed some space. He'd sprung his family on him and told him he loved him after amazing sex. Maybe the pressure got to him. Or maybe Casey had pushed things too far, too fast.

James had cheated on Myles, so of course he'd have issues with jumping into another relationship, especially something so unconventional.

Myles couldn't even leave the perimeter, so how normal could their relationship really be?

But Casey wanted to find a way to make it work with his ghost boyfriend, even though saying that out loud could get him a one-way ticket to Crazy Town. He didn't care. He had to push out the nugget of doubt that Myles only existed in his head before it worked its way too far into the open. He'd squashed the thought once; he could do it again.

CASEY HAD gone down to the beach to look around after a failed attempt at making breakfast—he'd overcooked the eggs and trashed them. He'd passed a jogger at one point but saw no sign of Myles or anyone else, so he gave up. His mood alternated from anger that Myles hadn't checked in with him, to fear he'd gone to the Beyond without telling him good-bye, to sadness for being left alone again.

As soon as he walked back into the house, someone knocked on the door. He glanced at the clock and realized he'd spent a lot more time on the beach than he'd thought. "Shit," he moaned when he heard Rachel's voice coming through the door. He'd missed their date.

"Hey, Rach," he said as he opened the door.

"Hey? What the hell, Casey? I've been calling you for half an hour. Why didn't you answer your phone?"

"I lost track of time." He took a step back to let her in, but she gave him a look and didn't budge. "What?"

"Is *he* here?"

Casey felt his heart stutter. "Who, Myles?"

"Yes, *Myles*."

He shook his head. "No."

"It took me a while, but I figured it out. Do you want to explain to me how my family had brunch with a dead guy? Jesus, Casey, I brought my kids here!"

"He's harmless."

"Harmle—he's dead! He's…." She ran a hand through her hair and blew out a heavy breath. "How is that even possible?"

"Do you think I know? I spent the first month in this house thinking I was crazy, well *crazier*, but I got to know him, and I've watched him get stronger to the point I can touch him now. And maybe I still think I'm crazy, but he's a good man, was a good man, and I don't care that he's technically dead because he's real to me."

"Casey?"

"You don't know him."

"I had brunch with him. I watched him build sand castles with my kids. I... I don't know how to deal with something like this. We need to find a professional."

"Why, so they can chase him away? I've already talked to a professional. She believed me, said he had unfinished business or had to help someone through theirs."

His heart sank at the thought he was the reason Myles had gone. He knew he should be happy for Myles if he'd moved into the Beyond, but why didn't he feel happy? Things had started to turn around for him, but what was the point of it all if he lost the amazing person he found along the way?

"Why didn't you tell me?" Rachel asked. Her shoulders relaxed a little, but Casey could tell she'd prepared herself to flee at a moment's notice.

"Would you have believed me? I didn't believe it myself for weeks. He's stuck in between Earth and the Beyond. He had no one but me and his uncle Joe for months, but he got stronger every day, and he helped me get back on my feet. We were getting closer...."

"Case?"

His eyes started to sting. Less than twenty-four hours had passed, but he couldn't shake the feeling that Myles had left for good. "I love him. I know you don't understand, nobody will, but I've never felt this way about anyone before, not Isabel or anyone else, and I tried to fight it, I truly did, because I know how crazy it is, but I couldn't do it."

"Are you forgetting the part where he's dead?"

"Don't you think I know that?" he growled. He pinched the bridge of his nose to conceal the tears threatening to fall. "I'm sorry... I know he's dead, and I know it's batshit crazy, but I'm in love with him."

"Okay, assuming it wasn't totally insane, how would that even work?"

"I don't know, Rach, but I wanted to find out. You met him, the kids love him, and you told me yourself Tony doesn't like anyone. That means something."

She sighed again and gave him a disapproving look, but he knew he could convince her. Until he remembered Myles had disappeared.

"But I guess it doesn't matter anyway, because I think he's gone."

"What do you mean gone?"

Casey couldn't answer around the lump in his throat, but the sympathetic frown on her face told him she understood anyway. And with that he let the dam break.

Chapter Twenty-Six
Land of the Living

MYLES HAD waited until Casey fell asleep before he slipped out of bed. Casey's confession had sent him reeling, but why did it feel more like a curse than a blessing? He couldn't imagine a scenario in which things turned out okay for them. They'd been doomed from the beginning. Casey deserved more than he could give, and he needed to make him understand that. But how?

He thought disappearing might work. Casey would miss him, but he'd eventually move on. Since Myles didn't know how to get to the Beyond, he'd have to avoid Casey until he grew tired of waiting for him and left on his own. Fred might let him crash at his house for a while, but he didn't trust himself to stay away from Casey. And he knew Jasper would alert Casey to his presence even if he stayed invisible.

But how could he avoid that kind of temptation? He had to do it, though; he had to try.

So he went down to the beach. Casey would have a hard time finding him among the crowd, so it would give him time to think of alternative plans.

He found a nice spot near the edge of his little slice of existence and sat down in the sand. The sun shone bright in the sky, and he could almost feel the rays of light dancing on his skin, but he knew he'd never feel that again. The illusion felt good, though, and he had to keep reminding himself that's all it was.

"Still having boy trouble?" Joe asked. Myles hadn't even noticed his arrival, his eyes too busy studying the ever-changing blue that stretched out in front of him.

He sighed and looked up to find Joe's smirk slipping into a frown. "Casey said he loves me."

"Oh," he replied. "That's a big step."

"It's too much. I need him to be happy, but I need him to find someone better, someone not…."

"Dead."

"Exactly."

Joe took a seat beside him, and they sat in silence for a while. Just having him close put Myles at ease from some of the turmoil in his head. Joe understood him better than anyone, and he knew his uncle would support him no matter what.

"I need to find a way to move into the Beyond."

"Oh, kiddo, I've told you it's just not your time."

"I can't do this, okay? I can't watch him get old without me or grow resentful when he doesn't have a normal life. I can't be the reason he wastes away in that beach house like Mrs. Walton. I love him, and I want more for him than that."

Joe hooked an arm around him and pulled him in for a long hug. "You're such a good man, Myles. I'm so honored that I got to be the one to raise you. And no matter what happens in the future, know that I've enjoyed every minute we had here together… but I think it's time for you to leave."

Myles straightened up. He wanted to cry, but he didn't even know if he could. He'd miss Casey with his whole heart, but being with Joe would lessen the sting. "So you're going to take me, then? Into the Beyond?"

"I'm afraid not."

"I don't understand," Myles said, his brow furrowing.

"I know, but you will. I've watched you gain strength over the past seven months, watched you fall in love with someone who truly deserves you, and as much as I worried about you when I died, I know now that you're going to be okay… but that means it's time for you to wake up."

Myles scoffed. "I am awake."

"No, you're not."

He had no idea how to reply to that. His eyes were clearly open, and he hadn't slept since he arrived. How could he wake up if he wasn't asleep?

"I love you, and I'll always be with you, but I need you to trust me," Joe said, repositioning himself on his knees in front of him.

"I do trust you," Myles insisted.

Joe took his hands, squeezing as he smiled. "Good, now close your eyes, and when I tell you to open them, I need you to try really hard, okay?"

"Okay, but you're starting to freak me out."

Myles didn't understand how opening and closing his eyes would help him move on from the Between, but he'd give just about anything a try. When he thought about it, he'd died and opened his eyes to this place in what seemed like an instant, so maybe jumping between realms wasn't as complicated as he thought.

He felt Joe press a kiss to his forehead as he whispered another "I love you."

"I love you too, you big sap," Myles said with a laugh.

"Are you ready?"

No, he didn't want to leave Casey, but he knew he had to, for Casey's own good. "Yes."

"Good. Then open your eyes."

Myles didn't realize how hard it would be, but his eyelids felt like concrete bricks. He saw light as they fluttered a little, but it felt like an exercise in futility to get that far. "Joe, this is ridiculous."

"Come on, you can do it," said a voice that most definitely was not Joe. Was it the voice of God? Gabriel, perhaps? Or whoever else manned the heavenly gates?

The voice shocked him enough to where he could get his eyes open a little farther. He tried to ask who had spoken to him, but his throat felt sore and scratchy, like someone filled his mouth with sand.

"Give it another try. We've all waited a long time to meet you," the voice said, the soothing masculine tone putting him at ease and piquing his curiosity.

Myles took a deep breath and, with all the energy he could muster, opened his eyes. The bright room had him squinting, but when things started to come into focus, he saw a man in dark blue scrubs and a lab coat leaning over him with a big smile on his face.

"Well, hello there, John Doe. Welcome back to the land of the living."

AFTER A much-needed dose of Ativan, Myles eventually calmed down enough to let the news the doctor told him sink in. Apparently a fishing boat had scooped him out of the ocean somewhere off the coast of Canada after he got swept up in the Davidson and Alaskan Currents. They brought him to the closest hospital in Vancouver, where he'd remained in a coma for the last seven months. Needless to say, the fact that he hadn't died hit him almost as hard as when he'd woken up on the beach.

The doctor ordered a bazillion tests after a quick workup. CT scans, MRIs, blood work, EKGs, the whole nine yards. He felt like a pincushion by the end of the first hour, and he hadn't even met with the occupational therapist or the shrink yet. His whole body felt sore, even his fingers, and he couldn't get comfortable in the lumpy bed. He'd lost a lot of muscle and didn't even know if he could walk. The staff refused to let him try until they'd finished poking and prodding.

One of the nurses asked if she could call anyone for him, but he only wanted Casey. He hadn't needed his phone number when they lived together, so he didn't know it. She smiled and assured him she'd look him up, but she found no Casey Norths listed in Land's End. Of course not, Casey only planned to live there temporarily.

He thought about having the nurse call James instead, but the idea soured his stomach… or maybe he should've blamed the Jell-O, the first solid thing he'd eaten in months.

They asked him a barrage of questions, but it didn't help that everything felt fuzzy in his head, the last seven months weaving in and out like bad reception. It had taken him several minutes to remember the name of the town he'd stayed in. And he only remembered Casey's last name because it was a direction, so maybe he'd gotten it wrong.

The psychiatrist didn't help much either. He almost had Myles convinced he'd dreamed the whole thing. The longer he stayed awake, the more he started to believe it. But it had felt so real; Casey had felt so real. And his heart felt broken, not knowing if he'd ever see him again. On the upside, he finally understood how Casey felt, unsure of reality to the point of insanity.

He didn't want to give up the possibility that what they had was real. Even if he could only see Casey in his dreams, he'd do everything he could to make that happen. He just had to figure out how to get out of the damn bed first. Or if all else failed, how to fall into another coma.

MYLES DIDN'T get much sleep that night. Half the time he feared he wouldn't wake up again, and the other half, he felt too ashamed that he hadn't said good-bye to Casey. What if he found Casey but Casey didn't know him? And what if he couldn't find him at all? What if he didn't even exist? Myles didn't know what was worse.

The hospital notified the detective in charge of his case as soon as Myles regained consciousness, but he didn't show up until later that morning. A knock on the door had him cringing at the prospect of more ridiculous tests, but much to his relief, the guy who walked in wore a badge instead of a stethoscope.

"Hello, Myles. It's nice to have a name to go with the face," the man said with a chuckle. "I'm Detective Lee Charles, and I was assigned to your case when you arrived."

"Forgive me if I don't shake your hand."

"No worries. The doctors updated me on your condition. I'm sure you've had a long couple of days already, but I want to make this as painless as possible."

Myles smirked. "Can you pass that idea on to the nurses?"

"I'll see what I can do. But for now, do you think you're up for a little chat?"

"I think I can handle that."

Lee pulled up a chair and reached into his pocket for a pen and notepad. "I'll try to make it quick.... So, when I got the call, the doctor gave me your name, and after a few international calls, I was able to locate your missing person's report. The fact you washed up on Canadian soil makes things a little messy, but we're going to get everything straightened out. Don't you worry." He smiled, and Myles nodded. "Okay, what's the last thing you remember before you woke up here?"

"Um... everything's kind of fuzzy."

"That's to be expected. Your doctor warned me your memory might be fragmented. And there are things you might never remember, but at this point, anything could help us piece together what happened to you."

Myles let out a long breath as he thought back. He remembered Joe kissing his forehead, but he figured Lee meant before he died, or rather, *almost* died. "I was at a beach house in Land's End with my boyfriend, James. It was early morning, and I was going to propose. We decided to go for an early surf, and that's it... but I think he might've been cheating on me."

"Oh, I see. Do you know with whom?"

"Uh, his agent, Logan."

Lee winced.

"What? What is it?"

"After I reviewed the case, I ran a background check on James, since he was listed as a possible suspect in your disappearance, and I discovered he recently married a Logan Winthrop."

"Did they even wait for a body to show up?" Myles asked, but he already knew the answer.

"I'm sorry. I know this must be hard to wake up to after so long, but I'm going to try and find you some answers…. Do you remember a riptide?"

Myles thought for a moment before nodding. "Yes, after we surfed for about an hour, but I've been caught in them before and know how to get out. I've spent half my life in the water, and I'm a strong swimmer."

"James claimed you were drunk and insisted on going surfing after sundown, where you were caught in a riptide and washed out to sea."

"No, I would never do that," Myles protested. He stopped trying to die years ago. "I don't surf drunk. It takes away from the clarity of it all. And I haven't surfed at night since college."

Lee let out a breath and leaned back in the chair. "I'm sorry, but I think—"

"The bastard tried to kill me?"

A heavy silence filled the room as Myles tried to process everything. His heart rate monitor spiked, and his thoughts immediately jumped to the previous day when Casey had sent his heart fluttering. That's what he'd heard, not the damn delivery truck. Casey had to be real. He had to find him.

"I also found a million-dollar life insurance policy James took out on you a few months prior to your accident," Lee added once he'd settled down a little.

He shook his head. "I don't remember signing anything like that."

"I figured as much, so I ordered the signature to be analyzed after I discovered James petitioned the court to declare you dead in absentia."

"What the fucking hell?" So much for calming his rage.

"It hasn't gone through yet, and all your assets are still tied up in a trust. No need to worry about that just yet, but have you tried to contact him?"

Myles almost succeeded in sitting up a little straighter, but Lee had to help him readjust his pillow. "No, I need to get stronger first so I can punch his cheating, murdering ass in the face."

Lee covered up his laugh with a cough. "Is there anyone else I can call for you, then?"

"Casey."

"Last name?" Lee asked as he jotted down the name on his pad.

"North. He's staying in the same beach house. He's a chef, and his restaurant burned down."

"Do you remember the name of it?"

"It's… no, I can't remember."

Lee put his pen and paper away before standing. "Okay, I think that's enough for now. Why don't you rest while I figure out how to proceed? I'd advise that you don't contact James just yet. The LEPD cleared him on lack of evidence, but if he did try to kill you, we need to see if we can build a case first. We might have better leverage if he doesn't know you're alive. I'll try to keep this out of the press for as long as I can so you can gain some strength."

"Thank you. And don't you worry about that. I want nothing to do with him, but please… just try to find Casey."

CHAPTER TWENTY-SEVEN
WHEREVER YOU ARE

CASEY HADN'T seen Myles in days, but he'd spent half that time at Rachel's. The beach house didn't feel the same without him, and Casey knew he'd fall back on bad habits if left to his own devices. Rachel had offered her couch, and he graciously accepted. He helped her with the kids during the day, and she made him one of his favorite comfort meals, chicken and dumplings, and bought him a few pints of mint chocolate chip ice cream.

It didn't help. How did you mourn someone who died before you met them?

Moping helped a little, and so did crying on Rachel's shoulder as she reminded him of all the other fish in the sea, even though the only one he wanted had already left the water. Myles had ruined him for everyone else, he just knew it, and the jackass had been dead their whole relationship. He'd let himself fall in love with a dead guy against his better judgment, and he didn't know how to pick up the pieces after Myles had gone.

But at least Rachel believed him. It felt strange to let her comfort him. They didn't have a close relationship growing up, and he knew she resented him for moving away and leaving her and their mother all alone. Now she and the kids were the only family he had left, and he'd learned from Myles the importance of that, of how quickly it could all get stripped away.

He'd blown off her suggestion to schedule a visit with Dr. Roberts, though. He didn't think he had it in him to explain everything to someone he knew wouldn't believe him. His own fears kept him from seeking out Bobbie and the Waltons. He couldn't face knowing the truth, that Myles had left him for good just when he'd realized how much he loved him. Avoidance meant he could pretend Myles needed space.

"If you want to get your stuff, you should probably do it before the storm pushes in," Rachel said as she cleared the table. Casey had made the boys some sandwiches for lunch and was in charge of wiping off their sticky little hands.

"Do you think I have time?" he asked, looking out the window at the darkening sky.

"You will if you stop dragging your feet."

"I'm not *dragging my feet*," he huffed, but they both recognized the lie.

"I told you I'd go with you after Gary gets home."

"No, I can handle it."

He wiped Will's face and got him out of the high chair. Tony and Ethan had already dumped out a box of giant Legos in the playroom, and Casey sat him down with his brothers, laughing when he grabbed a big block and tried to stuff it in his mouth. "You just ate."

"Casey, go!" Rachel ordered from the doorway, smacking him on the ass with a dishrag.

"Fu-udge, I'm going!"

MRS. WALTON'S door opened as soon as he pulled his car into the driveway. If it had been anyone else, he would've chalked it up to coincidence, but he had a feeling she came out to talk to him, or at the very least to glare at him.

"Good afternoon, Mrs. Walton," he said as he waved.

"Is it?" she hissed back, and Casey sighed.

"No, not really."

When she didn't move from her walkway, he moved closer to her so he wouldn't have to shout. "I don't suppose you've seen Myles around the last few days?"

"He isn't my responsibility."

"No, I guess not. Thanks anyway." He frowned at her and turned to walk away.

"But... Mr. Walton said he left," she added.

His lip quivered, but there were no witnesses around to see it. He nodded his appreciation and continued into the empty house, holding it together only long enough to shut the door behind him. He leaned back against it and let himself slide down to the floor, pressing the heels of his palms against his eyes in a sad attempt to keep the tears at bay. But he saw no point to it. Myles had gone, and he felt so unfathomably alone.

AFTER HIS pity party, as Myles would've called it, he picked himself up and started gathering his things. He had a month-to-month rental agreement that still had another week to go, but he couldn't stay in the house without Myles. He'd stay with Rachel until her family got tired of him and then move to a hotel or something if he hadn't decided to go back to Los Angeles by then.

He tried to hurry, blindly grabbing things out of the bathroom so he didn't have to think about the memories they'd made in it, emptying the dresser drawers in record time, and fishing out some of Jasper's toys from under the bed. He knew the faster he worked, the quicker he could leave.

Once he'd finished packing his and Jasper's things, he felt compelled to go down to the beach one last time. They didn't get the chance to say good-bye to each other, but he thought it might offer him some kind of closure. They'd spent a lot of time out there, especially after he learned how to surf—which he hadn't wanted to do the past few days—and he couldn't think of a more appropriate place to say good-bye to Myles than on the beach.

The dreary day fit his mood, and the dark ocean had an eerie calm to it. He walked toward the shoreline and sat down, stretching out his legs and letting his hands sink into the soft sand. He'd lost count of how many times he'd sat there with Myles, sometimes in complete silence and others where they'd bared their souls to each other.

He knew he should start heading back to Rachel's. The wind grew fiercer the longer he sat there, charcoal gray hanging just above the horizon, and the blue water had turned a choppy white from the offshore winds rolling in. He could see the beginnings of lightning ripping through the air and smell the ozone blowing in.

Myles would've loved it, but he didn't think he had the strength to weather it alone.

"Wherever you are now, Myles Taylor... I just hope you're safe and happy. And I hope you know how much you meant to me. Who knows, maybe we'll meet up in the Beyond for a beer someday, if they have those there," he said, chuckling to himself, mostly to keep from crying again.

"Well, I'm free now," he heard Myles say from behind him.

Casey froze, his heart leaping into his throat. Had he made it up? Or had Myles come back to say good-bye?

"But only if you want."

He slowly turned around, a hot tear trailing down his cheek, to find Myles smiling at him. At least he hoped it was a smile. He had trouble discerning it through all the moisture clouding his vision.

"You left me."

"I know. I'm sorry."

Casey scrambled to his feet, wiping his eyes with the back of his hand. "You could've told me you were leaving." The words came out harsher than he meant, but his sadness had turned to anger. He didn't want to say good-bye.

"I think you're missing the bigger picture here," Myles said, holding his arms out. That's when Casey noticed the scrubs he wore, dark blue and a striking change from the bright white swim shirt and red board shorts he knew he couldn't take off. He looked skinnier too, like he'd lost weight, his muscles less defined and his cheeks more hollow than Casey remembered.

"What happened to your clothes?"

Myles laughed. "It's a long story, but the short version is I'm not dead."

"Wha'? What?" Casey sputtered, his mind having trouble comprehending the words. "But you died. You, you were dead. I read your obituary myself."

"I was in a coma. Some fishermen pulled me out of the ocean seven months ago, and I woke up in a hospital a few days ago—in Canada of all places. No wonder they hadn't found me, but I knew I had to find you. The doctors said you weren't real. They said you were all in my head, like yours said about me, but I knew that wasn't true. Even when Detective Charles couldn't find you, I knew."

"But you're a ghost, Myles. I've seen you disappear and walk through walls. How can you—"

"I don't know how."

"If this is a joke, it's not funny!"

"It's not a joke," Myles said, frowning at him. "I thought you'd be happy to see me."

"Of course I'm happy to see you. This is just a lot to take in."

Casey hadn't realized how close they'd gotten or which one of them had moved, but he ached to touch, to reach out his fingers and *feel* him. It was the only way he'd know for sure. He raised his arm but hesitated until Myles gave a nod. Myles closed his eyes and leaned into the caress when Casey's fingers brushed against the stubble of his cheek. That was new.

The electric feeling he'd gotten used to when they touched didn't register, only the heat coming off him, the searing sensation like a brand when Myles gripped his forearm. Myles opened his eyes and looked at him, deep blue pools taking his breath away, all his features sharp and clear, different yet so much the same.

Casey had no idea how they'd found each other, how Myles had been with him and in a hospital bed in a different country at the same time, but he didn't care because he was real and perfect and standing right in front of him.

"Oh, and I love you too," Myles said, a shy smile sending Casey's heart into spasms.

Myles licked his lips, and Casey took it as an invitation. He cupped his cheeks and pulled him close until their lips all but touched, relishing the feel of every puff of air from Myles's lungs as he greedily breathed him in. Casey couldn't do that before, nor had he been able to feel the way Myles's body heat sent tendrils of warmth snaking through him like vines as they grew together.

But he could now.

"Don't ever leave me again," Casey whispered, swallowing up any chance of a reply when he smashed their lips together.

The storm raging offshore had nothing on the one brewing between them. A thunderous moan rumbled in his chest as Myles's hands slid from his hips to his back, fingers trailing up his spine to cut canyons through his hair. And everything flashed white-hot when Myles angled his head, deepening the kiss and diving into him with all the determination of a hurricane wind.

His skin crackled with the electricity dancing around them, and he had no idea if lightning had lit up the inside of his eyelids, or if Myles had with that thing he'd just done with his tongue, but fuck it—he was going to open them to find out. This was real; Myles was real. He had him in his arms again, and he never wanted to let him go.

He'd fallen in love with Myles's spirit, and he could've had a happy life with that version of him. They would've had to work a little harder to reach some kind of normalcy, but he would do it for Myles. But now his heart wanted to burst, knowing they could have it all: a family, a future, and a normal life. Myles was real, which meant they had a chance at real happiness. And he couldn't help but think of that kiss, on a beach under a thousand-foot thunderhead, as a damn good place to start.

Myles eventually pulled back, just enough to catch his breath, and Casey had to steady him when he wobbled. Though Casey needed the steadying when a hellish combination of thunder and lightning set the sky on fire above them.

"I think we should get you inside," Myles said, the smirk evident when he pressed a sweet kiss to Casey's lips.

"I won't argue with that."

"And I have some people for you to meet." Myles turned around and almost toppled over, Casey catching him with both hands around his waist. "Sorry, I'm still rather weak."

"I gotcha."

"I told you not to overdo it, Myles," chided the woman who was striding toward them, wearing blue scrubs that matched Myles's.

"Jesus, Rita! Did you have to embarrass me right after my big romantic gesture?" Myles asked.

"If you had listened to me in the first place, I wouldn't have had to."

Myles huffed and draped an arm over each of their shoulders. "Casey, this is Rita, the evil nurse the hospital insisted accompany me against my will. And obviously, this is Casey."

"Uh, nice to meet you?" Casey half asked as they started back to the house.

"Told you he was real."

"Hi, Casey. I've heard a lot about you," Rita said, smiling around Myles. "But I must ask, is he always this stubborn?"

"How do you mean?"

"I told him walking out onto the beach with a storm on the horizon wasn't the best idea for someone who woke up from a coma less than a week ago, but he insisted on dragging his weary bones out here."

Casey chuckled. "Yeah, I've been trying to break him of sitting on the kitchen counter for months. The cat learned, but not him."

"Hey, I'm right here, guys," Myles said.

"And trying to give him his medicine is like wrestling with my rottweiler," Rita added.

Myles scoffed. "I have trouble swallowing pills."

Casey did his best not to laugh at his pout, but Myles's glare said he didn't succeed. "Sorry," he said, punctuating his apology with a peck on the cheek.

Myles and Rita spent the short walk bickering back and forth. Casey had worried at first, but he soon realized they fought like he and Rachel did, without malice and mostly to get a rise out of the other.

"Okay, now I'm regretting this decision," Myles said once they'd reached the stairway. "Did you add more stairs while I was gone?"

"You need help down there?" a man called from the deck.

"No, I got it, Lee," Myles yelled back. "I think."

"Just go slow," Rita said, positioning herself in front of him. "One step at a time."

Myles nodded and took the first step, Casey hovering behind him just in case. They had to stop for a moment halfway up so he could rest, but they eventually made it to the top just as it started to sprinkle. Myles swayed a little when his feet hit the deck, and he shook his head.

"Are you okay?" Casey asked, wrapping both arms around his middle.

"Yeah, but I think I just remembered what happened to me."

CHAPTER TWENTY-EIGHT
JAMBALAYA

"WHAT IF they don't buy it?" Myles said, staring at his pale reflection in the bathroom mirror. He'd woken up from his coma a week ago, so the white knuckles on the edge of the sink had as much to do with his lack of strength as it did with the nervous energy thrumming through him.

Casey slipped his hands around him and rested his chin on his shoulder. "I think they will, but if they don't, we'll have to figure something else out." Casey planted a kiss right behind his ear, and he shivered.

"I guess there's only one way to find out."

"Hey, guys, they'll be here soon," Lee said from the doorway.

They followed him into the guest room, where the undercover team had monitors set up for the cameras they'd placed around the house. Detective Mathis stood behind a tech manning a computer. Since Lee didn't have jurisdiction in the States, they had to turn to the local police department for assistance. Mathis had run the initial investigation into Myles's disappearance, and as soon as they told him what they wanted to do, he took their plan and ran with it.

The team spent the last three days setting up the cameras and going over ways to coax the truth out of James and Logan. Casey came up with the idea for Myles to dress in white and pretend he was dead to trick them into confessing to his "murder." Hopefully they would buy it, but the whole thing hinged on how convincing a ghost he made.

"You both know the plan," Detective Mathis said. "Just get them talking, and hopefully Myles can catch them in a lie. Press them if you think you can, but we'll be right here if you need to use the safe word. Either way, they're leaving here in cuffs."

Myles nodded. He didn't fear them, but knowing the police had their backs gave him more confidence he could pull it off.

"Any questions?"

"We've got a car pulling up," interrupted one of the techs.

"Looks like you're up," Lee said, patting Myles on the back.

Casey squeezed Myles's hand and gave him a peck on the lips, careful not to rub off any of the makeup Rita had put on him. "It's going to work."

"I know," Myles said with a smirk. He had Casey by his side; he could do anything.

The doorbell rang, and he stayed in the guest room, watching through the monitors as Casey shuffled to the door. With help from Bobbie, they'd set up a table for a fake séance, complete with her glass ball and an accompanying light show. Despite the fact it took him almost a month to convince Casey of his presence, he had confidence that the ambiance would work in their favor to speed up the process if James and Logan had doubts.

Myles watched Casey open the door, and as soon as his eyes landed on James, anger flooded his veins. The last time they'd seen each other, Myles almost died, the hazy memory bubbling up to the surface. He pushed it down, knowing he'd need to stay calm to win them over. But he couldn't help that James's arm wrapped around Logan had him seeing red.

He'd found a better man in Casey, who he had them to thank for, but the pain of betrayal stung like an old, festering wound split open. The ache felt different than it had when he thought he'd died, mostly because he knew the same hands that used to hold him close now held the man who'd tried to kill him. But he'd deal with that later. Right now he had to set the trap.

"Casey?" James asked.

"Yeah, that's me. Come in," Casey said, waving them into the house.

"This is my husband, Logan."

Casey scoffed. "That was fast. He's been dead less than a year."

"The heart wants what it wants," Logan replied with the most fake smile Myles had ever seen stretched across his face. "Who's she?"

"Oh, that's Bobbie. She's a medium, and she'll be helping us contact Myles."

"I thought you said he was a ghost?"

"He is," Casey snapped back.

"Sometimes the dead need help navigating the celestial planes," said a calm Bobbie from her elaborate chair. She'd insisted on bringing it, and Myles had to admit it added a certain flair. "Shall we begin?"

"This is ridiculous," Logan whispered, but Myles heard him through the hidden microphones placed around the house. "He probably doesn't know anything."

"You promised we'd see it through," James replied, ushering him over to the table.

They sat down, Casey making sure to sit by Bobbie so James and Logan would have their backs positioned toward the bedroom doors. Once Bobbie began, Myles would slip out and make himself known, and hopefully scare them to the point of confessing.

"First, I must place a protection spell around us to ward off any unwanted visitors," Bobbie said. "Please hold hands, and whatever you do, do not break the circle." He could sense Casey's reluctance to hold James's hand, but he did. "Now, I'll need you to close your eyes." Once they had, Bobbie began chanting in Latin. They'd done a dry run before, but it still sent a chill down Myles's spine.

James jumped when a cabinet door shut in the kitchen. Myles had to hold in a laugh, knowing it was Jasper. The hairy bastard had scared him with that trick a time or two since he'd been back.

"It's just the spirits making contact," Bobbie said. "Nothing to fear.... Everyone ready?" After a few mumbled yeses, she continued, "Oh, blessed spirits of the Beyond, we wish to commune with Myles Taylor. Let him be guided into this world by our light so that he may bless us with his presence."

Myles took his cue and snuck out of the bedroom. They had dimmed the lights to help dull his features, and the smoke machine billowed out a sweet-smelling fog to distort his appearance even more.

"Myles, are you with us?"

"Yes, I'm here," he said from behind Bobbie, his voice slightly altered by a microphone hidden in his collar.

"Myles?" James shrieked when he opened his eyes and saw him.

"I'm dead, you idiot. Not deaf."

"You're... but you're—"

"A ghost, yes, I'm well aware of that fact." He glanced at Logan to find his mouth hanging open. "Logan, it's good to see you too."

"M-Myles," he stuttered. "How is that possible?"

"I really don't know," Casey said. "He just showed up in my kitchen one day and wouldn't leave."

"People who are murdered have trouble moving into the Beyond," Bobbie said. "Their spirits can sometimes get stuck in the Between."

"Murdered?" Logan asked, shooting a look James's way.

"What? Did you forget pushing me down the stairs?" Myles asked. "Because I did at first." But then he'd woken up in the hospital and found his way back to the house, the surroundings triggering memories he didn't want.

"That was an accident," Logan said, his shoulders stiffening in defense.

"Was throwing my unconscious body into the ocean an accident too?"

"We don't know what you're talking about," James cut in. "You got caught in a riptide. I tried to save you, but the current was too strong."

"That's what I thought too, but the longer I lingered around here, the stronger my memory became until it all started to piece itself together." He suddenly remembered Logan showing up on the beach and the argument that followed.

"Myles, I loved you. It was just an accident. We panicked when you wouldn't wake up."

"Innocent people call the cops," Casey hissed.

"You were cheating on me, James. I partially blame myself for refusing to see it, but I was going to propose to you that day. And then *he* showed up to *our* romantic getaway."

"I just wanted him to know he didn't have to settle for someone who couldn't keep him satisfied," Logan said.

Myles had woken up the previous night, a cold sweat coating his skin and Casey's arms stretching around him as the memory of teetering at the top of the stairs hit him again like a ton of bricks. His chest still ached where Logan's palms had smashed into him, the force sending him into a free fall. Now he wished the riptide was all he could remember.

"Well… you could've just said that instead of pushing me down two flights of stairs."

"Logan, shut up!" James pleaded. "He didn't push you. He didn't push him," he said to Casey. "You fell, and we thought you'd want to be buried at sea."

"What the ever-loving fuck is wrong with you people?" Casey snapped.

"It was an accident."

"Give it up, James. They already know," Logan said.

"So you admit it?" Myles asked, brow arching in surprise at how easily he confessed.

"Yes, I saw an opportunity to get rid of you and took it. And I must say, it's working out pretty great for me. We even got the ring you bought resized for me."

"I'm calling the cops," Casey said.

"Go ahead and try," Logan challenged, standing up and pulling a gun out of his jacket.

"Jambaah," Myles shrieked, the safe word mangled in his throat.

"Logan, put it away," James said.

"This was your idea, James. 'See what he knows, then get rid of him.'"

"That was before we had another witness!"

"Well, we'll just have to kill her too."

"Jambalaya!" Myles yelled, this time getting the word out despite his shock.

A second later, the bedroom door swung open, as did the front and back doors, and the room flooded with cops. James threw his hands in the air, but Logan spun around, taking aim at the two detectives.

"Logan Winthrop, James Avery, you're under arrest for the attempted murder of Myles Taylor and conspiracy to commit murder," Mathis said. "Lay down your weapon and put your hands behind your head."

Two cops had grabbed Myles, Casey, and Bobbie and started ushering them out onto the deck. Mathis yelled again, but Myles saw Logan drop the gun just before he went through the door. He had mixed feelings about that. Logan deserved a bullet to the balls at the very least, but he didn't want to risk his ghost hanging around the house if he died.

"Are you okay?" Casey asked, throwing his arms around his neck.

"Yeah, I'm okay. Are you okay?"

Casey smiled. "Of course I'm okay. I have you."

They melted into a kiss that had Casey looking like he'd blown a box of powdered donuts when they broke apart.

"My makeup rubbed off on you," Myles said as he laughed.

Casey scrubbed his mouth. "Thanks a lot."

"Looks like it worked, though."

"Yeah, they fell right into it. I thought it'd take longer than that."

"Logan always had an ego problem. I think he let it get the better of him. But it's over now. I'm alive, we're safe, and they're going to jail. Couldn't have done it without you."

"Once you get your strength back, you can show me just how much you appreciate me."

Myles chuckled and pulled him close. "Count on it."

IT TOOK a while for the police to clear out. Detective Mathis took all their statements and assured them they had enough evidence to put James and Logan away for a very long time. Myles didn't care that much about jail time. Justice had been served, but he'd gotten something much more precious out of the whole ordeal.

Mathis said he'd keep in touch about how to proceed with trial prep and things like that but told them they did an excellent job. He offered to let him speak with James or Logan before they got carted away to jail, but Myles couldn't think of anything he wanted to say to them. The sting had taken a lot out of him, so he'd stretched out on his favorite deck chair and let Casey take care of the loose ends.

They thanked Bobbie for helping out and said good-bye to Lee, who had to get back to Canada. Rita offered to stay until he could gain more strength, which he appreciated even though he seemed to be getting better every day. The hospital had made arrangements for him to take rehab at the medical center in Land's End, but he had a long way to go before he'd be back to his old self.

He'd already contacted his agent, and the next big step was to hold a press conference about him turning up alive. The police did a great job of keeping it under wraps until they'd taken care of James and Logan, but he couldn't wait to catch up with some of his friends. He didn't know if he'd ever surf professionally again—he'd have to see how rehab went—but every time he caught a glimpse of Casey smiling at him, he knew it would all work out in the end.

"Do you hear that?" Casey asked as he squeezed into the deck chair with him.

"The sound of waves?"

"Yep, and the sound of an empty house."

The long day and the even longer seven months had worn him out, but Myles felt like he finally had time to breathe. The quiet came as an added bonus. "Sounds nice."

"Uh-huh... I'm going to make dinner. Any special requests?"

"I know anything you make will be spectacular."

Myles let out a hum of contentment when Casey pressed a tender kiss to his lips. He watched him walk back into the house, thankful for such a wonderful view. The sun had set hours ago, and he hadn't realized how hungry he'd gotten. Though watching Casey walk away whetted his appetite for something else entirely.

He heard someone clear their throat and jerked his head around to see Joe sitting on a deck chair. "Joe!"

"Hey, kiddo, just thought I'd check in."

"I... didn't think I'd see you again," he said as he sat up a little.

Joe huffed out a laugh. "Why? Because you're awake now?"

"Well, yeah."

"If you want me to go—"

Myles rolled his eyes. "Not what I meant. I just assumed I wouldn't... it doesn't matter. I'm happy you're here."

"Sometimes all it takes is for you to open your eyes a little wider."

"I'm already awake, Joe," he teased. "But seriously, did you know?"

"Not exactly, but I wouldn't have told you even if I had."

"Guess I had to fall in love first, huh?"

Joe snickered. "I didn't know you were such a romantic, Sleeping Beauty."

"Also not what I meant," Myles said with a sigh.

"I came to say I'm proud of you, but I hope you already know that."

"I do. Am I going to see you again?"

"I think you know better than I do that nothing's set in stone, but it's difficult to get a day pass here. I had an excuse to visit the Between when you were there, but it's harder to come all the way through. I'm already feeling weak."

Myles frowned and blinked away the beginnings of a tear. "I'm going to miss you."

"I'll miss you too, but I'll always be watching over you. And maybe someday, when you get back on your board, you'll catch a perfect wave and look over to find me riding right alongside you."

"You always did like stealing my waves."

"Love you, kiddo."

Joe vanished in the time it took him to blink.

"Love you too," he whispered into the wind. Getting to say a proper good-bye to Joe meant everything to him, but he had a feeling he'd see him again in the future—hopefully sometime before he died.

"Myles, it's ready," Casey yelled from the kitchen.

"I'll be right in."

After a dinner he knew would send his taste buds into overdrive, he and Casey were going to climb into bed and cuddle until they fell asleep tangled in sheets he could feel on his skin. He'd wake up in the morning with lips fluttering against his collarbone to the promise of a new day, and if he was lucky, a hand job, but he didn't want to push his luck. He'd settle for Jasper making biscuits on his belly. After all, he'd already died once. Everything else was just icing on the cake.

EPILOGUE

CASEY HAD just handed over the last order of the night to a server and started shutting down the stoves. Getting back into a professional kitchen took longer than he'd expected, but he and Myles had taken things slow during his recovery. The first several months were filled with rehab, press tours, and even a spot on *Good Morning America*. They kept the ghostly aspects to themselves, but Myles had made news simply for waking up.

Once they'd caught their breath from that, James's and Logan's trials started. It caused quite a few sleepless nights, as Myles had to recount the events leading up to his near death several times during trial prep and then in open court. Casey did what he could to comfort him, and everything paid off when the jury found James and Logan both guilty. The judge gave them the maximum sentence.

Things settled down after that. When Myles could surf again, they spent every morning in the water. Casey had continued to run his blog, which amassed him a decent following, and thanks to their encouragement, as well as Myles's, he decided the time had come to open another restaurant.

Myles said he'd move to Los Angeles with him if that was where he wanted to go, but Casey had grown quite fond of Land's End over the past year. He didn't want to leave his sister after they'd reconnected, nor the nephews he absolutely adored, and he had kind of fallen in love with the beach house to the point of asking the owner if he'd sell.

But one thing at a time.

The last several months, their focus centered on getting the restaurant up and running. Since Myles had officially retired from surfing, he had all the time in the world for Casey to teach him the ins and outs of the restaurant business. But Casey didn't think he'd be happy stuck inside all day when he'd spent most of his adult life in the ocean, so he came up with a great compromise.

The grand opening of the Backside Cafe & Surf Shop blew them both away. The whole town came out to show their support. Casey's food got rave reviews from the local critics, food blogs, and even got a mention in a national newspaper. Myles ran the shop side of things, and as soon as he opened sign-ups for his surf school, the classes filled to capacity. He had to make a waiting list, which neither of them had anticipated.

After the initial excitement waned, they established a nice routine. Casey looked forward to having the day off for themselves tomorrow, even though that meant he had to close the restaurant tonight. Myles had already left, and knowing him, a yummy dinner awaited Casey when he got home. All the private cooking lessons he gave him had really paid off.

"Thanks for your hard work tonight, guys," he told the staff as they cleaned up. They'd taken care of everything by the time the last patrons left, and he made sure everyone got to their cars safely before driving home.

Jasper greeted him at the door with a meow and a nice long rub against his calves. "Nice to see you too, buddy," he said as they walked toward the delicious smells coming from the kitchen. "And you too."

"Hey, love," Myles replied with a smile as he leaned in for a kiss. "Dinner's almost ready."

"Smells good. What is it?"

Myles chuckled. "A BLT pizza."

Before Casey had a chance to respond, the kitchen timer went off. He watched Myles slip on an oven mitt to pull a sheet tray out of the oven. "That looks amazing." And he didn't just mean the pizza.

"I aim to impress."

Myles sliced it with the pizza cutter and plated a few pieces for each of them. He took the plates to the table while Casey grabbed them each a beer.

"How was work?" Myles asked while they waited for the pizza to cool.

"It was good. We had a late party arrive, but we got them in and out pretty fast. Jessie deserves a raise. Best manager I've ever hired."

Myles hummed in agreement as they both took a swig from their bottle.

"Okay, I think I'm going for it," Casey said, picking up the smallest slice on his plate. He blew on the end before taking a tentative nibble. "Hot." He knew Myles was waiting to hear the results. "Really good, babe."

"Yeah?"

"Yeah, think I might steal the recipe for the restaurant."

"Think it might need some garlic and a thinner crust," Myles said after he'd taken a few bites.

"Oh yeah, that would really push it over the top."

They polished off every bite and decided to leave the dishes for tomorrow. In the bathroom, Casey took a quick shower to rinse away the sweat from the day before they elbowed each other for control of the sink as they brushed their teeth. Jasper beat them to bed—he looked a little put off when they forced him to move—but the three of them soon snuggled in for a good night's sleep.

He'd had a long day, but he loved every minute of it. He considered every night he got to fall asleep with Myles's arm flung over his chest a good one. And if everything went to plan, tomorrow would be even better.

MYLES AWAKENED to the low roar of the waves pummeling the beach. Casey magically turned into a starfish most nights, so he'd grown used to the leg sprawled over his most mornings. He thought about letting Casey sleep—they'd had a later night than usual—but he just couldn't help himself. He ran a hand up Casey's thigh, fingers burrowing into the fabric of his boxers to tease the sensitive spot just under his ass.

Casey's breathing stuttered as he woke, sleepy eyes finding Myles's. "Morning," he muttered through a yawn. He stretched and ran a hand over Myles's chest.

"Morning, beautiful," Myles replied as he moved closer to kiss him.

"Mmm... how's the swell?"

"Don't know about out there, but in here the *tide* is rising."

Casey laughed, and he had to join in. "Imagine that."

Myles waggled his eyebrows. "See for yourself."

He felt Casey's hand slide down his naked body to palm his growing erection. Casey gave a gentle squeeze that had his body shivering, goose bumps forming on his skin. But then it was gone, and Casey rolled out of bed.

"Where you going?"

"Surfing."

"Casey," Myles whined, frowning when Casey smirked at him over his shoulder.

"Don't worry, babe. The only wave I want to ride right now is you. I just gotta pee."

Myles glared at his retreating form as he disappeared into the bathroom. Casey's muffled "Don't start without me" went in one ear and out the other. He rolled over and dug out the lube from the nightstand before positioning himself so Casey would get a good view of his ass when he exited the bathroom. Then he got to work prepping himself, fingers working open his tight hole while he rutted against the mattress for that added bit of pleasure.

"Jesus, Myles! Are you trying to kill me?"

"Most definitely not, but you were taking too long."

Casey huffed out an amused laugh as his hands landed on Myles's ass. "So impatient."

"Can't help it."

Myles moaned when hands skated up his back. The bed dipped beside him, and he felt the heat of Casey's cock press against the back of his thigh. Kisses tickled his shoulders before Casey licked a path up his neck. He blew on the cool trail left behind, causing Myles's skin to crawl in the most salacious way possible.

"Did you need help?" Casey asked in a low, silky tone.

"No, I'm... just need you."

Casey's fingers twisted in his hair and guided his head back far enough for them to share a kiss, sloppy and wet but full of want. He heard the cap of the lube pop open and decided he was loose enough. He mourned the fullness when he pulled out his fingers, but he knew Casey would feel even better once he pushed into him.

He loved that part: the initial burn, the ache, the fitting of their bodies together in such a scintillating way. He'd almost come from that alone the first several times they'd been together, but he'd gotten better at holding back, letting Casey chase his pleasure before unleashing his own. But fuck if it wasn't hard. Especially when Casey told him to roll over, because then he'd have to look into his eyes blown wide with arousal when he entered him, and if a more beautiful sight existed, he didn't know it.

"Ready?" Casey asked, lining them up.

"Always."

Casey bit his lip, the look of concentration on his face ridiculously adorable. Myles wrapped his legs around his waist as Casey slid inside, neither breathing until he'd reached the hilt. A few easy thrusts later and they were both reduced to grabby hands and mouths pressing kisses, teeth grazing over skin.

The beautiful morning called for slow and easy, but then Casey hooked one of Myles's calves over his shoulder, and the change in angle had him hitting his prostate with every thunderous crack of his hips. He must've fed off the unintelligible gibberish Myles had started spouting, because every forward strike had him speeding up their rhythm.

"Can't... hold on... long," Myles managed to get out.

"Good," Casey said, wrapping long fingers around his cock. "Wanna watch you come."

Myles arched his body, head rolling back. He opened his eyes to find an unimpressed Jasper staring at him upside down. He thought about shooing the little shit away, but then Casey squeezed him just right and he forgot all about it. His body tensed, muscles tightening, before he spilled out between them. Casey leaned over to kiss him, fucking him through it until Myles felt his cock pulse inside him.

"Fuck," Casey panted when he came, both too winded to say much else.

They basked in the euphoric haze for a few moments, soothing hands moving tenderly over sweat-soaked skin. Myles loved morning sex. James had always made it feel like a chore, but everything with Casey came a helluva lot easier. They just fit. And he wondered why he had ever settled for James when *this* had been waiting for him all along. The answer didn't matter; they had each other now.

Myles groaned in protest when Casey got up to grab a washcloth to clean them off, but Jasper kept him company by climbing on his chest. "Yeah, yeah, I know you love me."

"I love you too," Casey said when he returned.

Myles grinned. "I know. The feeling's mutual."

"Sure hope so," Casey muttered as he tossed him the washcloth before walking out of the bedroom.

"Now where are you going?" Myles hollered after him.

"I have something for you."

Myles pushed himself up onto his elbows, sending Jasper jumping off with a perturbed meow. "You got me something?"

"Yeah, it's nothing much, but it's the one-year anniversary of our first *real* kiss."

"Casey, I didn't—"

"No, don't worry about it," he said as he came back into the room. "This is something I've been wanting to give you for a while. Guess I'm just using that as an excuse."

Myles sat up when Casey joined him on the bed.

"I, uh, couldn't decide how to do this, but Rachel said to just grow a pair… so here."

He thrust a small box at Myles, and his heart sputtered. He didn't have to open it to know what it held inside. "Casey?"

"The past two years have been the craziest time of my life, with the fire and a breakup and the depression, but I got through it all because of you, because of the ghost in my kitchen who turned out to be the best thing that ever happened to me. I'm still amazed every day that you're here, and I can't imagine not having you in my life. I love you, you love me, and so I was hoping you'd agree to spend the rest of your life with me."

"Just this life?" Myles teased, bumping him with his shoulder.

Casey shrugged. "And whatever comes after."

"Yeah, I can absolutely agree to that."

Casey kissed him before he took the box back and opened it up, then pulled out the white gold band to slide on his ring finger. It fit him perfectly, not that he had any doubts, but he thought he'd be the one to propose. Casey surprised the hell out of him.

Myles threw his arms around him and kissed him so hard they fell back in bed.

"But we're getting married on the beach."

"Definitely."

Myles had no idea how much his life could change thanks to a tumble down two flights of stairs, but he was grateful for it. He and Casey met in what felt like the middle of a hurricane, but the sea had finally calmed. They'd made it past the breakers, and now Myles hoped the rest of their lives would be easy sailing. And if not, at least they had each other.

LUCIE ARCHER is a student of the universe who is obsessed with the stars, in love with beaches, and crazy about dudes falling in love. Her weaknesses include a big heart, the sun, self-doubt, and kryptonite… probably. Not the exact recipe for a supervillain, but she has plans to take over the world nonetheless.

Her first foray into nonacademic writing started with fan fiction—hardly an original origin story—but after a few years of honing her craft with other people's characters, she realized she was perfectly capable of creating her own. Her underground lair, somewhere in Texas, is now overflowing with them as she prepares to unleash them on an unsuspecting world one book at a time.

As a realist, she works hard to write stories that are as honest and accurate as possible, regardless of whether that means staying up till 5:00 a.m. researching circumcision in the Ol' West or refusing to quit until she knows exactly what the runway in Circle Hot Springs, Alaska, consists of. (It's gravel, in case you were wondering.)

When she's not writing, she can be found tending to her garden, playing with her four-legged children, procrastinating, or planning world domination. Although she does spend an awful lot of time fending off random plot bunnies that threaten to derail her WIPs.

Website: LucieArcher.com
Twitter: @Lucie_Archer
Facebook: facebook.com/writerluciearcher

When two very different men are stranded on a deserted island, will opposites attract, or will they end up killing each other—if the elements don't get them first?

Marc Reed is an expert scuba diver and leads underwater tours of the infamous shipwrecks scattered around Bermuda. When a robbery forces him and his boss's son—a man he despises on principle—to take shelter on an uncharted island, he might have to reassess his opinion of the spoiled snob.

Ian Blythe-Darcy II lives a life most would envy. He's a trust-fund kid being groomed to take over his father's empire of hotels and resorts. But it's not a life that matches what's in his heart. He's in the closet and engaged to a socialite he doesn't love, but he's about to get a crash course in being true to himself—and maybe learn money can't buy happiness after all.

World of Love: Stories of romance that span every corner of the globe.

www.dreamspinnerpress.com

TAMING
THE *Wyld*

LUCIE
ARCHER

The Witness Protection Program dumps JD Smith practically at the ends of the earth—in Two Pines, Alaska—to protect him until he can testify against a dangerous gang. He tries to stick to his story and keep his head down, but it's impossible to ignore bush pilot Jake Wylder, a sexy loner with quite a reputation around the small town.

Flying medical supplies around Alaska suits Jake's wild streak and love of freedom. He's perfectly content to keep his romantic encounters casual—at least until he meets JD. Something about the nurse makes Jake think settling down might not be such a hardship. Now he just needs to convince JD he's serious—which won't be easy, given his past.

For a relationship to stand a chance, JD must testify so he can return to Two Pines as the man he really is—and Jake must grow into the man JD needs him to be.

States of Love: Stories of romance that span every corner of the United States.

www.dreamspinnerpress.com

Also from Dreamspinner Press

THE HAUNTING OF TIMBER MANOR

F.E. FEELEY JR

www.dreamspinnerpress.com

www.ingramcontent.com/pod-product-compliance
Lightning Source LLC
Chambersburg PA
CBHW070114260626
47160CB00004B/1468